Someone to
Watch Over Me

Also by Paul Wilson

The Fall from Grace of Harry Angel
Days of Good Hope
Do White Whales Sing at the Edge of the World?
Noah, Noah

Someone to
Watch Over Me

PAUL WILSON

Granta Books
London

Granta Publications, 2/3 Hanover Yard, London N1 8BE

First published in Great Britain by Granta Books in 2001

Copyright © Paul Wilson, 2001

Paul Wilson has asserted his moral right under the
Copyright, Designs and Patents Acts, 1998, to be
identified as the author of this work.

A CIP catalogue record for this book
is available from the British Library.

1 3 5 7 9 10 8 6 4 2
ISBN 1 86207 419 4

Typeset in Palatino by M Rules
Printed and bound in Great Britain
by Mackays of Chatham plc

Contents

Prologue   1
1 The Geometry of Miracles   3
2 Providence Street   24
3 The Difference Engine   44
4 Jack's Book   72
5 Buggerfuck   93
6 Almost Debbie Reynolds   110
7 Defence and Counter   125
8 The Testament   147
9 Letters from God   170
10 Reaching the Hearts of Men   192
11 It Ain't Necessarily So   221
12 The Bells of Parte Vieja   237

There's a somebody I'm longing to see
I hope that he
Turns out to be
Someone to watch over me

George and Ira Gershwin

Prologue

People saw the parchments falling through the smoke like a benediction. They had the quality of dried leaves. It was hard to say for certain how many fell at the time because of the panic. The blaze, and the aftermath of the explosion in the school, had formed a gauze that was too dense for the television news cameras to be able to pick them out definitively, but a reporter from one of the news agencies would confirm that he saw four of them coming down, and that he broke ranks past the police cordon onto the school's playing field to retrieve one of them. A woman whose son would survive the siege said she saw half a dozen falling. Each parchment had a separate verse inscribed on it in a language no one recognized – people guessed at Arabic or Sanskrit – but which would be identified later as Hebrew, each one falling separately, softly, to the earth. A couple of them caught on draughts of spiralling hot air as they veered too near the still-burning boilerhouse on their journeys downward and jolted like doves scattering.

In the days to come, more of them would be found in Heslop Bridge as far away as the fields under Holker Fell and in the yard of Cottee's builder's merchants a mile down

1

the road – the Cottees whose son had been one of those shot inside the school by Jason Orr. Keith and Karen Cottee weren't the only ones. Most of the families who lost children in the siege would wake in the days to come to find that brittle and yellowing parchments had been gifted to them. The last of the parchments to fall on Heslop Bridge was gathered up from where it was found beneath the altar of the church on the morning of the town's remembrance service. By then, Brendan Moon – a man with a record of uncovering fraudulent evangelists and the simple wishful thinking of grieving lovers – would be assigned to the case by his employers to disprove the miracle.

Eighteen parchments in all were recovered. No one was sure whether they all fell at the same time and lay waiting to be found, or whether they had continued to fall onto the small town in some preordained sequence through the dark hours following the massacre, once dusk had bruised to mulberry and cobalt blue the undersides of the ships of passing cloud, and then in the quiet sanctity of the nights which followed. But everyone agreed that they had fallen. From the sky.

1

The Geometry
of Miracles

Brendan Moon was thirty-eight. It was an age at which all things should still have seemed possible. If he chose, he could surely start again. He could follow in Hemingway's footsteps, he sometimes reasoned, and rent a couple of rooms in San Sebastián on the hillside overlooking the harbour and teach English to pay the rent and watch the sailing boats nudge their way back into port each honey-coloured evening past the sardine trawlers. He could pack an overnight bag and leave to run a bar on a Greek island. He could travel the Silk Route in a battered jeep, or hitchhike across America. He could quit Mercantile Municipal, for whom he had worked for twelve years, for whom he had been transferred to London and promoted twice, and do any of these things. He was unaware as yet of the sound of doors softly closing on the possibilities of his future life.

Yet, there is a point at which the gradual momentum of a life reveals itself to be a subtle tide too strong to swim against. There is a point at which the chance to start *everything* again becomes an illusion. The weight of what has gone lies heavy. Having reached the age of thirty-eight, certain things held true. In imagining his future, it barely seemed to matter that there were parts of the work that he disliked, or that he had no responsibilities outside of his job that might lead people to regard him for more than a couple of hours as irresponsible if he rang the office one day to say he was leaving for Provence or Tuscany. The fact was, he was a success story in Mercantile Municipal's business fraud department. He had a talent for what he did, and he was paid well. He liked the business of driving out to cases, the freedom, the unmasking of flaws, the revelation of the disappointing truth. He had done it for such a long time that the difference between *him* and *it* was sometimes hard to see.

It was also true that he had a suspicion of grand gestures, of rash decisions. He had seen enough people brought to their knees to know that simply to come through intact was an achievement beyond the reach of most of the people he dealt with on a daily basis. Brendan Moon himself had settled for coming through intact.

Brendan wove his way between the lines of morning pedestrians. People's true lives, he knew, were happening secretly inside them even as they passed him. This was the real battleground. Preoccupations and half-edited replays tumbled messily in that inaccessible place from which everyone, in truth, was forced to view the world in monk-like isolation. These private thoughts, he knew, were disconnected from the imperative of their hurrying through these London streets. Here, inside people's heads as they shuffled past him on the Marylebone Road, was the nagging, not-quite-adding-up past, the restless residue, far removed from those few sharply incandescent turning points that lit up a life. He passed along these city streets daily, feeling the scurry of other people's private urgencies quicken with his into a single tension gripping all their hearts. This, he understood, was to do with being out of doors and vulnerable, with staying alert for that unforeseen split second of malevolence which everyone imagined was coming somewhere soon, out there on the streets. But this wasn't ultimately what mattered. These public passages of life weren't, in the end, what brought people to their knees.

People were less impressive than they seemed. That was Brendan Moon's view. If you got to know them well enough, their lives could usually be summed up by simple enough equations that had to do with money or loneliness. They appeared braver than they turned out after you'd dug a little. Except for those who were lucky, or stupid, people seemed destined to reach a point of critical tension in the shape of the lives they were trying to construct which broke them and left them forced to travel the rest of the way carrying the remnants in pieces.

Brendan Moon stepped out of the crowd, into the side street housing Mercantile Municipal's private car park. He slid into his car – a muddy blue tank of a Volvo – and began the morning's drive north to Lancashire.

People were less impressive than they seemed. Take the woman he had investigated after she had sold her story to the *Express*. While things were going her way she was sweetness and light. She said that she felt blessed. She showed him the X-rays and reports from the Chinese herbalist who had reported the remission, while they sat on her lawn amid the garden's gentle summer hum. But when he uncovered a specialist who had treated her previously and who disagreed with her version of the nature of the tumour, and then discovered that there were identifiably malignant cells still active in her body, she began leaving increasingly agitated messages on his answerphone about her damaged *karma*, and finally started stalking him, as if the reality of her failure to fully escape the clutches of the cancer was *his* fault.

Take the church-goers in Donegal who had reported their statue of the Blessed Virgin Mary to be weeping tears of blood. The report had followed hard on the heels of other articles in the English and Irish press about a statue in the Italian port of Civitavecchia that had wept blood fifteen times. In Brendan's view, such claims usually followed each other like sheep out into the open and, sure enough, within a year, a dozen statues all over Ireland had been reported as either weeping or moving. In Italy, the Vatican had declared the tears of Civitavecchia to be genuine. In Donegal, at least, Brendan was able to commission laboratory tests on the statue. The report had confirmed that beads of condensation had been forming overnight due to a chemical reaction within the cooling plaster and then gathering in the ducts of the eye indents. Despite this, writs in Ireland had been taken out for slander against both Brendan and the laboratory in the face of clear-as-daylight scientific evidence.

It hadn't surprised him. Nothing surprised him. It was the way of the world. When he gave thought to these things, as he occasionally did late at night, it brought to mind the parish priest of his boyhood, an earthy and practical Leinster man, who had nevertheless been a stubborn champion of such miracles.

'The Roman martyr Sergius', Fr Wynn liked to tell his annual Confirmation class, 'was decapitated in Syria in the fourth century. At the moment of his death, boys, a halberd fell out of the skies over the city of Trieste.' His class would gasp at the thought of the gleaming double-headed axe being cast down from Heaven to mark the martyr's passing. 'That halberd', the priest would add after a moment's delay, and in the whisper of a natural Gaelic storyteller, 'is preserved to this day in the city's cathedral.' The fact that people believed such things so many centuries ago seemed understandable, even reasonable. After all, for a thousand years after the martyrdom of Sergius, primitive science had continued to prove that the world was flat, and that mankind had begun with Adam and Eve. And even throughout the course of the Rennaissance, the compatriots of Michelangelo had believed devoutly that St Minias had carried his own severed head out of the city from the Piazza della Signoria and set it down on the hill where the Florentines had afterwards built a church in his honour. But how people could still continue to believe such things at the outset of the twenty-first century amused and defeated him. Yet Brendan knew that pilgrims still wound their way up to Florence's hilltop shrine of San Miniato; and that thousands of people still converged on Trieste each year on the feast day of Sergius to pay homage to the halberd exhibited on the altar of the church of San Giusto. Not only that: people seemed intent on imagining *new* miracles. The closing years of the twentieth century had seen more reports of statues moving, of visions making proclamations, of apparitions confiding heavenly secrets to a chosen few, than in the whole of the previous two centuries. People would believe anything in order to bestow upon their personal worlds a geometry and a sense of meaning which, in reality, were not there. And always, in Brendan's experience, after you'd dug a little, after you'd listened to them tell their tales, people were less remarkable than they seemed.

So it was that he found himself heading for East Lancashire where, seventeen days before, an assault by a twenty-two-year-old man on a primary school during its morning assembly had resulted in a six-hour siege, nine fatalities, and subsequent claims in the town, in the days that followed, of a miracle. The man responsible for the shootings was now in custody. He'd been led out of the school, handcuffed, relaxed, smiling. He'd said they'd remember him now.

So much of life, Brendan had reflected, was made up of failure, and the impulse to seek refuge from it.

It wasn't until he'd been driving for an hour that he felt across in the glove compartment for the tape. The radio station had been only too happy to supply copies of the recording to anyone who wanted them. Brendan pushed in the cassette. The flute concerto playing on the radio cut out. There was a hiss and a series of clicks, then the end of a music jingle and a presenter's voice. The next caller on Line One was Jason.

'Jason, what d'you want to say?'

No one answered.

'Jason? You're through to Danny Megson's *Night Time Phone-in* on Radio North. Speak now or forever clear off and stop bothering me.'

There was still no answer.

'A nation waits and holds it's breath, Jason. The stage is yours.'

'Is that Danny Megson? Am I on?'

'It's like threading a needle with a spatula, Jason, isn't it?'

'What?'

'For the love of God, Jason, just talk to me – I've already

lost forty listeners to *Prisoner Cell Block H* in the time it's taken so far to crank up your motor.'

'It's about my step-mum.'

'So tell, Jason, tell. Thrill us with your insight.'

'Can I say about your show, Danny? It cracks me up.'

'Flattery will get you everywhere, providing the station manager's listening which she isn't cause she's sunning her bum in St Lucia, so get on with it.'

'No, I like it when you get those slags coming on who think they know everything and you wind them up. When her that said she was a social worker rang up the other night to have a go, saying she was gonna get you taken off the air and you cut her off cause you said she was talking out her arse.'

'Well, I cut her off, I seem to remember, because she was trying to tell me that every time some woman got sexually abused in Milford Haven or Timbuktu it was *my* fault because I was a man – like I'd *personally* held each of the bitches down. Now cut to the chase, Jason.'

'Well, that woman was making out how it's always men's faults – all this stuff. And that's bollocks.'

'How do you know?'

'Because I've been sexually abused – by my step-mum. That's what I rung you about, Danny – to tell you about me being sexually abused.'

'By your step-mum? What about your dad in all this?'

'He was always on nights.'

'That was handy. For your step-mum, I mean. What do you think made her do it, Jason?'

'Well, I dunno really. It's hard to say. My friends say I've got a really big donger. Huge. Biggest they've ever seen. They reckon it might be that. Women have fainted before now when I've put it all the way in.'

'And you think it was that, eh?'

'My step-mum, she couldn't get enough – from when I was about eleven, twelve.'

'It must have been pretty traumatic for you?'

'Are you kidding? I was knackered.'

'What's your stepmother called, Jason?'

'Cheryl. I don't live with her and my dad now, but I still help him out on his market stall, and she still comes around.'

'Have you had any help with this thorny problem Cheryl seems to have handed you? Anyone tried to intervene?'

'Course, but she won't stop. She says she'll shop me to the dole if I don't give it to her regular like. It's not like she's not a good looker. Blonde. She's got a big pair on her, and these long legs. Men are always after her, but she says she prefers me. Sometimes she makes me tie her up on the bed and lick stuff off her before, well, you know.'

'What's the psychologist say?'

'Psychologist? Piss off, Danny – I'm not letting anyone like that get inside my head. I'm like you – I don't take no crap off no one. When they used to come around to the house – the welfare and stuff – they were just after giving her one themselves, but she wouldn't have it.'

'Except from you.'

'Yeah, except from me.'

'Can I tell you something?'

'Course you can, Danny – as long as you're not gonna cut me off.'

'I can't see that anyone would want to get inside your head.'

'I told you, I won't let no one. Well, you wouldn't take no messing from them either, Danny, would you?'

'Let me ask you something, Jason.'

'What?'

'What would you list as the significant achievements of your life to date?'

'Achievements?'

'Things you're proud of. Things you'd use to measure how far you've come. How have you made your mark? In between getting laid by Cheryl.'

'Well, you know *Tekken 3*. I've got through all the levels on that – at Christmas – and I only lost three lives. Four days it took me. God, I was crapping it near the end. No psychologist could get to the end of *Tekken 3* if they did it for a year. A hundred years.'

'You know what?'

'What?'

'That's why no one would want to get inside your head.'

'Why?'

'Because there's nothing in there, Jason. It's just a big, dark, empty space.'

'So have you done *Tekken 3* then? Or what about *Tomb Raider*? Not the first one – that's a piece of piss – the newest one, without using the cheats.'

'I tell you, Jason – anyone with agoraphobia should keep clear of your head.'

'What gives you the right to talk? Just because you use fancy words!'

'What gives me the right to talk? Well, the fact that it's me sat here in a warm studio with the headphones on, and it's you in a public phone box sticking tuppences in the slot while the wind's blowing through the crack in the door up your backside.'

'I'm not in a phone box.'

'Well, you've got me reeling on the ropes with that one, Jason, haven't you?'

'So what's so hard about sitting in a studio talking? Anyone can do that. That's not such an achievement. Anyone can just sit there talking all night. That's not so special.'

'Is that so? Tell you what, Jason, I'll just go and put the kettle on for me and the producer and you take over the calls for me until we get to the news at midnight. What d'you say?'

'Talking on the radio's nothing.'

'Talking on the radio's nothing?'

'I bet when it comes down to it you're nothing, Danny.'

'You bet I'm nothing?'

'I bet in real life you're probably a little runt with glasses who's balding.'

'In real life? Oh, Jason, you're killing me. How much do you know about *real life*? I've got news for you, Jason – real life is out here amongst the grown-ups, not shooting space invaders with a ray gun. Come out and join us one day.'

'Or else you're a fat git with a beer belly and an old man's beard . . .'

'. . . and a Range Rover the size of your back-yard sat in my space in the car park, and a five-bedroomed detached in Cheshire that's paid for, and a daytime series on cable this year, and a contract you'd wet yourself for. And you've done *nothing*, Jason. If you died tomorrow, no one on this planet would remember you by next week. Jason? they'd say. Don't remember any Jason. You know what, Jason. Here's some advice for you from a man who's made it. Stop sitting there in that smelly little hole of a bedsit you're sat in day and night with no friends, fantasizing about having it away with

women when you've probably never had a sniff: go out and
do something with your life. Get a job, climb a mountain,
make a statement. Make people notice you. Do something to
make them sit up and think – something they'll remember
you for when you've finally gone. If you're never gonna
make it, Jason, make sure you've made the attempt and go
down fighting, then at least the world will know that you've
actually been alive while your lungs have been going in and
out. Because up to now, Jason – judging by the last five minutes – you've just been a waste of space on this planet. And
one more thing, Jason, before we break for a commercial . . .'

But the line was already dead.

The recording kept running for a while but there was just
the smooth hiss of the blank tape. The Mozart concerto
Brendan had been listening to in the earlier part of the journey resumed partway through the *Adagio*.

In the aftermath of events in Heslop Bridge, Danny
Megson of Radio North was already said to have made six-
figure sums from tabloid exclusives. 'My Heartache By
Phone-In Host Danny'. He had appeared on two national
chat shows, and his own deal to host a daytime cable TV
series was being renegotiated by his agent.

You could drive through Heslop Bridge in three minutes.
The approach off the M65 East Lancashire motorway was a
reservoir, fields, the yard of a builder's merchants, then the
signpost for the town just past a couple of industrial units
and a petrol station. Lower Heslop Bridge was signposted
right at the lights by the cricket ground.

Heslop Bridge itself ran for about a mile either side of the
main road. The better houses – the gardened semis with
bow windows set back from the road by public crescents of

grass, and the new Barratt estate – were at the motorway end. The shops beyond the cricket ground ran either side of the main road. The bottom end of the town was the former weaving district where streets of narrow terraced houses formed short irregular grids back to the foot of Holker Fell on one side of the main road, and as far as the slipper factory in the former Heslop Bridge Mill on the other side. Then the road climbed again, between fields guarded by unruly hedges and irregular corrugated fencing, and split into two at the brow of the hill – one road leading to Clitheroe in the Ribble Valley, the other to Burnley and the narrowing line of hill settlements between Heslop Bridge and the inexorable rise of the Pennines.

Brendan drove through the town once, slowly, to gain his bearings. Even with a stop on red at the traffic lights, it was a short drive from the edge-of-town 'Heslop Bridge' sign-post by the petrol station to the other one on the far side of the town, and after that he swept the car around on the Burnley road to bring him back onto the M65 slip road, back to the reservoir, the fields, Cottee's builder's merchants. He pulled in at the petrol station.

The roadside signage and the lights of the kiosk were starting to stand out in the last dull hour of daylight. Brendan got out of the car. The movement took a swill of blood from his head. He stood still, taking long breaths of air. He stretched some of the cramp out of his shoulders from the long drive, broken only once at a service station north of Birmingham. He sat back down in the driver's seat sideways on and checked the sequence of messages from the office on his mobile phone. As he did so, he watched the bulky woman sitting hunched at the window next to the petrol station's kiosk. Every so often she turned the page of something she was reading. He tried to guess what it would be – a TV listings magazine, a shopping catalogue. When he was done checking the messages he unhooked the petrol pump's nozzle to fill up the car. The engine of the pump began to hum.

A man appeared in the doorway of the workshop next to the kiosk. He looked about sixty, with a sharp, indifferent face. He wore overalls and was wiping oil from his hands with a rag.

'We're closing,' he said.

Brendan paused. 'The lights are still on,' he observed.

'Joyce must have forgotten the lights.'

'And the pumps.'

'Is that so?'

'So can I fill her up?'

'She'll have been cashing up,' the man objected. 'You'd better ask. She's probably reckoned up by now.' Then the man walked back over to the workshop, still wiping his hands.

When Brendan went into the kiosk, a bell rang and the woman came out of the side office where she'd been reading. She was a large woman, wearing elasticated leggings and a black smock smothered by a vast knitted cardigan that stretched down to her knees. There was a roll to her walk as she drew the weight of each leg in turn around a central point of gravity.

'The man says you're shut,' Brendan said. 'I've got to ask you if I can use the pump.'

'Course you can use it, love. The lights are still on.'

'I was told you were cashing up.'

'You mean Jim? Oh, never mind him. You wouldn't think we run a business here, the way he goes on.'

'Does he work for you?'

'I work for him. He's my father-in-law. It's his business – not that you'd notice. Go on, you fill her up.'

Brendan went back outside. The man in the overalls – Jim – was standing at the door of the workshop, watching him. Brendan walked over to him. 'She said it was OK,' he said. He noticed that the man's overalls didn't quite fit, as if he'd borrowed them from someone larger.

'It's mine,' the man said, observing Brendan looking past him into the workshop.

'Sorry?'

'The car. It's mine. I'm just checking the suspension.' The old Rover was raised up over the inspection pit.

Brendan filled his tank. Back in the kiosk, Joyce processed his credit card payment and told him how her father-in-law paid her eighty pounds a week to work in the kiosk and to do the books; how he had gradually ceded all responsibility for the business (the ordering, the book-keeping, the *worrying* about the business) to Joyce while he played assistant to the string of mechanics half his age who sub-let the workshop from him on six-month leases. Brendan listened. She talked quickly, happy, it seemed, to have company.

When she stopped talking, he said, 'He told me it was just his own car he was fiddling with.'

'He says that to everyone in a good suit – in case they're a spy from the oil company. You're not a spy, are you?'

'Do I look like a spy?'

'I don't think so. I can usually tell. I think Jim's secret is safe for now.'

'Why does he do it?'

'I think he just likes the subterfuge. He likes the idea he's getting one over on the big guys. I can't say I blame him. I suppose eventually, when they remember that they even have a filling station in Heslop Bridge, they'll either close it down or turn it into a Stop and Shop mini-market franchise that we won't be able to afford to lease. It's ironic, really. While he's worrying about getting caught for cheating a multinational company out of a few hundred pounds a year, he hardly notices that he's losing weight too fast for comfort. I've had to put new holes in his belts so his trousers won't fall down. The trouble is, he thinks he's still in his thirties to hear him talk. He thinks he's invulnerable.'

'Have you worked here long?'

'Six years. I was a supervisor in the slipper mill until Jim asked me to help out. That was about the time my husband upped sticks with a woman half my size. I'm not sorry I said yes. Jim's been a good help with things. And you get to see the weather every day. You get time to read in the quiet spells. I never got that in the slipper mill. I miss the crack sometimes – the other girls on the line. That's a regret. You know he still pays me what he started me on. I love him to bits. And he'd do anything for me, except pay me a decent wage.'

She handed him back his credit card and the receipt.

'You driven far, B. Moon?'

'London.'

'London? Why didn't you get the train?'

'I don't like trains.'

'Is that so.'

'It's just a personal thing.'

'TV or newspaper?'

'Neither.'

'But you're here for the remembrance service tomorrow, right?'

'What makes you say that?'

'We don't get many good suits in these parts. Or we didn't till a fortnight ago.'

'I work for an insurance company,' Brendan said.

'So what's that, something to do with the shootings? The school burning down?'

He nodded.

'You have to talk to people about what happened?'

This time Brendan shrugged in confirmation.

'I bet you're good at your job,' she said.

'What makes you say that?'

'Your face,' Joyce said. 'You have a comfortable face – the kind that makes it easy to talk to you. A sad face.'

'Is that right?'

'But you don't give much away yourself.'

'No?'

'Just because you've lived in the same town all your life and you're the size of a barn door, B. Moon, it doesn't mean you don't see things.'

'What sort of things?'

'A challenge, huh? Haven't had one of those in a while. Well, I suppose, like I said, you're probably good at your job. And I'd say you haven't done anything rash in about a million years, B. Moon. I mean, for one thing, I still don't know what the 'B' stands for, and you're not going to tell me, are you?'

'Rash?'

'Rash, spontaneous, irrational.'

'Like what?'

'You want my example? You want me to confess my irrational extravagance first? I decided to learn how to play the oboe.'

'You what?'

'Oboe. Bloody long useless wooden howitzer of a thing with a reed stuck on the end. Two years ago, I decided I wanted to learn to play it. Woke up one morning at the age of forty-six and just decided. Never done anything musical before then. Someone told me it would help me to control my breathing. I have asthma.' She produced a blue salbutamol spray from the pocket of her cardigan for him to see. 'I go on the bus to Burnley once a week to take lessons,' she said, ' – sod to get on a bus is an oboe. Me and the oboe together on a bus seat – there's a hoot. Impossible to master. No decent tunes written for it. How irrational can you get? There, that's my confession. Now, what about yours?'

'Mine?'

'You know – I show you mine, you show me yours. What's the matter, you never played that game in London when you were little?'

'I wasn't brought up in London. I only work there.'

'Where were you brought up, B. Moon?'

'Salford.'

'Salford! Almost a local boy.'

The discovery made her happy. It made it easy to persuade her to do more of the talking, and she was happy to talk about Heslop Bridge. She told him how awful it was – the things that had happened. She said she knew some of the families. She said some of the women had worked on her line in the slipper mill when she'd worked there. She said she couldn't imagine what had possessed Jason Orr to do what he did. She said it was a remarkable thing about the parchments. She said you pray for things like that to help you get through such a tragedy but you don't expect it, so when it happens – when it happens in a little place like Heslop Bridge and you realize that God has remembered you're here, even if the oil company has forgotten all about you – it helps you to cope. Did he know, she said, did he know that one of the parchments had been found next door to where they stood now? Keith Cottee had found it in the yard of his builder's merchants the day after Keith's son had been shot dead by Jason Orr. She herself had joined the support group that was running once a week in the cricket club in the aftermath of the tragedy. She'd slept better herself, thinking about the parchment that was dropped inside Keith Cottee's yard next door.

He asked her about Keith Cottee's version of finding the parchment, what time, who was with him, what kind of man Keith Cottee was, whether she believed him. She told him that she did believe him. She said that Keith Cottee was a friend of her father-in-law – they played cards together and drank beer one night a week. Brendan asked her what book she had been reading in the office. She said it was about how people's lives were shaped by astrological events. She said she'd known since being a child that people's lives were governed by their horoscopes. You could understand a lot about a person from knowing their star signs. You could tell a lot from them about what made people *tick*; you could make sense of things. And she told Brendan again that he had a sad face.

The school looked smaller than it had done on the television. It was tucked away two streets behind the cricket ground. According to the reports, when news of the siege broke at Heslop Bridge's slipper factory at the bottom of the main street, the one hundred and thirty workers downed tools as one and ran out into the street and up the hill half a mile to the school, where the police had already cordoned off the roads.

The drive leading from the street to the school entrance was carpeted with flowers and written messages. This was the path down which Jason Orr had walked before entering the school's assembly hall and starting to shoot. Brendan tried to guess at the number of bouquets. Seven hundred, eight hundred, maybe a thousand. Maybe more. He read some of the messages tied to the flowers.

In the days following the assault, parents and friends and teachers had come to this spot and laid flowers and hugged each other, and a hundred TV cameras had pointed their lenses from their perches beyond the railings, and commentators had asked how such a thing could come to pass in a small Lancashire town you could drive through in three minutes. Surely, they pondered, the world should have been more carefully ordered than to allow so many lives – young, as yet unlived lives – to be snuffed out in that way. It was hard to know what else to do other than to bring flowers and to embrace and to weep, and to have the reporters eat it all up and conduct their two-minute inquests live to camera before handing back to the studio for the sports news and the weather.

The explosion had been around the back of the school. Jason Orr had set it off using a homemade chemical bomb with ingredients he had bought from Chettle's hardware shop on the High Street the day before the assault. His plan had seemed to be to blow up the entire school, himself included, but the explosion had not been big enough. The school had been built in an 'L' shape; as a result of the fire, one of the two blocks of classrooms had been completely blackened, and that part of the school was fenced off with temporary steel sheets wedged in breezeblock feet. The windows of most of the classrooms had been blown out.

Everything was covered in black soot and black ash and black grease. Pieces of roofing had collapsed. The hidden skeleton of the school protruded through the walls of seared brick that remained – strands of insulated wire and steel joists and warped piping. Three walls of the boilerhouse, and the caretaker's storeroom at the end of the building, had been blown down. No one had died as a result of the explosion. The ones who had died had been shot by Jason Orr. But the fire made it *feel* like a place where people had died. Twelve days on, the black charred classrooms with no roofs felt to Brendan like a more accurate memorial to what had happened than the miraculous sweep of flowers. The blackened classrooms didn't *look* like classrooms any more. They didn't feel like they were part of a school, or ever had been. They didn't feel like lessons had ever been taught there, or simple prayers recited. They felt like part of a war. And yet. And yet.

And yet in this dowdy town, in the middle of a scatter of small green hills and old farms, was the public possibility – delicious to the media who, initially, had been frenzied with the scent of it – that God might have been touched sufficiently by this tragedy in the middle of England to have intervened, to have shown Himself to this community of people who, by and large, spent their working lives in Heslop Bridge's slipper factory, and shopped at Kwik Save, and toured car boot sales, and where elderly couples watched Lancashire League cricket on Sundays from May to September, with blankets over their knees, after setting the video for the episode of *Eastenders* that they'd watch after supper.

It was difficult to believe, but not the hardest thing. The hardest thing to accommodate, Brendan Moon knew, was the unimportance of it all. The very hardest thing, but the bravest thing, was the acceptance that humankind was spinning on a small blue-green planet unnoticed and inconsequential and randomly evolved, and that such atrocities as those committed by Jason Orr went unlamented in the wider scheme of things, because that was the adult truth of the matter. People needed the soothing comfort that *someone somewhere* was in control of events, even as their own lives were being warped by the corrosives of missed chances and irretrievable loss, although what they yearned for was not out there.

2

Providence Street

'Our Father, who art in Heaven, hallowed be thy name . . .'

In primary school, the miraculous and the mundane swam side by side. Brendan Moon remembered that. He could recall himself beseeching God in one and the same breath, during silent prayer in assembly, for an improvement in Grandad Walter's bad chest and for Manchester City's away form to hold up. Prayer had been an immediate and straightforward currency when he was a boy. It was a kind of slot machine into which wishes were submitted, then scrutinized, and finally granted or not according to a rational but complex formula – akin to algebra – hammered out between God and Fr Wynn.

'In the name of the Francis Lee, and of the Bell, and of the Summerbee, Amen.'

That's what the boys had liked to recite as they were following Fr Wynn in making the Sign of the Cross, before they trooped into class for the day's lessons to begin. That's what Brendan had liked to whisper, offering it up as a plea for Manchester City to win their Saturday fixture. It was a brave mantra for a boy to chant in such a tightly constructed universe, even when it was mouthed silently in an assembly hall humming with children and crammed with the smell of wood polish and the sweetness of the school's old, ripening damp. There seemed, Brendan could recall, a genuine risk of being thunderbolted, or at the very least of being unmasked in the act by some heavenly searchlight. A small squad of angels were, assuredly, hovering at the windows of the school, and out on Abbott Street and Providence Street, and drifting zephyr-like within the assembly hall itself, just a few feet above the children who sat cross-legged on the floor. The angels were making notes. They were keeping a celestial score for Fr Wynn. Sometimes, Brendan had realized as a boy, if he sat still enough in those morning assemblies, amid the slats of sunshine and shade falling on him from the morning sky outside, he could feel an angel's breath as it ghosted over him, assessing his state of grace.

'*In the name of the Francis Lee, and of the Bell . . .*'

It was a world which contained the Catholic school of St Joseph's and a neighbourhood of a dozen Salford streets. It was a world in which the goodness of Brendan's next-door neighbour Mrs Lynch, who gave him sweets, could be measured by her guaranteed place in Heaven as a result of her attendance at the nine First Friday masses of nine consecutive calendar months. It was a world in which what was right and what was wrong were absolute and irrefutable and could, if God chose, be daubed in vast and permanent painted letters on the walls of the hospital grounds which rose at the end of Abbott Street. It was a world whose edges blurred into hearsay and indecision past those same hospital walls, and at the far end of the boating lake of the corporation park, and beyond Fr Wynn's boxing gym on the big road which served, in Brendan's world, as a definitive full stop.

In such a world, it was understandable to the eight-year-old Brendan Moon, natural even, that God should take a personal and detailed interest in the lives of those who lived in this small kingdom of His. These were the streets which invited God's special interest. Whatever lay beyond mattered less. Whatever lay out there was, anyway, shrunken and made neutral by the inexactness of the images which represented it on the black and white television in the front parlour at home, and by the map on the classroom wall which, in embracing the totality of the world, travelled from just beyond Catherine Yallop's coat-peg across to the dark green casing of the door frame.

In such a world, apostolic saints and first division footballers, and the boxers in black and white on the walls of Fr Wynn's flaking gym walls, were robust kinds of men known personally to his father and to Fr Wynn, who bestrode city-centre Manchester and the other metropolises, blue-eyed and long-limbed and needing to duck their heads below lintels to enter rooms that, one day, Brendan too would enter. Until then, his place was here in these preparatory Salford streets that were regulated for God by Fr Wynn in the same way that he refereed the school's football matches and the boxing bouts held in his evening gym on the Cheetham Hill road. Fr Wynn's whistle, which hung permanently on a rope around his neck nestled in the folds of his cassock, regularly brought things to a standstill when an infringement against the rules of any code – sporting or moral – took place. It stopped the universal clock going around for that breathless moment. Then the impatient drag of his Leinster voice gave out the admonishment, and (for all Brendan Moon knew) injury time was calculated and added to the end of the world.

That God intervened seemed obvious to Brendan. That miracles were enacted as a necessary way of adjusting the daily balance of this small and closely scripted play was taken for granted. He had parted the Red Sea for Moses; He had turned Lot's wife into a pillar of salt; He had fed five thousand people with five loaves and two fishes. In the same way, He had punished Kevin Eatough for whacking Brendan's football into the boating lake by giving him measles for a fortnight. He had gifted 'Colin Bell' to Brendan amongst the weekly six-pack of collectable football cards Brendan had bought from the newsagent's on Duckworth Street three days after confiding to his father his decision to give up chocolate for Lent. He'd let Manchester City become league champions at the end of that season of 1967–8 as a way of making it seem more reasonable that Manchester United would be allowed to win the European Cup at Wembley four days later.

The result was an established rhythm to life. It was a rhythm that found expression in the Christmas and July tests in which Brendan would emerge (each time to his vague astonishment) near the top of the class and in which, anchored at the bottom, was dough-faced Gordon Clough, sitting in front of him, who cribbed the answers from Brendan in spelling tests and who Brendan, five pounds lighter but quicker on his feet, sparred with in the gym. Gordon Clough lived in one of the rented houses on Abbott Street with his mum and a man who wasn't his dad. Abbott Street was the place boys lived if they got free school meals and did PE without plimsolls and in yellowing vests tucked into their underpants instead of in PE kit, and whose back-yards played host to rats coming in off the hospital fields – and where Brendan's mum and dad said he'd end up if he didn't work hard at school. It was a rhythm that ensured that, although the Cronshaws smelled and had poor teeth, they were provided with the ballast of their mother's regular wins on the bingo; it ensured that Gordon Clough, whose ancient, ill-fitting sweaters rode up on his belly, was provided with the consolation of wearing vast wooden clogs whose metal soles clattered like gunfire on the hard school floors; it ensured that Catherine Yallop, as a counterpoint to her frequent headaches and haughty, day-long moods when she wouldn't speak to Brendan at all, had a china-doll prettiness that made Brendan breathless when she looked at him.

Even the local villains – Gordon Clough's older brother Frankie, Billy Cronshaw's cousin, Vincent Guppy – were part of this seamless tableau. Even the villains (people said they were villains) boxed in Fr Wynn's gym in the evenings, or came to talk with the priest about their families, their run-ins with the police, the goals they'd scored, or nearly scored, against St Anthony's or St Bede's a decade before.

Once, when Brendan was waiting to meet his father after work, he found himself cornered at the end of Abbott Street by one such apprentice villain – the fifteen-year-old Frankie Clough. Brendan smelled Frankie Clough's tobacco breath and the unfamiliar tartness of aftershave.

'You're Brendan Moon. I seen you in the gym. I seen you sparring with our Gordon.'

Words were an unfamiliar currency to Frankie Clough. He'd gone to the slow school. He was holding Brendan by the shoulder as he spoke.

Brendan nodded, his face pale with apprehension.

'Our Gordon says Fr Wynn's going to put you in for the scholarship exam,' Frankie Clough said gravely.

Instinctively, Brendan waited for the retribution. Frankie Clough had boxed at bantam-weight for Fr Wynn's club against Wythenshaw Amateur; he had stolen birds' eggs; he had been drunk; he and Vincent Guppy had been to Borstal. He had once knocked a full-grown man to the floor for calling him stupid. Brendan realized that the stylish jabbing Fr Wynn tutored in the gym wouldn't help him against an opponent so much bigger and stronger. Who knew what special torments Frankie Clough had learned to inflict in his short and chaotic life. Pressed back against the hard stone of the terrace's windowsill, Brendan had felt himself light-headed, disengaged from the realities of the passing street-life around them. Was this a kind of ending? Brendan would recall thinking afterwards, as Frankie Clough leaned casually over him in Abbott Street. Was Frankie Clough some designated instrument of change? Was this the consequence of Brendan's failure to go the full six weeks of Lent, having succumbed to a fifth-week pear drop from Kevin Eatough? He tried to imagine what those tall, blue-eyed saints, or Manchester City's doughty, hard-as-nails full-backs Glynn Pardoe and Toy Book, might have done in such a situation as this, cornered in some dark corridor of the football stadium, leading to the dressing room.

But Frankie Clough said only, 'Our Gordon says you might be going to the grammar school next year.' He said it solemnly, and with astonishment, that in a world centred on Providence Street, such things might be.

Brendan gradually came to realize that other influences must be at play somewhere beyond this tight kingdom. As a curious boy, he worked hard to incorporate them into the tapestry he had created. Thus, he came to calculate for himself that there must be mile-high factories somewhere up on the moors which manufactured the Saturday football results, the changing canvas of daily news items which his father followed, and the production line of new babies. As for what else lay out there, he was unsure, but he knew that he wanted to know. He envisaged himself – just like Odysseus had done in the school library book he had taken out four times in one term – sailing out to deal with high seas and remarkable multi-headed Hydras, partnered in his mind's eye by his father in a ship crewed by square-jawed centre-halves and brave inside-forwards, before returning one night in a squall, bearded and sun-tanned, with the boating lake providing a kind of harbour for his ship. Fr Wynn would be waiting for them with a flask of vegetable soup, standing atop the rain-washed tiles of the roof of St Joseph's, guiding them in with a lantern, with pretty Catherine Yallop standing breathlessly beside him.

How easily it came to him; the business of knowing capitals for countries, the rules for spelling certain words, the voyages of Odysseus and Marco Polo and Alexander and Columbus that he read about. Brendan was astonished at the thought of Alexander the Great having an army that only went forward, like a relentlessly ticking clock, amazed at how it simply went on conquering one new land after another – Syria, Egypt, Persia, Mesopotamia, Samarkand, India – without ever returning to its starting point. *He* was like Alexander – conquering knowledge like lands. One day, Brendan would reach the end and have all the knowledge there was to know, as his father had, as Fr Wynn had, and until then, until he understood everything and could rest easy, his life would be a voyage towards that constant, distant, lighted port.

It was only gradually that his vision of the port diminished. He realized slowly that he wasn't any good at praying. He closed his eyes and spoke the words, and there was no one there. No voice. No guiding light. No connection with anything. Whenever he forced himself to imagine the recipient of his petitions, he realized that God's bearded face was actually that of Fr Wynn, and so he found himself, in his mind, praying to the small red-bricked house three streets away, behind St Joseph's church, beseeching his boxing coach – the parish priest.

In *Lives of Great Men*, borrowed from Salford Library's junior section, Brendan read about Galileo's discovery that the Earth moved around the Sun, and how for his troubles the scientist was found guilty by the Catholic Inquisition of heresy and threatened with torture if he didn't confess that the Earth was still at the centre of the universe.

On the early evening television news, he watched images of Biafra and Belfast and Vietnam, and puzzled over why God didn't spend a little of his time helping the people there instead of lavishing all his days co-ordinating the carefully worked out lives of Providence Street.

He watched the first Pakistani family move into the top end of Providence Street and observed his next-door neighbour Mrs Lynch organizing a petition, demanding that the Council move them out as undesirables. She went up and down the street, persuading people that the family ate dog food and didn't wash, and had a dozen more relatives hidden away in the loft where they roamed the full length of the street's connected attic spaces. Twenty-eight householders, including Brendan's mother, signed the petition. One of the signatories shovelled a dog turd through the letter box of the house. Frankie Clough lobbed a half brick through the living room window one evening after tea. The man who had bought the house came down to see Mrs Lynch. He knocked on the door and asked if he could come in to talk to her about the petition. Brendan and Gordon Clough were sitting on the pavement's edge swapping football cards. Brendan turned and saw Mrs Lynch's face tighten.

'I'm not having a pakkie setting foot inside my house,' he heard Mrs Lynch tell the man in a voice he barely recognized as hers. 'Why don't you and your tribe just clear off back to that mud hut you came from.'

Frankie Clough wasn't the instrument of change; Brendan's father was.

Brendan's father worked in the loan store at the hospital. The store sent out items of equipment needed by patients who were leaving a hospital ward to return home after surgery or some debilitating course of treatment. Brendan pictured the hospital's doctors in their white coats queueing at his father's door with dockets requesting items of his father's equipment; he pictured people taking up the regular shapes of their lives after their hospital treatment thanks to his father's work; it seemed to Brendan to be a *kind* of sainthood.

Each day, his father finished work at four thirty and walked down the hill to the end of Abbott Street. More days than not, Brendan would make his way to meet him there so that the two of them could walk home together, and Brendan, walking alongside him, would carry his dad's rucksack containing the book he'd taken to read in his lunch hour, and the empty flask, and the day's lunch wrapper. The weight of the bag on his shoulder through the three streets to home – Abbott Street, Duckworth Street and Providence Street – depended on the size of the book his father was reading that week. *Animal Farm* he had barely noticed. *Around the World in Eighty Days* had been fairly heavy by the time they reached the end of Providence Street. *The Ragged Trousered Philanthropists* (which had been a hardback) had been terrible to carry and Brendan had been grateful when his father had finished reading it and taken the book back to the library.

As they walked, Brendan would imitate his father's fatigued and splay-footed – and mysteriously grown-up – gait. It was the time they were closest. It was the time his father seemed most free of the formality of his role as parent which made him awkward and blustering. The walk back home was the time his father shared things with Brendan. It was the time his father had told him the only two things Brendan knew about his father's childhood when he had been evacuated to Lancashire from Clapham in London during the Blitz. He told Brendan that he had needed to use a shovel and barrow to scrape up the remains of a cow which had been killed by a stray German bomb falling on the edge of Sturrock's farm where he'd been placed after being evacuated. And once he had talked about the two wartime land girls who had been posted to the farm and who he watched strip down to their waists at the end of the day to wash at the water pump behind the barn – each one taking turns to pump the arm up and down while the other doused her hair and torso and hanging breasts in blue-white water that puddled on the bare earth and would be lapped up afterwards by the dogs – before they dressed and were picked up at the gate by a man in a red car who drove off towards the town.

Once a month, on Saturday mornings, Brendan's father took him into the loan store. The store was a long single-storey warehouse in the grounds of the hospital, with a sluice and a loading bay at the back and an office at the front. There were only ever the two of them there on these Saturdays. Brendan's father explained that only he was allowed to check the monthly inventory of items the store held. While his father was out in the warehouse, Brendan sat on the leather swivel chair in the office, surrounded by all the paperwork and piles of dockets, pretending to be his father in his father's chair, giving out orders on the weekend-dead telephone in the way that his father did each weekday.

The two of them spent the bulk of these Saturday mornings walking around the warehouse together. Brendan carried the clipboard with the inventory sheets fastened to it. His father led him down each aisle, saying out loud the name of the item stored on the stacking shelf and how many were in stock, and Brendan ticked the box on the inventory sheet with a pencil and noted how many there were.

This wasn't always to have been his father's job, Brendan knew. His father had told him how he had been called for trials for Manchester City and Preston as a youth, and then had been signed on schoolboy forms as a full back by Burnley, but he had hurt his knee playing in a Forces match while he was doing his National Service and couldn't tackle after that. Having this office and the work he did there with the hospital doctors seemed a kind of reasonable consolation for the injury in the same way that the Cronshaws were allowed to have their mother win so often on the bingo.

The day the children were sent home from school because

the boiler had broken down overnight was Brendan's tenth birthday. Brendan's mother told him to play outside until after lunch – she had arranged to take Grandad Walter to the doctor for more tests for his bad chest – and Brendan decided to meet his father at the loan store for lunch. He ran from the bottom of the hill, curious to see if he could keep going all the way there without stopping, now that he was ten. There was a chill of sweat in the small of his back by the time he arrived and he was panting. Two secretaries sat at desks in the outer room that connected to his father's office. The plain one was typing. The pretty one with blonde hair and a small, hard mouth had put the cover on her type-writer and was sharing a cigarette with a man who was perched on the edge of the desk. The door between the two offices was open and the blinds were up. A second man sat in his father's swivel chair with his feet up on the desk. It was Vincent Guppy. Brendan stood at the door. He asked what they were doing in his father's office.

'Who, old Stemp?' the one by the window said, ' – he's gone home poorly.'

'No, he means Sluicy Lucy,' Vincent Guppy said from the other office.

'Sluicy Lucy Moon? He has a son?'

'Sure he does. Goes to St Joseph's. You've come to see your dad, have you?'

Brendan nodded.

'And *this* is his office?'

Brendan nodded again.

'He's in the sl—' the one by the window began.

'He's, ah, out on deliveries at the moment,' Vincent Guppy said. 'Come in, sit down. Take your *dad*'s seat. Be about twenty minutes, won't he, Fitzy?' He stood up out of the swivel chair. 'What do you suppose we'd better talk about with the boy, Fitzy, to pass the time while we're waiting?'

'What do you think, Vince?'

'Leave the boy alone, Vince,' the older of the two women, the one who was still working, said.

'I know what,' Vincent Guppy said, ignoring her. 'We could talk to him about his dad, couldn't we? Being as how this is his dad's office. And with his dad bringing those big books of his to read in his lunch break. There'd be plenty to talk about.'

'Vince!' the woman said again. She sounded cross with him.

'Leave off, Moira,' Vincent Guppy said, ' – you're too soft with him.'

Vincent Guppy ushered Brendan through into the manager's office and sat Brendan down in the swivel chair. The other man came in as well. They shut the door. Brendan's stomach felt funny.

The hospital employed a manager, two drivers, two secretaries and a warehouseman in the loan store. Vincent Guppy and the other man were the drivers. Brendan's dad, they explained, was the warehouseman. His job, Vincent Guppy took pains to explain, consisted mainly of washing down the equipment in the sluice with scrubbing brushes and a hose once it had been returned to them. Brendan's dad, Vincent Guppy explained, spent his days scrubbing the hardened shit from the commodes of incontinent spinsters.

How could he have been the manager of the loan store? He couldn't read much beyond his name. It had taken the drivers a good while to work out this fact. After that it had become a game for them. The business of stock-taking had formerly been a task for the drivers, when they weren't out on deliveries or collection, but they had persuaded the loan store manager, Benny Stemp, that it was a job that should really be done by the warehouseman. Then they'd sat back and watched him wrestle in silence with the dilemma, refusing from shame to confess to any of them that he couldn't actually read because he'd spent his evacuated school days bailing hay and shovelling cows' innards for Sturrock the farmer who wanted his money's worth from the evacuee he'd taken in. Finally, he had taken to coming into the loan store on his own on Saturdays to concoct the inventory when no one else was around.

Then there was the business of the books. Brendan's dad took out his book each lunch break and sat on an old wicker chair he'd set up in the corner of the sluice room while the two drivers lolloped around the secretaries' office for the hour, or took the two women to the Stop and Rest for half a bitter and a sandwich. They'd ask him with a smirk what he was reading that week. It was always a week – a book would last Dennis Moon exactly that long. He'd tell them the title, and who it was by. Then they started asking him about the plot, and the characters. What was the hero called, Dennis? What was his mother like in the book, Dennis? How did he meet the girls? He found himself having to make things up to satisfy them, to keep them away from the secret they'd already guessed. The game was the interrogation each day, and the frantic battle he was confronted with to explain the plot developments of books whose titles he knew because he asked at the library but whose words he couldn't read. He told them that *Death in Venice* was a murder mystery about a gondolier who killed his passengers to rob them. *Brighton Rock* was about the people who worked on a seaside pier each summer. What happened to them? Vincent Guppy asked. They organized a show. Why did they organize a show, Dennis? To raise funds because the pier was falling down. What was the show about? Dennis Moon told them. Does anyone fall in love in the book? they asked him. Brendan's dad told them the names of two people who fell in love. Do they have sex in the book? And so it went. Most days, Vincent Guppy and Fitzy were in hysterics. They'd laugh about it in the Stop and Rest. They'd spend their lunch hour planning what to ask him about his book that afternoon when they got back.

In the end it was Moira, the plain secretary, who took pity on him. She started telling him secretly what books to get. They were the same books she herself was reading in her flat at home. She told him what they were about. She told him what happened in the books, and Dennis Moon told Fitzy and Vincent Guppy.

Brendan would come to guess in time that his dad knew something of this episode – of Fitzy and Vincent Guppy telling his son what his actual job was, and how he couldn't read. If he did, though, he never spoke to Brendan about it. Instead, each of them carried the knowledge as a secret beneath the surface of the days and years that followed. The following spring, Grandad Walter died. In the hospital he went glassy-eyed like he'd drunk sherry, then grey and skeletal. Finally he formed into the small shape of a hurt animal under the sheets, his cheeks hollowed out by the absence of his dentures, but in Heaven, Brendan's mother said, he would be his filled-out shape again. They closed the curtains in the house for three days and Brendan couldn't play out.

'I'm sorry Grandad died,' Brendan told Grandma May.

She looked at him as though he'd asked her a question that she didn't know the answer to.

Grandma May moved in with them and they sold her house. The plan was to use the money they made to buy a corner shop business in the neighbourhood – a sweet shop or a hardware store. It occurred to Brendan – from what he had learned from Vincent Guppy – that his father would be anxious to escape the regime of the loan store, but buying a shop seemed to be such a difficult decision to make. Spending money they'd never been used to having seemed to require a leap of imagination too big for them. Every now and then they'd go and inspect premises that had come onto the market, but nothing came of it and his father continued to walk up the hill each day to the loan store, with his lunch wrapped in newspaper and his book for that week, and the money stayed in the bank. In the end – for reasons far beyond Brendan's own small orbit of reasoning – it came to pass that Brendan's dad went to live with Moira, the plain secretary, who somehow contrived within a year to spend all the money. There was a holiday in a hotel in the Isle of Man, and a Morris Minor, and a business they were going to be partners in which sucked out the rest. After that she threw him out and he had to rent a widow's upstairs rooms in a house on Abbott Street because Brendan's mother and his Grandma wouldn't let Dennis back home and, gradually, Brendan became a go-between, learning about the disappointments of the world through the brittle messages his parents passed to each other through him. Then Dennis left unannounced. No one knew he had given a fortnight's notice to the manager of the loan store. His landlady found his week's rent on the table in his room. He wrote to Brendan twice in the next month. Brendan's last contact with him was a card his dad sent him on his sixteenth birthday. It said 'Best Wishes Son', as if the two of them had only yesterday walked home to Providence Street together, talking about Sturrock's cows and Manchester City.

Afterwards, Brendan came to see his childhood as a rehearsal for the business of choreographing a safe kingdom for his own son, avoiding his own father's mistakes, learning from the imperfect past, plotting against the vagaries of the world.

By the time he married Carol, the last vestiges of any religious faith Brendan once held had fallen away. He felt only relief, now that the world made better sense.

'But what would you say,' Carol mused one evening as they were struggling to open their third bottle of wine and Brendan had been coaxed reluctantly into talking about such things, ' – what would you say if you died and you found yourself standing in front of God and he wanted to know why you hadn't believed in him?'

Brendan pondered her question, eyeing her through the tint of the Burgundy in the bottle. 'I would say to him "God, why did you bother to give me a brain to think with and then give me no proof that you were real and no evidence of a plan we were all being guided by?"'

Carol considered his reply. She held her glass out for another refill, then adjusted herself against his shoulder. 'But what if he told you that he was going to send you to Hell because you hadn't worshipped him on Earth?'

Brendan put the bottle down on the carpet in front of him. 'Then I would tell him that he was the kind of God I wanted nothing to do with and I would be glad to go to Hell.'

Jack was born to Carol, vigorous and red-faced, a week

after Brendan's twenty-fifth birthday. He weighed five pounds and seemed to smell of goat's cheese and cried vehemently for the first ten minutes of life. He grew into a coltish boy with a slow, wide smile when it came and a flop of white-blond hair. Each summer his mother's freckles spread across the bridge of his nose and in a sweep across the paleness of his cheeks.

Brendan taught his son to shadow box on the lawn, he encouraged him to value the accrual of knowledge, and to doubt wisely, and he watched his son absorb everything with good grace except his father's pleadings not to support Manchester United. In McDonald's one day, Brendan told him about the prayer he and Kevin Eatough and Gordon Clough used to offer up and they laughed together about it and slurped their milkshakes because Jack's mum wasn't there to scold them for the habit, and they imagined together what kind of life Jack would have when he grew up.

Yet it was a wonder to Brendan all the while Jack's small life slowly unfolded that the boy's sparrow chest was strong enough to pound sufficient oxygen around his body to sustain him. Like any sensible parent he took steps to protect his son. He moved his family out of London to a quiet village in Kent, into a double cottage with a garden, with a village school a hundred yards away and sheep in the field across the road. He was careful in the construction of the tree-house he made for Jack at the end of the garden, making sure that the wood was planed smooth and wouldn't splinter in the boy's hand, and took pains to ensure that the handle to the stepladder climbing to the tree-house was the right height for Jack to grasp as the boy climbed in and out. He took Jack to the swimming pool once a week and taught him to swim a satisfactory breaststroke and an untidy front crawl. That was nevertheless good enough, by the time he was nine, to beat his father when they were on holiday and challenging each other to races with running starts from the lounger on which Carol was arranged, with her holiday thriller resting on her flat stomach while she tanned. Because Brendan understood that some people were lucky with their lives and other people were not.

In such a world, it would always be remarkable to Brendan (and now and then a source of anxiety) that Jack had somehow never forgotten to breathe in his sleep, was never lost to his father through such simple absent-mindedness or some previously undiagnosed irregularity that might have brought the simple rhythm of his heart to a dead stop unnoticed during the night. Sometimes, Brendan would come home after a day spent walking in the ashes of some gutted factory insured by Mercantile Municipal, and he would lie there on his sleeping son's bed, listening for each next indispensable beat of blood from the boy's contracting ventricle in the dark of his room, beseeching Jack's heart to run on in something that fell a little short of prayer but with that same fervour and lack of real comprehension.

Mercantile Municipal was Brendan's third company. For Brendan, it felt part of the unenunciated plan – to earn enough to be able to nurture and protect his family, to keep them all safe together. It was not selfish or complacent but cautious and clear-headed and proof of love. It was with Mercantile Municipal that he made the move into the field of fraud. There was something in the work that suited him – some necessary alliance of intelligence and the stamina required to uncover human duplicity, and the way Brendan had of inviting people to talk to him that came from his being softly spoken and from his ability to handle silence.

There was also something deeper at work. There was a cleanness in laying bare the extent of disorganized and unsatisfactory life. Investigation, he had come to understand, diminished people, but the act of investigation was a cleansing agent. Nothing disturbed Brendan Moon more as he grew into maturity than the ignorance of a well-off man proclaiming that God had reached down and contrived to guide him towards the stocks and shares, the property transactions, the market niche that stoked his comfortable life – as though everyone deserved what they got. Such belief was childish egotism. It was the religion of the playground in which God in a white robe now sat on some tubby oaf's bitumined Rolexa garage roof, worrying for him over his company's market capitalization and his daughter's gymkhana scores while remaining blithely indifferent to a house fire in a damp council flat in Hume, or the slaughter of the Rwanda Tutsis, or Srebrenica.

And so he would occasionally wake at three in the morning and go into Jack's bedroom and see the vulnerability in the boy's face, looking so much like his, the guilelessness, and listen in the hanging silence for his son's breathing, and the thin beat of his heart. And listen, and listen. And then it would be morning.

3

The Difference Engine

The way Harvey Maslow explained it to Brendan in the brothers' minimalist office the size of Fr Wynn's old gymnasium which looked down on the grey Thames, it was like this. Until the nineteenth century, science and religion had, for the most part, been mutually reinforcing. But this established view of the world had gradually been undermined by the advent of new sciences. The church had responded by emphasizing those things that science couldn't account for – the historical evidence of the life of Jesus and the existence, through the ages, of miracles that were not subject to natural law.

In this heady atmosphere of discovery, scientists and their patrons fell into two camps: those who wanted to use new knowledge about the natural world to challenge religious belief, and those who wanted to see the integrity of the church's teachings preserved.

The latter camp included the Duke of Bridgewater whose will gave £8,000 to the Royal Society for the production of works 'On the Power, Wisdom and Goodness of God, as Manifested in the Creation'. Bridgewater's bequest to the Society gave rise most famously to the essay by William

Whewell, which concluded in 1833 that science and religion were simply incompatible and that scientists were automatically disqualified from pondering theology. Others, notably Charles Babbage, were keener to reconcile science with God.

The prickly Babbage, Harvey Maslow told Brendan, would later be revered as the forefather of modern computer science. In 1837, however, Babbage was overlooked when the Royal Society awarded eight academic commissions as a result of Bridgewater's bequest. Upset at this slight, Babbage produced his own unofficial Ninth Bridgewater Treatise which deliberated on the nature of - miracles and led him to the creation of his miracle machine.

Babbage's *difference engine* was a mechanical forerunner of the computer. The machine sought to reconcile the two ideas of rational order and miraculous events. Even before 1837, he had already accounted for the Resurrection, through his version of probability theory by calculating it as a 200,000 million to one event. His machine went one step further.

At his regular dinner parties, Babbage liked to demonstrate his theories to his guests using a scaled-down version of the difference engine which he would himself never manage to build in full. One of the notables at Babbage's dinner parties was a young naturalist named Charles Darwin, recently returned to England from a five-year expedition on the *Beagle*, who attended to witness the prototype of Babbage's difference engine in action. The demonstrations involved the machine throwing out random, miraculous (i.e. highly improbable) numbers in the middle of the lengthy, apparently standard numerical sequences it had been generating. In the same way, Babbage explained to his admiring guests (and in his Bridgewater Treatise), God had also programmed random, inexplicable miracles into our world as a way of nurturing religious faith.

Not every Victorian man of science was as anxious as Babbage to see religion accommodated into the new scientific understanding of the world in this way. Joshua Maslow, for one, was famously disappointed by Babbage's wish to preserve rather than destroy the validity of theological teachings. Maslow, a patron of scientific research and another regular attender of Babbage's London dinner parties, was a self-made man of Jewish extraction. He had fled Russian Lithuania as a boy with his grandmother in the aftermath of a series of pogroms in their town. Such assaults on Jews – led by the local police and actively encouraged by the Russian Orthodox Church – were frequent occurrences in the Jewish Pale region. It was during one such assault on the Jewish community that Joshua Maslow's parents and brother had been murdered.

Maslow had come to establish a business in London based on brokering sugar imports and other commodities. As a man whose family had been decimated because of the bigotry of Christian intolerance, Maslow believed that any chance of undermining the hold that religious faith had on the general populace should be grasped with both hands as a duty to humanity. Anxious to restore a balance in light of the Bridgewater bequest, he finally responded in 1846 by establishing a prize of his own – whose terms were lodged with the Royal Society and published in *The Times* – for any Englishman offering firm evidence of a miraculous phenomenon which none of the modern sciences, given leave to investigate it, could explain or refute. His aim, as church teachings about the natural world fell victim to the breakthroughs in biology, palaeontology and geology, was to mount an assault on the last safe bastion of religious faith – the proof of miracles. The prize consisted of an award equivalent to 10 per cent of the annual operating profit of Maslow's own business (a little less than £4,000 in 1846), to be offered in perpetuity for as long as the company he had founded continued to trade. Until his death in 1871 – the year Darwin published *The Descent of Man*, in which the theory of evolution by natural selection was explicitly linked for the first time to mankind – Joshua Maslow took great delight in pointing out to bishops, politicians and scientists alike that no one had successfully laid claim to the prize.

Not up to 1871. And not since then, either, as J. C. Maslow Ltd expanded into cocoa, molasses, coffee, onto LIFFE – the financial futures exchange – and into the management of commodities funds, with £700 million under its control by the time Brendan Moon was summoned by its two executive directors. There had been a few sporadic submissions over the years, Harvey Maslow explained to Brendan – a few opportunists and cranks in search of Joshua Maslow's elusive crock of gold – but nothing to have worried them unduly.

'Take as a premise,' Louis Maslow said, making his first contribution to the conversation from over by the long window, 'that the company has no intention of paying 10 per cent of £70 million to anyone as a consequence of this facile clause.' He had not looked at Brendan as he spoke but out of the window at the passing river.

'So why am I here?' Brendan asked. 'If you don't want to pay, don't pay.'

'Until now, we were happy to adopt the line which the

family has done since 1871 – to take our chances with any occasional challenges for the money that our founder staked so publicly,' Harvey Maslow said, 'and if necessary threaten to fight the claimant in the courts on the basis of contesting the legal validity of the clause.'

'When it comes to the long slog of litigation,' Louis Maslow said, 'we are not, after all, without resources.'

Louis Maslow was the older of the brothers by two years – swept-back blond hair, fiercely intelligent, physically very slight. Harvey Maslow was the stockier of the two, more businesslike, less cold, more calculating. On the day Brendan was summoned to see them, the two brothers wore charcoal-grey suits which seemed to him to be identical. It was said the Maslow brothers owned a Caribbean island. It was said they were obsessive about their privacy. It was said neither had married. It was said that Louis Maslow always declined to shake hands, that he washed his hands whenever he used the phone or moved rooms, using an anti-bacterial solution the brothers had flown in regularly from a health spa in Berne. Here were people, it occurred to Brendan, bounded by so few defining restrictions, so free of mundane rules, that they had been forced to invent their own.

Until recently, Harvey Maslow said, their approach in relation to the Maslow clause was sufficient to ward off all but the most pig-headed of opportunists. But the arrival of the Americans had changed that.

'Have you heard of Fellowship TV, Mr Moon?'

Brendan shook his head. No matter, Harvey Maslow said. Fellowship TV was a cable television channel making inroads in the UK. It was funded by its American parent company, a Christian fundamentalist organization which had run its own university in South Carolina since 1927 as a safe educational haven for children who might otherwise be corrupted at secular universities, and which had run franchised religious cable stations across America for years. It was Fellowship TV which, having stumbled across the existence of the Maslow clause, had begun to publicize the existence of the prize and to champion certain claims for their own commercial ends. These people, Harvey Maslow explained, had the financial muscle to slug it out in court over the full fifteen rounds. It would be a war of attrition. Of course, he said, J. C. Maslow would pursue that course if they were obliged to, but they felt that a more opportune approach would now be to kill off claims before they resulted in a legal challenge for the money. In other words, do precisely what Joshua Maslow wanted when he set the challenge – ensure that any claims of miraculous phenomena were investigated thoroughly and discredited as efficiently as possible to avoid any threat of litigation. Which was where Brendan Moon came in. They had wanted a fraud specialist. Someone whose assistance they could call on if a claim was made. Someone discreet. Someone they already had knowledge of, who had carried out work for them before. Someone employed by the insurance company which J. C. Maslow themselves had used satisfactorily for more than a hundred years.

'Why me?' Brendan asked. 'There are others in the firm.'

'We have done our research,' Harvey Maslow said. 'We've looked at your record. We've spoken to your employers who have allowed us to make this approach.'

'I took time off work last year. Maybe you want someone more focused.'

'We think we have our man.'

'What makes you so sure?'

Louis Maslow spoke. 'Your son died last year.'

The sentence was dropped casually, or seemingly casually. But then, it had occurred to Brendan, men like this did nothing casually. Nothing in their lives, even down to the eliminating of bacteria, was matter of fact.

'What does that have to do with anything?'

'Nothing,' Harvey Maslow said. 'It has nothing to do with the situation. Except to say that we know something of your time away from work. We know the background to it.'

'What else do you know?' Brendan asked. 'Have you been investigating me?'

'No more than we would do prior to any significant appointment,' Harvey Maslow said.

'Though we have a further question we would like to put to you.' Louis Maslow touched the side of his mouth with a finger, and Brendan saw for the first time across the room that the man was wearing thin cotton gloves.

'So ask.'

'Do you believe in miracles, Mr Moon?' Louis Maslow asked him. It was that same light, game-playing tone.

'Why?'

'It would be useful for us to know where you stood on the matter, given the nature of the task we are discussing.'

'What sort of miracles?'

'Whatever you perceive them to be. It was more our founder's field than ours, you understand. We are merely the executors of his private and particular obsession.'

'Humour me,' Brendan said, 'give me some examples.'

Louis Maslow thought. 'Levitation. Making the lame walk. Raising the dead.'

'I see no evidence of miracles,' he said.

'How do you explain occasional reports of such things?' Harvey Maslow asked.

'Weakness. Wishful thinking. Fraud. Mischief-making. Do I pass the test?'

'No test, Mr Moon, no test. Simply a testing of the waters.'

'One more question,' Louis Maslow said. 'Do you believe in God, Mr Moon?'

'No,' Brendan said.

'You are so definite?'

'I didn't know intelligent men believed in God any more.'

'There is an energy in your answer, Mr Moon. Perhaps there is more to it than that.'

'You mean my son? Is that what you mean? My son was nine when he died. He was alive and then he died. There was no reason for it. There was no purpose in his death. There is no God. It's a story we tell our children to make the unbearable bearable.'

That had been four years ago. Brendan had not spoken to the Maslows since then. From the following month, however, he was paid a subvention by them in addition to the salary he received from Mercantile Municipal. He continued to carry out his role for the insurance company, but every so often he was asked to investigate a case which related to the Maslow clause. He learned how swift and simple it almost always was to uncover the duplicity of public evangelists. He had a nose for the self-deception of the poor in spirit. And now he was in Heslop Bridge where Jason Orr had gunned down nine primary school pupils, and someone somewhere had begun persuading the citizens of a backwater community that the papers wafting about on the breeze in the aftermath of the siege eighteen days before represented the miracle they craved to make sense of their tragedy.

It was dark when Brendan woke. His neck hurt from a draught. The quilt on the bed had been too thin and in the end he'd got up and put a sweater on over the T-shirt he was sleeping in. Then there'd been the noises – doors being opened and closed until well into the night, someone coughing every few minutes beyond the thin wall, the sound of a television playing low somewhere in the building all night, which he couldn't block out to get to sleep. He had tried several days before to book a room in the out-of-town conference hotel on the road to Clitheroe but it was full of media crews camping out in readiness for the remembrance service, and he had to settle for one of the two bed and breakfasts in Heslop Bridge.

At about six o'clock he got up. He switched on the radio and sat in the stand chair by the window, listening to the courteous tones of the morning newsreader on Radio 4. There was mention of the Heslop Bridge service of remembrance three items into the news. He watched the milkman make his morning deliveries down the high street as the day's light ebbed into the sky over the houses. The drizzle patterned the window and dampened the pavements and polished the black tarmac of the road. Eventually, the people of the town of Heslop Bridge, sober-faced, began to walk past his window in ones and twos. But instead of making their daily way to the shops and to the slipper factory, they were making their way early to the church, because the town of Heslop Bridge was closed for the day.

All the seating in the pews of the Holy Souls church had been reserved for the bereaved families and for those who still had children at the school, and for the staff. Outside the church, loudspeakers had been erected. A bank of cameras had been set up beyond the wall of the churchyard. On either side of the path leading to the entrance were ranks of people from the town who did not have reserved seating inside the church. Across the road, beyond the television cameras, more people were gathered in rows that banked back another thirty or forty yards. Some of them had umbrellas up against the drizzle but most simply stood in the soft rain bareheaded. Here and there, as he looked around from his own position in the crowd, Brendan could see people holding hands. There were crash barriers erected both within and outside the church grounds, but there was no jostling for position. People let each other by. Perhaps it was the shock. More likely, Brendan thought, it was the sense that after a hundred generations of anonymity, this was the morning in which Heslop Bridge was at the fore-front of the nation's consciousness. No one after today would ask 'Where is Heslop Bridge?' After this morning, after the Sky news bulletins and the BBC and ITV's tea-time round-ups and Channel 4's *News* at seven and tomorrow's press coverage, everyone would know where the town was, if they didn't know already because of Jason Orr. And the image they would bring to mind forever was this one – of a soft drizzle falling on Heslop Bridge's Holy Souls church, and the townsfolk waiting, hushed, for their public service of remembrance to start.

Brendan had found a spot across the road from the church. From there, he felt close enough to take in the scene but far enough away not to feel he was intruding. Whether Joyce had spotted him there or whether it was coincidence he wasn't sure, but shortly before the service was due to start she manœuvred her bulk in beside him at the barrier. In a rug of a coat that fell to her ankles she seemed even bigger than she had done the previous evening at the garage. As people with places reserved for them inside the church were escorted up the drive, she gave Brendan a murmured commentary on who they were: Karen Cottee from the support group, and her husband Keith in his bleakly unfamiliar and ill-fitting suit; Lewis Chettle's parents holding hands, Kieren Sewell's mother, a small, white-faced woman huddled in a borrowed coat and surrounded by Kieren's remaining family, one of whom, with a half-shaved head, gobbed onto the flower bed on his way into the church; Wilf Wardle, the cricket club groundsman who also maintained the school grounds, whom Brendan watched instinctively deadhead the brown stump of a dying flower as he passed the flower beds on his way into church.

'It's a terrible day,' Joyce said, wrestling her inhaler from one of her many pockets and taking a puff, ' – people'll remember this day forever round here, don't you think, B. Moon?'

There were things, Brendan knew, that they would remember. Small things that would always stay with them. Trivial things they would observe, then disregard – a voice in the crowd, the nine single rings of the Holy Souls church bell, the way one of the two loudspeakers crackled now and then with static, the way the water captured from the night's rain gently lipped over the gutter where it was blocked to one side of the vestry – but which, half a lifetime later, would have stayed with them; small, meaningless pieces of the day unaccountably hoarded in the vaults of memory while the important things ran through their fingers.

There were things that Brendan remembered: the scent of

the year's first cut of grass in the grounds (it had been April); the bluebells in the wooded gardens leading to the crematorium; the wrong shoes he'd worn (Carol had said they were wrong) but not which suit, or any memory of having got dressed; his watch being fast, which made it seem that Jack's funeral had begun at seven minutes past eleven; the way the tops of the trees were so still, coming out afterwards; the warmth of the day following the chill of the crematorium.

And things he didn't remember. Couldn't remember afterwards, no matter how he tried. How many people were there. *Who* was there. A single thing he did in the month that followed. A single solitary thing. He could remember the service had started seven minutes late but not what Jack's favourite ice cream had been. He would lie awake, willing himself to remember until he realized his fists were clenched. Then the gear of memory would slide into place. Mint choc chip. Relief. He must never allow himself to forget again. Mint choc chip. He wrote it down. Carol found it. They quarrelled about why he would write such a thing down. He couldn't explain, not in a way that made sense to her. But he knew he wouldn't forget what flavour any more. Then he forgot what date the funeral was on. What size shoe Jack was. What size shoe Jack would always be. Then his son's face. For half an hour. He was out of the house. He couldn't remember where. But for half an hour he couldn't bring to mind his son's face. Unforgivably. Obscenely. He ran home from wherever he had been. Ran all the way. At home, got an album out. Pored over the photographs. There. There was Jack's shining face, returned to him.

That was the worst day. Of all the days that one was *the* worst, because he saw then how Jack was ebbing away from him, small piece by piece, and how one day soon there would be nothing of him left except the seven minutes, and the bluebells, and the wrong shoes Brendan had worn.

After Jack's funeral, Brendan had taken to sitting in the tree-house at the end of the garden. It became the place where he kept the hardbacked notebook in which Jack had liked to write and which they'd found in his luggage along with the stones they'd collected on the beach the day before he died. The tree-house was where Brendan pinned up the note that said *'mint choc chip'*, and the other notes he wrote as reminders. On that worst day, when he hadn't been able to remember what his son's face looked, the tree-house was the place where he had sought refuge. That was where they found him eventually, twelve hours after Carol had reported him missing to the police, sitting on the wooden floor, surrounded by sixty or seventy photographs of Jack which he'd taken from the family albums and pinned up all around him.

That had been the last straw for Carol. He wasn't the only one with needs, she'd said. He wasn't the only person in this marriage who'd lost a child. Dave McCosker from the college was with her when she found Brendan. Dave – who taught alongside Carol – had been a big help through all of this, she'd said. When they'd found Brendan in the tree-house, he'd had his mobile phone beside him. He'd been ringing numbers from the local Ashford phone book, talking to people. Carol didn't recognize any of the numbers he'd scrawled down before ringing them. He wouldn't say who he'd been talking to or what he'd been talking to them about. He wouldn't go into the house.

The voice of the primary school's headmaster coming through the loudspeakers carried on the swell of silence outside the church. The man spoke about the children who had died in Jason Orr's assault on the school. He remembered Kelly Dyer as a vivacious and outgoing girl – a budding actress. He remembered Jordan Holmes as inventive and articulate and always courteous. He spoke of Luke Swan and Kieren Sewell as being lively and boisterous friends – typical boys who were sometimes in trouble for boyish and ultimately forgivable pranks. He remembered Sam Cottee's cheekiness, and Stacey Greenalgh's smile, and Leanne Kellett's recorder-playing, and placid Lewis Chettle's enthusiasm for looking after the school gerbils during holidays.

Short epitaphs, Brendan thought, as he stood in the quiet Heslop Bridge ranks outside the church while the television cameras whirred. Short epitaphs for full and intricate lives, no matter that those lives had run only eight years. What of the *rest* of them? What of the rest of Sam Cottee and Stacey Greenalgh? What of the rest of Lewis Chettle? Was Lewis Chettle *always* placid? Was he ever peevish, or excitable, or spontaneous? Was he ever resentful that his parents worked long hours in the hardware shop on the high street – the shop where Jason Orr had bought the ingredients with which he had blown up half the school? Was the *only* thing he'd be remembered for the way he volunteered to take care of the class gerbils each term's end? What other aspects were there to Lewis Chettle that would now be lost insidiously as days went by? What made him the remarkable individual that he was? What complex and unique characteristics made it a tragedy that Lewis Chettle's life and Jordan Holmes's life and Sam Cottee's life and Stacey Greenalgh's life had been cut short and would never now be lived out, shaped as they were like partially constructed sentences, left forever unenunciated and incomplete?

He had cried when his son was born. What he remembered mostly was the sheer ordinariness and rhythm of the process – the way the crown of Jack's head slipped into sight, and the small amount of blood, and Carol's pain in bursts and then her tiredness afterwards in the high, hot room in the old hospital.

He remembered Jack starting school and anticipating his first PE lesson, and Brendan forgetting to pack his son's PE kit. He realized as he got to work. All day he was sick with the feeling of betrayal. That night Jack explained that he'd had to sit on the side of the hall while the rest of the class did PE, and Brendan cursed himself.

He remembered the times when Jack reported that his coloured star had been pinned on the teacher's classroom noticeboard as a sign of achievement. It was the most wonderful thing that could ever happen. Each time, the star was allowed to stay on the wall for a whole day. It meant that Mrs Worden loved him best. It meant that on those days Jack was the most deserving.

He remembered Jack explaining about the *Titanic*. How it had struck an ice cube; how people had taken to the deck chairs to be saved.

He remembered how much Jack loved pencils. They could visit nowhere without the need to buy a pencil to add to Jack's collection.

The minister said, 'Sometimes, we look about us and we see only darkness.' Brendan disliked his reedy voice. It hovered between the obsequiousness of a college porter and the ready-reckoning of a bank clerk, tallying up the accounts of his investors. He was wary of the man's claim to his obvious and simple truth.

'Sometimes,' the minister said, 'we can lose sight of God's plan. This is such a time. We are gathered together inside – and outside – the church of the Holy Souls, and everything seems dark. It is as though we have lost our way. It seems that there is only pain. Worst of all, it seems as though we are alone with that pain. What our faith teaches us, however, is that we are not alone. Not even at such a time as this. Especially not at a time such as this.'

Brendan remembered the two of them watching a holiday programme together soon after Jack had started at primary school. Jack liked seeing all those faraway places. He liked deciding where he and Leanne (a girl in his class) might go when they were married. He worried out loud about how they'd get to the airport for the flight because he wouldn't have a car. Brendan said he could drive them. Jack said no, he couldn't. Brendan asked why not. Jack said because Brendan would be dead by then. Then he burst into tears. I don't want to die, he had said. Brendan said it was all right – he wouldn't be dead. Eventually, Jack was persuaded. So will you take me to the airport with Leanne? Brendan said yes, he'd take him. They had snuggled up together. They had watched Minorca, and Dublin, and snowboarding in Colorado.

'It is not always for us to be able to see God's purpose at every turn,' the minister said, 'but be assured that he is there. He remains in control. He continues to see things through to His own divine ends. Although those curious and perplexing parchments which have exercised us all have provided some comfort to our community, their origin, in a way, is immaterial. It is our overwhelming faith in God which is the ultimate comfort to the members of His Church on Earth. However tragic it is for us to lose a little one, be assured that, in the end, we will be allowed to see God's purpose in cutting short these young lives. Be assured that all of us will be together again, reunited in eternal bliss in the Kingdom of Heaven.'

He was under the water when Jack fell. He was under the water when the parapet gave way and Jack fell. What he had wanted to know was whether Jack was still alive when his body finally hit the ground. He was under the water, and when he rose from the blue silence of the water and looked up at the azure blue of the sky, Jack wasn't there, and people were screaming because the masonry had given way and the English boy had fallen from the high hotel balcony onto the concrete patio below.

Brendan felt a touch on his arm.
'It's you, isn't it?' Joyce said, still beside him at the barrier.
'Sorry?'
'That's why you're here,' she said.
'What is?'
'The parchments. You've come to check that they're genuine. They said at the support group that someone was going to come from an insurance company.'
He looked away from her. He noticed that people were folding up their umbrellas. Joyce took his arm with her large white paw of a hand and squeezed it. 'It's you that's going to be able to say for sure that it was a miracle,' she said.

'God bless you, B. Moon. God bless you for what you're going to do for these people.'

It had stopped drizzling. The sky over the town was lighter.

There was a meeting of the support group that evening at the Heslop Bridge Cricket Club. The group had been set up in the aftermath of the tragedy. Some of the people who had started attending had lost children, or had children who attended the school. Two of the school's teachers came. Others, like Joyce McCready, were simply friends or neighbours of the bereaved.

They had appointed Karen Cottee as chairman. She had been hesitant and stumbling at first. She had thanked people for nominating her. She had apologized for how much harder it felt to chair this group than to run the playgroup she was involved with in the town. People had smiled. She had spoken at first about the daughter she and Keith had lost, and then about the bereavement suffered by other people around the room. Then she had written out 'WHAT WE WANT' on the flip chart one of the teachers had brought from the school, and asked people to say what they wanted from the group.

Jordan Holmes's father had been angry at the school. He felt that the security had been too lax if just *anybody* could walk in off the street. He wanted the support group to consider forcing the school to organize better security, or even taking the school to court for failing to provide adequate care of the children. Kelly Dyer's father wondered what good it was to think about security now? Luke Swan's mother said it was Jason Orr they should take to court, once his criminal trial was over, to make *him*, not the school, pay compensation. Karen Cottee pointed out that this might not achieve much since they all knew that Jason

Orr had no money. There had been one or two shrugs of resignation.

Stacey Greenalgh's father said he just wanted his daughter back. People knew Gary Greenalgh hadn't returned to work at the slipper factory since the shooting. People knew the doctor had prescribed him tranquillizers. Was it too much to ask, Gary Greenalgh said, that he should have his daughter back? Could somebody explain, he said, *why* it was too much to ask? Leanne Kellett's mother, sitting next to him at that first meeting, had put her hand on his shoulder for a moment. Mrs Kellett herself said she wanted to be able to sleep a little again. Karen Cottee asked what they could do to help with that. Mrs Kellett said she just wanted to be able to talk to people about Leanne without feeling as though she was embarrassing them. Even her husband, she said, wouldn't talk any more about Leanne, and whenever she tried to sleep she lay thinking about her daughter and wanting to talk about her. If she could talk openly about Leanne somewhere, she said, maybe she would be able to sleep a little. There had been a murmur of agreement around the room. Standing at the flip chart, Karen Cottee had written, '1. Talk About The Children.'

Lewis Chettle's mother said she didn't want Lewis to have died in vain. She said she was glad about the parchments, even though it couldn't bring Lewis back, because it helped her to understand there was a purpose to what had happened. She said this was something that would help to keep the memory of the children alive. Karen Cottee had written down, '2. Acknowledgement of the miracle.'

The few meetings so far had divided evenly into two parts. During the first hour, people talked about the children and about what they felt in the aftermath of the tragedy while the others in the room listened. Of those who spoke, some talked and talked while others had to squeeze small words out from somewhere in the pit of their stomachs or the high, tight cages of their chests, and those listening held their breaths to see if the effort would break their comrade. Sometimes people cried. Sometimes one member of the group held or nursed another one.

It had occurred to Joyce McCready that she had found out more in a few evenings about the people who sat with her in the clubhouse than in the lifetime she had shared with them in Heslop Bridge, and she knew there were things they had said that she would never repeat beyond the confessional of the support group. Her horoscope had prepared her for it. 'Despite your concerns and misgivings,' it had said, 'despite conflict and disorganization, you will be part of a process of reconciliation. It will require perseverance on your part, but impressive results are within your grasp.'

During the half-time break at the meetings, it had naturally fallen to Joyce to brew the tea, and people helped themselves to the buns or biscuits she had baked. After the interval, they dealt with issues that the group needed to take decisions about. It was in this part of the proceedings that they had decided to commission a service of remembrance for the whole community to attend, and to ask their MP why Jason Orr had been able to get hold of a gun so easily despite the law on guns, and to discuss setting up a sitting service to take care of bereaved families' surviving children for an occasional hour or two as respite. They had also discussed the approach they had received from an organization called Fellowship TV, asking permission for its representative to address the support group and offering to assist the group in their efforts to have the authenticity of the parchments somehow recognized.

From his position on the back row of the chairs shaped into a semi-circle, Brendan had watched Joyce organizing the tea whilst people discussed the details of the remembrance service earlier in the day and, when the queue had died down, had gone to speak to her. Now he watched as Karen Cottee introduced Madeline Geller to the meeting. Madeline Geller had a girl's figure and pale skin, and long red hair that fell in waves down the back of her sober suit.

'It must kill her, poor thing, to stay looking like that,' Joyce had confided to Brendan as they had observed her during the interval, without a trace of envy in her voice. 'No good for survival in eskimo weather.'

'My name is Madeline Geller,' the speaker said. 'I work for an organization called Fellowship TV.' She had an American accent with a southern drawl. 'I want to thank you for letting me be with you today.' Her big, dark eyes looked all about her. She spoke serenely. She smiled fleetingly.

'God decides,' Madeline Geller went on, 'how and when He reveals Himself and His purpose. What we know from history is that He does not always do it to the highest and mightiest. Our Lord, after all, was born in a stable in a poor country far from the centre of power and influence. And when he has chosen to reveal himself, that has often been to ordinary people.'

She opened a leather folder. Inside was one of the parchments. She held it up for the audience to see. The ceiling lights in the clubhouse illuminated it so that the dense Hebrew lettering could be seen through the back of the manuscript. 'Now, it seems a possibility that He has opened his heart to Heslop Bridge over the loss of its children. It seems as though God may have chosen your tragedy to speak to us.

'You all know, of course, that a number of these parchments were witnessed falling onto the school. You also know that, in the days which have followed, more of them have been gifted to families who were bereaved in the assault. What you might not know is that a further parchment, inscribed in similar fashion, was discovered in the church this morning. It was found beneath the altar stone some time before the remembrance service began.

'There are some things that we all know about them already, simply from their translations and from what has been written about them in the newspapers. We know that the language on each of the parchments is Hebrew. We know that each of the parchments has a different inscription on it – each one a short philosophical meditation of startling beauty and simplicity. It seems likely that the parchments form a connected series of verses. Each one seems separate, but together they make a complete whole. Perhaps the most ready comparison for me to make would be to compare these meditations with the Old Testament Psalms.'

Seven minutes. The bluebells. The wrong shoes. The funeral of his son. The end of his son. The phone calls made to strangers in the dead of night that he continued to make for six months after Jack's death.

Each afternoon on the holiday, Jack had taken a siesta back at the apartment. Some days, Brendan would glance up from his lounger and see Jack high up, standing on the balcony, having woken from his sleep. He would wave and Jack would wave and smile, and drift back into the apartment. Sometimes Brendan would swim slow lengths of the quiet pool while Jack was up in the apartment sleeping. Sometimes Brendan would dive into the blue water of the pool beneath the blue of the sky and when he rose from the water Jack would be there, looking down, hands resting on the parapet of their balcony. It became a game during the course of the holiday. Brendan would dive, and the world would be blanked out for the three or four seconds of the dive while he was under the water, and then he would rise and Jack would be there, silhouetted against the orange-pink wall of the hotel, beneath that azure blue sky.

'I would go as far as to say this,' Madeline Geller said in her sad, sweet, lilting drawl. 'These parchments seem designed, in the way that they are written, to respond to the pain that we all know is being felt in the aftermath of Heslop Bridge's tragedy. They seem to speak directly to you – and through you to others – as you struggle to comprehend what has befallen you – as you ask yourselves *Why*?

'I believe these parchments assure us that God remains amongst us,' she said. 'These parchments seem to speak words from Our Lord that are more direct and personal than anything He has chosen to communicate to us since He sent His only son to live amongst us, and to die amongst us, two thousand years ago. It is this which persuaded Fellowship TV to contact your support group. It is this which has persuaded us to agree to champion your cause. Since there are sceptics and doubters outside your community who are happy to dismiss or to denigrate what has happened, we feel that somebody should stand side by side with you in your struggle. This is what has persuaded Fellowship TV to work, on your behalf, to get the parchments authenticated in the eyes of the world.'

She paused, and several people in the room applauded. Others joined in, slowly at first, and then with swelling certainty. Madeline Geller waited until the room quietened again. 'There is one further thing we know, of course, about these parchments,' she said, ' – one further thing that reaffirms our faith in the Christian vision, that drives us on in our shared hope of creating a fitting memorial for your children by having the events of the past few weeks recognized by a doubting world for what we know them to be. It is the title of this series of parchments. Each one, as we know, has its title scrawled faintly but decipherably in the top corner. The title, as you are all aware by now, translates from the Hebrew as *Letters from God*.'

In the week following his meeting with Harvey and Louis Maslow, Brendan had gone to the Science Museum in Kensington. He had concluded in his mind that the story Harvey Maslow had told him was just that – a story. He felt certain that Charles Babbage was fictitious. He was sure that even if Babbage *had* existed, then the story of his difference engine was surely bogus; that the Science Museum in London would contain no such exhibit when Brendan went; that the founder of J. C. Maslow, the brothers' Victorian predecessor, had been involved in no such scientific patronage, had offered no such prize, had made no such provision in his will and in the company papers. These men were rich enough, and disconnected enough from the world as Brendan understood it, to find amusement in toying with anyone they saw fit. Louis Maslow's questions had at least convinced him of that.

He was wrong. He found Babbage's device just as Harvey Maslow had told him he would, constructed by the museum authorities to mark the bicentenary in 1991 of Babbage's birth.

After that, Brendan returned every so often if he had an hour to spare. The spent cathedral air of the museum served as a kind of balm. He had always liked museums. As a man who made a living digging at things that were hidden or obscured, he liked their probity. Sometimes he would nose around in other galleries, but mostly he was drawn directly to the difference engine. He would stand in front of the complex steel contraption the size of a large closet, made up of cogs and vertical rods, which had been built to Charles Babbage's exacting design – too exacting for its construction to have been possible in Babbage's own lifetime. Brendan liked to take the handle and turn it gently in a single revolution. He liked to feel the weight of the gearing and the tension of the cogs as their teeth rotated the steel arms of Babbage's machine. He liked to watch the cogs engage and the arms turn as he moved the handle through another revolution, and another. He liked to hear the click of the number change on the wheel at the bottom of the machine after each full revolution. He liked to watch for the number rising sequentially by two each time as it computed its mechanical calculation, and to imagine generating that single intuitive, random and miraculous discontinuity that he understood the machine was capable of, because that was how it had been programmed. But whenever Brendan turned the handle, the numbers on the bottom wheel only ever rose incrementally, stubbornly, by another two.

*

He waited for the phone to be answered. It was dark and he was cold. He was sitting with his legs pressed up to his chest, still wearing the coat in which he'd driven back down south after the support group meeting in Heslop Bridge had concluded. He'd had to peer myopically at the Ashford phone book and then at the digits on the mobile in order to dial the number. He shivered. The number rang and rang. Finally someone picked it up.

'Hello?' Brendan said.

'Hello. Who is that please?' It was a woman's voice, an old voice.

'I was wondering if there was somebody there called Marmaduke,' Brendan said. 'I need to speak to him.'

'I'm sorry, there isn't. Are you sure you have the right number?'

'I thought I had,' Brendan said. 'I'm sorry. I didn't wake you, did I?'

'No, you didn't. I don't sleep much any more.'

'You don't?'

'Not at my age A little during the day. Cat naps, my mother would have called them.'

'You're retired now, then?'

'Oh, long since. I was an infant school teacher. Forty-two years. They call them reception classes now, you know.'

'Is that right? I'm sorry, I don't know your name.'

'My name? Connie. I'm Connie. Yes, yes, live alone. Never married. I like my own company. I like my own routines. At eighty you get rather stuck in them, I'm afraid.'

'I know what you mean about routines.'

'Do you, dear?'

'I'm keeping you up, Connie.'

'No, not at all. I'm grateful to hear the sound of another

voice. Nobody rings me up any more, I'm afraid. There's only me and the cat. That's all. And the radio.'

'You listen to the radio at night?'

'Radio 4, dear. Then the World Service. Whatever I can find to keep me company. The house is far too big for me, of course. All right when I had friends around. When I could get about more – when the arthritis wasn't so bad. Too big for one. It was the old rectory, you know. My father's. He bought it. Now it's mine. Too big, though. I have a little help to clean it on Tuesdays and Thursdays. Apart from that, it's just me and Bagpuss.'

'Bagpuss is your cat?'

'Yes, my cat. Just the two of us here. What is it that *you* do, dear?'

'Me?' Brendan said. 'I'm an engineer.'

'An engineer!'

'I help to build bridges,' Brendan said. 'In the Middle East. It's contract work. I travel a lot. My name is Sam Shepherd.'

'Hello, Sam Shepherd,' she said. 'I wonder why it was that you needed to speak to your Marmaduke. Such an old-fashioned name.'

'I'm trying to find someone,' Brendan said.

'Who, dear?'

'I think Marmaduke and the others might know where he is,' Brendan said.

They talked. He didn't mention the remembrance service earlier in the day. He didn't say anything about Heslop Bridge, or the fact that he had driven south on the motorway for the last four hours and was sluggish with fatigue. Brendan Moon – who understood that the anguished and gullible people of Heslop Bridge had been taken in by some sly charlatan, and who would now set about the task of proving that the Heslop Bridge parchments were fakes – didn't say that he had not resorted to such random phone calls for almost three years, or that he was sitting in his coat in a child's tree-house, or that everywhere on the walls surrounding him were photographs of his son.

4

Jack's Book

The motion of waking found Brendan scurrying to catch up with his soul. He went on such remarkable journeys asleep. It was a nightly exodus in which, it sometimes seemed, he went scavenging over all the darkened rooftops of the world. At some point in his dreams, something always fell. He was never sure what – only that his heart reared at its dullish drop.

He had read somewhere about the necessary nocturnal twenty miles travelled by the fox. It was a phrase that seemed to catch some sense of the compulsion of his dreamed voyaging. Afterwards, he would wake confused, like a man climbing from a crashed car, relieved and shaken, in sheets that were damp with sweat and wrestled into rope. For that one slurred moment he had no sense of self at all. For one moment, paroled by forgetfulness, he was part of some general, larger motion, some sweet migratory flock of souls, until remembering jolted him back into his own fixed position in the world.

He had been back in Heslop Bridge for a week. He was booked into the hotel just outside the town on the Clitheroe road, which had been too full to accommodate him three weeks ago on the night before the memorial service. His initial reservation there was for a fortnight. In accordance with the routine he had settled into, he pulled on faded grey jogging pants and a T-shirt, and laced up his trainers. In the lobby, still wreathed in sleep, he wandered past the 7 a.m. shift change going on at the check-in desk. Outside on the gravel drive, he walked half a dozen steps in air made cool and damp by the dawn. He reached the first of the tended flower beds by the long lawn and started to run.

He ran two miles. He liked to run before breakfast whenever he could. It made him feel less prone to that anxious work-day tightening of the chest. He ran out as far as the bypass and back to the hotel. He arrived back for his shower, his heart pounding with exertion, his mind – as it did each morning now – preoccupied with formulating explanations for the parchments.

The regular table he had been given for meals in the hotel overlooked the rear gardens. Eating his breakfast, Brendan watched one of the hotel's uniformed cleaners appear from a side door and walk slowly down the gravel path. He recognized her as Kieren Sewell's mother. She stood quite still on the edge of the hotel lawn, arms crossed. Her face was small and tight and expressionless. She looked straight ahead, past the garden, to the fields beyond the hotel's ranch-style boundary fence. She hadn't wanted to speak to him about the tragedy when he had approached her, and so he had left her alone. He imagined that Kieren Sewell's mother, like the others, would think of her suffering as special; he imagined that she would have an explanation for him as to why she deserved a miracle for her particular loss.

The hotel itself was still busy with media people, but they were mostly specialist reporters from magazines, periodicals, the foreign press. These were people who came for one or two days and then left to write 2,000 words, increasingly sceptical in the tone they used, all the while pretending to know intimately the Heslop Bridge community they wrote about back at their desks. Sometimes these articles got the names of local people wrong. Sometimes the writers made details up.

The first wave of tabloid hacks had left the hotel a fortnight ago. A number of them were now in pursuit of a Premiership football manager, who was alleged to be hiding out somewhere in North Wales after the fifteen-year-old sister of a former reserve team player at the club (now released) had professed her love for him. Her current boyfriend had passed on a home video and two rolls of film (taken when she was fourteen) to one of the tabloids as proof of his love. The feeling among the hacks was that they had *done* Heslop Bridge. The content of the manuscripts, in the end, had disappointed them. The newspapermen had hoped they might have contained more explicit instruction. They had hoped to be able to report on clear-cut solutions to the ills of the world – a world which surely needed solutions after going so badly wrong in Heslop Bridge. They had anticipated some latterday Ten Commandments setting out how to put things right. *That* would have been good copy. *That* would have persuaded them that maybe the parchments were worth pursuing further. The manuscripts themselves had been good copy for a few days, but without further revelations, without visions or cures or more letters from God appearing with more definitive instructions to the world, they lacked the narrative drive that was needed to maintain the increase in circulation which Heslop Bridge had given their editors for the last month. But there were no such events, and the number of parchments remained eighteen and there were no headlining edicts from the translated verses and so the media, resorting increasingly to tones of knowing incredulity, had started to drift away.

Brendan's laptop was open in front of him on the breakfast table. He worked sporadically on his notes while he ate: he was drafting elements of his report for the Maslows. He asked for fresh tea while he tried to establish in his own mind whether someone could have acted in concert with Jason Orr to plot the hoax. The first parchments to have appeared were the ones which had descended onto the school in the immediate aftermath of the explosion. Brendan could see how Jason Orr might have been responsible for these. He could have planted them somewhere in the school and, instead of being uncovered later by the rescue services as he had perhaps intended, they had been sent spiralling skywards above the school by the explosion. He struggled to accept, however, that Jason Orr was capable of composing the verses on the parchments, let alone translating them into some obscure foreign language. He had spent some time tracking down the man's school reports and his former English teacher. Jason Orr, it turned out, had been an anonymous student, with no close friends. He had been no better than average academically, and had struggled for a small clutch of unspectacular GCSEs. His English was a Grade D pass; he had failed French; he had shown no affinity for any other language.

Brendan also had difficulty in accounting for the way that the parchments continued to be uncovered around the town for several days after Jason Orr's arrest and detention for questioning at the central police station in Accrington. That was why he had begun to believe that the deceit could not have been perpetrated by Jason Orr alone. He had made little progress, though, in establishing who that second person might be, except for discovering that, with only one exception, everybody's movements within the school in the immediate aftermath of Jason Orr's arrival could be confirmed.

Brendan had spoken to the Heslop Bridge desk sergeant and been given information on who was in the school at the time. Of those, he had met with the headmaster and several of the primary school's teaching staff. In addition, he had spoken to the caretaker (who worked a split shift and had left the site half an hour before Jason Orr had arrived). What had become clear was that, at the time of Jason Orr's arrival, most people within the school were either gathered with the children in the assembly hall or were in the school's office. No one, with the exception of a man with profound learning disabilities who helped the school gardener with some of the landscaping chores at the school was alone in the school at any point during the siege, and he had fled the grounds in terror as a result of the explosion.

By nine-thirty, Brendan was the last guest left in the dining room. When he finally shut his laptop and stood up to leave, all the other tables had been cleared and freshly laid. There were two messages for him on his mobile. One was confirmation that the officer-in-charge was available to see him at the hostel where Brendan understood the handicapped man was housed. The second was a call from Cambridge, confirming that the results of the forensic report on the parchment which Karen Cottee had lent to Brendan for the purpose of examination would be completed that morning and sent through to him. There was a further message for him at reception, from Madeline Geller, asking Brendan if they could meet that evening.

*

The officer-in-charge of the Atlas Street hostel was a pallid man in a knitted cardigan. His shoes were scuffed. He polished his glass with the ribbed edge of the cardigan while he complained to Brendan about the paperwork he was expected to get through.

'Investors in People, Best Value, Risk Management, Business Plans, Service Objectives.' He spat out the phrases.

'You find it difficult?' Brendan asked.

'There's no recognition for it,' the man said. 'The problem with me is that I'm not a yes man, and they don't like that.'

'How long have you worked for social services?' Brendan asked him.

'Eighteen years,' the man said. 'From the early days of resettlement. These days, I put in applications for promotion to senior management just to wind them up. I know it won't get me anywhere. It's a joke. A bloody joke.'

'Resettlement?' Brendan asked.

'From Calderhall and the like – for those released back into the community.'

'What is Calderhall?'

'A hospital colony, set up under the Mental Deficiency Act. That's where Oscar Brigg came to us from. Calderhall is five miles from here. Most of those coming out had no family to return to, they'd been in so long, and they were settled around here. Hence the extra resettlement grant from the government to help the local authority cope – not that you'd know it from the resources we're actually given to run the services. Oscar Brigg was one of those moved out under the resettlement programme.'

'This . . . man, he lives here in the hostel?' Brendan enquired.

'With five other men. Six clients for us to manage. And for

the last eighteen months I've been two members of staff
down and with the budget for only one replacement casual
who won't do sleep-overs. I'm sick to the back teeth of complaining about it, but nothing gets done. I have bits of kids
half my age managing me from County Hall who are too
busy with business planning seminars to come out and see
me.'

'This Oscar, he helps someone with gardening chores?'

'A man called Wilf Wardle employs him. He's an example
of what I was saying. It took weeks to get the benefits side of
things sorted so that he could go out to work. Yet the department still refuse to let me go back to full staffing. I mean,
how are you supposed to go and speak to Welfare Rights or
some bureaucrat at the Benefits Agency *and* be available to
answer the phone here at the same time? Answer me that?
You can't, can you? No, nor can they, but do they *do* anything about it?'

'What's wrong with him?' Brendan asked.

'How do you mean?'

'I mean, why is he here? What was he locked up for?'

'He has a learning disability.'

'What does that mean exactly?'

'Learning disability is the term that's used now instead of
mental handicap.'

'He got locked away for that?'

'Yup. I don't suppose he saw the outside world until he
was in his late forties.'

'Can he read?' Brendan asked.

'No.'

'He can't read or write?'

The man shook his head.

'What, not at all?'

'No.'

'What else can't he do then?'

'He can't tell the time. He couldn't catch a bus on his own. He can't count money – he has no understanding of money. He couldn't cook for himself, or shop, or communicate very much at all.'

'And you're sure he can't read?'

'Oscar Brigg has lived here since he was let out of Calderhall. Until a couple of years ago, he didn't even use language. Apparently now he says a couple of words to this man who employs him, but even then it's only names, not sentences or anything. I've never heard him speak myself. He lives very much in a world of his own. He's an odd fish. I've never really taken to him myself.'

'Is there a file on him?'

'We keep some basic information here on our people. The main file was apparently missing from the archive at Calderhall when he was released. That's what they told me. It happened a lot during the upheaval of the resettlement process.'

'Could I look at the file you keep here?'

The man smiled, happy to be in a position to thwart Brendan's enquiries. 'Outside of the department, only family would be allowed to look at it.'

'Family?'

'No one's ever been in contact with him here,' the man said. 'I don't suppose he has any.'

'So what do you know about him? About his past? As a person?'

'We know he's in his fifties. We know he was admitted to the paediatric unit at Calderhall in 1955, when he'd have been nine or ten, then transferred to an adult block later on, and that he came out in 1987. Three years ago, one of the staff here got him a job.'

'Is that it?'

'Pretty much. It's not much of a biography, is it? Why is it that he interests you so much, anyway?'

'Like I said on the phone, it's to do with the tragedy at the school. With the insurance.'

'So what's the connection with our man?'

'The connection is that he seems to have been the only adult present in the school during the siege who was alone at any time in the building.'

'You thought our Oscar Brigg might have been implicated?'

'I just wanted a sense of what he could and couldn't have done during that time. It's about covering all the angles.'

'Well, I'm sorry to disappoint you. I think with our Oscar Brigg, what you see is what you get.'

'I hope you get your staffing sorted out eventually,' Brendan said at the door when the meeting finally concluded.

The man sighed bleakly. 'I'll expect it when Hell freezes over.'

The length of the room in the hotel was eight paces from the door to the window on the far side. Brendan knew the paced measurements of his quarters by heart now – as he moved about the edges of the space in a familiar effort to settle. He would stand at the door to his room looking about him, then drift slowly around the space, passing through to the bathroom, re-emerging, looking out of the window or into space, moving back inside the room, always standing, even after he had taken his coat off, even after he had put the kettle on and made a cup of tea. Sometimes he would run the taps, or feel the need to try the lights, even though it might be the middle of the day. Sometimes he would make a noise in the silence – tapping his fingernail on a glass lampshade, or touching the surface of a wall mirror with a drinking glass – and stand there, listening to the sound ripple out and fade. He would drink his tea standing at the edge of the room looking in.

It was a single man's observance. He did the same thing back at the house. He had done it for as long as Carol had been gone. It hadn't mattered that the house was the one that the two of them had bought together – bought in anticipation of things ahead, when Jack was three. Ever since Carol had left, rescued from Brendan's grief by Dave McCosker from the college, Brendan had been cast adrift in the house. It was no longer a sanctuary. There was no sanctuary any more. At home – as in the hotel – Brendan walked the rooms over and over before he could bring himself, for some short period, to settle into a temporary truce with his surroundings. He knew lesser people fell apart under that kind of pressure. He believed he was strong enough to tough it out. He believed that, eventually, it would pass.

The chambermaid had made his bed and straightened the duvet. Everything else was where he had left it. A street map of Heslop Bridge, unfolded on the table, was marked with blue inked circles showing the locations where the various parchments had been found – the seven at the school and the remainder around the town. The relevance of each location, where Brendan could identify one, was noted in the margin of the map, though with some he had not yet been able to identify a possible connection. Next to the map on the table there were keepsakes which Brendan had brought with him: two photographs, a small mascot-sized teddy bear, a notebook with the words 'Jack's Book' printed diligently on the cover over the top of a picture of a fat and smiling ginger cat. There were lists on sheets of paper left on one of the chairs, of those who had died in the school, and of those present in the school on the morning Jason Orr had walked through the gates. There were two piles of interview transcripts on the dressing table. There were lists of telephone calls he had made with notes in the margins. Some of the calls related to Jason Orr's shootings, some were more personal. There was a reference in one marginal note to the old lady he had spoken to on the evening after the remembrance service. *Kindergarten*, Brendan had written, *Bagpuss*, *rectory*. Brendan picked up the hardback notebook from the table where it lay and flicked through the pages. There was a child's spidery writing throughout the first half of the book, then the dense script of an adult hand took over. Several pages at the end of the notebook were blank. He examined the blank pages at the end of the book for a while, then he put the book down and picked up the forensic report he had printed off.

He sat by the window sipping a beer he had taken from the minibar as he read through the details. The report told him what he wanted to know, confirming what the police had said about the parchments. The paper, despite having yellowed with age, was not ancient. It was less than fifty years old. It was certainly not the vellum of biblical days – the shaved and scraped calfskin on which, for example, the Dead Sea Scrolls had survived for 2,000 years – and which some of the tabloid headlines had made comparisons with in screaming headlines on the first day of press coverage. The meditations were in Hebrew, but the ink which had been used to write out the verse was also 'consistent with modern chemical compositions of writing inks'.

Brendan put the document down and finished his beer. He began mentally to run through draft versions of the summary of the report he would submit to the Maslow brothers. Soon he would return south, navigate the M25, and drive back to Kent. He would wander the rooms of his own empty house. He would finish his report. He would confirm to the Maslows that their money was safe. He would be back in the office, overseeing the investigation into some case of industrial arson in a lock-up in Catford or Woolwich. And so it would go on. He would return to it because that was the routine that kept him going. Like a shark needing to keep moving forward in the water or it would die, he needed the routine of the work that he did because, if he stopped, something bad would happen again; because it was hard to know the difference between him and it. Something bad would happen. It was hard to know what, but he knew and he lived in its shadow.

He sat on the floor at the edge of the room, his back pressed to the doorframe of the bathroom. In his lap was the stiff-backed notebook with the picture of the ginger cat on the front. The cat's name was Marmaduke. Brendan knew because Jack had told him. This had been Jack's book, containing Jack's story. Jack had added to it diligently each day in the months before he died and had even taken the notebook to Corfu and added to it there as well.

'What is it?' Brendan had asked him.

'It's a story, Dad.'

'What about?'

'About a boy called Jack,' he had smiled, bashful, proud, 'and he lives in a flat above a pizza shop and he has a cat called Marmaduke, and a stuffed rabbit and a bear who've never been outside the flat, and two mice in a cage who squabble about whose turn it is next on their running wheel.'

'Who runs the pizza shop?' Brendan had asked.

Jack had thought. 'Joe Salt. People ring him up with their orders, and Joe Salt has a van that he delivers them in.'

'And what happens in the story?'

'Well, the cat and the stuffed animals who belong to the boy, they all decide to go searching for him when the boy doesn't come back to the flat one day. They don't know where he is because he's forgotten to tell them where he's gone. So they get Joe Salt to help them look for them. They ring people up on Joe Salt's phone to ask if anyone knows where he might have gone. But he's just forgotten to leave them a note to tell them where he's gone. That's all. They go looking for Jack because he's forgotten to leave them a message. At the end of the story, they'll find him, but they haven't done yet.'

To Carol it was unimportant – just a boy's teasing scribbles, just nonsense amid the wider business of getting on with life. But to Brendan, the highlight of each evening was asking Jack what he had added to the story that day in the book that he kept under his bed bedecked with its Manchester United duvet cover. Maybe, Brendan had suggested to his son, he could be a writer when he grew up. Nah, Jack had said – a footballer, playing wide on the right whipping crosses into the box like David Beckham, or poaching goals like Dwight Yorke. But still Jack continued to add a little to his story each day, and to read it to his father at bed-time each night, working his way through the story one page at a time. But it wasn't complete. And now, it seemed, it was Brendan's task to finish it, to find out how

Jack's story ended. To find Jack. He couldn't explain it. It didn't make sense, and yet he did it. There was no why; there was only a how. Whenever he found himself alone in the months after Jack's death, he would take out the book and read through Jack's story and make phone calls in the night to complete strangers and make notes of who they were and what they said and use it to continue the story that his son had begun, because the important thing was to finish the story and to find Jack. As he added to the story page by page, he felt he was keeping the book alive, following a trail that he supposed might be there to be followed, leading to a truth, revealed, that Jack had merely forgotten to leave a note saying where it was that he had gone, working towards that moment which might occur any day, when Brendan would walk into a room and Jack would be there, smiling sheepishly at him, enquiring about the possibility of a Big Mac and fries, as if to prove that what had gone before had been nothing more than a misunderstanding, an error of sequencing, and that all along he had been alive and well and only temporarily misplaced.

He had seen Madeline Geller several times in the week he had been at the hotel. Usually, she was making her way to or from the fitness suite in baggy jogging bottoms, Lycra top showing a tanned, flat stomach, hair tousled, a white towel draped around her shoulders. He had heard her instruct the hotel management about which spring water she wanted to be served in the hotel restaurant as an alternative to the hotel's proffered brand. He had seen her use her hands fulsomely in gestures to emphasize points as she talked.

In the hotel restaurant, she had ordered a Mediterranean lamb dish. Brendan had asked for sea bass. They talked as they ate.

'I imagined you'd be steak,' Madeline Geller told him brightly.

'I thought you'd be a vegetarian,' Brendan said in flatter tones.

'Really?'

'I thought you'd be apologizing for just ordering a bit of green salad and then pushing it around on your plate.'

'Yeah, I guess it would have been like that at one time,' she said happily. 'I had problems with my weight in college. I was real big for a time. I fasted it off, but that's only ever half the battle. After that, you have to keep it off. I went through every fad going. You know, all those secret diets, the one that's going to work for you, the one that everyone says has been smuggled out of a private clinic somewhere. The Montignac Diet. The Hay Diet. The heart attack one with the vegetable soup. The ice cream one. The chlorella one.'

'The what?'

'Chlorella. It's a seaweed extract. The thing was, I was always frightened of food. There was always some particular set of rules I had to abide by. Because, as a woman, you have to look a certain way. It always seemed a tyranny, but it was always necessary. You know what I mean?'

Brendan didn't.

'Sometimes the rules I was sticking to would change, but not my need to stick scrupulously to them. Ways of eating, times of eating, combinations of foods that you think are deadly.'

'Like what?'

'Like what? Like not mixing proteins and carbohydrates.

Like only eating fruit on an empty stomach. That sort of thing. The thing was, they never really worked. I always felt empty. I was always hungry. It wasn't until I made the connection with God that I got a handle on it.'

'With God?'

'It took a while before I saw how I was missing the connection – that what I was really hungry for was the Lord. Punishing myself with all those sets of rules about what I could and couldn't eat, and craving food the whole time while I put myself through it was just me confusing stomach-hunger and heart-hunger. It was only through God that I was able to find a peace with food – to eat only when I'm hungry, and to know when that is. To run to the Lord, not the refrigerator. That's how I got into Fellowship TV. I'd been working as a journalist while I was having these battles all the time with food, and the *Feed on the Bible* programme I signed myself up to was managed by the same organization that ran Fellowship TV. God really does work in wonderful ways, just as He did in Heslop Bridge. But you don't believe that, do you?'

'I have the results back from the tests on one of the Letters,' he said.

'Let me guess,' she said, 'you can prove that the parchments aren't two thousand years old?'

'You knew that already.'

'It's not hard to figure the Maslows would come up with something like that.'

'It doesn't bother you?'

'Why should it bother me?'

'Isn't that meant to be the miracle?'

'Surely the miracle is that God has spoken to us at all?'

'I suppose you're going to tell me it doesn't matter that

the parchments are made of twentieth-century materials? That it doesn't matter that they aren't hide, or that the ink hasn't a trace of plant dye, or blood pigment, or charcoal?'

'You think the parchments should be made of some glow-in-the-dark celestial material, Mr Moon? You think God should perform made-to-measure stunts to satisfy cynics like you? He'll do it His way. Why can't He do things quietly if he chooses? Why shouldn't He do things in a way that rewards belief without fanfares and trumpets and the walls of Sodom and Gomorrah having to fall down each time, just because you say they have to?'

'But don't you think they should have been halfway to being *old*, if they were going to be genuine. They're 150-gram zeta matt paper that has probably just dried out after being stored badly for twenty years. It's a surface preparation ink made of some synthetic chemical. You're telling me that God shopped for it in some wholesale stationer's before he manufactured his Heslop Bridge miracle? Of course he didn't. It's a hoax. Someone planted those parchments. As much as you want a miracle here, you can't have one. There wasn't one. There was just a terrible thing that happened in that school. Your organization should just accept that and leave these people to get on with their grieving.'

'There's more to it than that.'

'No there isn't. Fellowship TV can make-believe all they like. You can shoot all the footage you want of the school, and of people hallelujahing about a miracle. Maybe they swallow this kind of thing more easily in the States, I don't know. It doesn't change anything.'

'Can I ask you something?' she said.

'Sure.' Brendan was slicing a side of flesh off the bone of the fish.

Madeline Geller had put down her knife and fork. She was looking at him closely. 'Why is it so important that you discredit what happened?'

'It's my job. It's what I do.'

'Something that needed to happen *has* happened, yet your instinct is simply to tear it down.'

'But what you say happened *didn't* happen. Isn't it important to tell the *truth*?'

'So how do you explain those letters? How do you explain the voice that speaks to people so personally about the tragedy in those verses? If you're so interested in the truth, explain the whole of it. You can't. Because you know what? I think you're frightened of the truth. Something's making you frightened to acknowledge the truth of God's love. What you want isn't the truth, its confirmation of how *you* need the world to be constructed.'

'So do I take it that you're intent on pursuing the Maslows for the money, then?'

'I want them to confirm what took place in Heslop Bridge. There is already enough evidence; there are enough witnesses prepared to say what they saw, and what they received. Like the Maslows, I would be happy to avoid going to court, so I'd be happy to negotiate a settlement on behalf of the support group.'

'You want the Maslows to cough up money on the say-so of Fellowship TV? Is that meant to be an offer?'

'That way, both sides can cut their losses and we can all go away happy.'

'My job is to provide an explanation for the parchments.'

'But you can't explain them.'

'You want an explanation for them. All right, I'll give you one. They didn't fall from the sky – they were taken up a hundred feet or so in the backdraft from the explosion in the boilerhouse.'

'But Jason Orr was in custody when, according to you, all the other parchments starting appearing around the town.'

'There was a second person.'

'So why does Jason Orr keep on saying that he acted alone? That's what the police told us at the press conference.'

'If there was an accomplice, the police may want to keep quiet about it. After all, it's going to be the autumn at least before they're ready for a trial.'

'And what motive could have persuaded someone with the literary prowess needed to compose the verses to be involved with someone like Jason Orr? Someone with the humanity that is so evident in the writing? You surely can't deny *that* of the verses. Even by your standards, they must at least represent remarkable literature. What could possibly have persuaded someone like that to compose spiritual laments – in Hebrew – in readiness for a tragedy which hadn't yet unfolded and which, at the time of their composition, was entirely preventable?'

'The alternative,' Brendan said, 'is that someone else – someone who wasn't known to Jason Orr, who wasn't directly connected to the assault – perpetrated the hoax. That would at least account for how the parchments could have come to have been composed after the event.'

'But that person would still need a motive for the deception,' Madeline Geller protested.

Brendan shrugged. 'Maybe it wasn't intended to be malicious. Maybe the hoaxer wanted people to feel better.'

'And more than that,' she went on, ignoring him, ' – that individual would have to be local. They would need to know the addresses and places of work of all those people, of everyone who, having been touched by the tragedy, became recipients of the parchments. That argument still doesn't explain the seven parchments falling onto the school at the time of the tragedy. So your hoaxer must be someone with the foresight to *have known* that Jason Orr was going to shoot nine children and blow up part of the school and to be ready for it. Mr Moon, it's not me being unwilling to accept the truth, it's you. It really happened. Here. In Heslop Bridge, Lancashire. Just because the paper and the parchments are man-made doesn't make this any less a miracle.'

'Of course it does, and if you're not prepared to explain that to the support group you've managed to hijack, then I'll have to convince them.'

'The fact that the loaves and the fishes that Jesus fed the five thousand with were real loaves and real bread didn't make *that* any less of a miracle, Mr Moon. That's all Fellowship TV are saying. That's all we'll be saying if we have to take on the Maslows.'

'You'd persuade those people to go to court?'

'As long as that's what they want.'

'As long as you can carry on telling them that that's what they want.'

'Like I say, Mr Moon, as long as it's what they want, our organization will continue to offer support to them, just as it's done with others like them.'

'What about what you want? Fellowship TV just needed an event. They just want it to make money. They want a vehicle to consolidate their UK expansion. And having found one, they're happy to dupe any poor sods in the battle to win customers and make more money. I presume you're not *giving* channel subscriptions away yet?'

'There's nothing wrong with making money, Mr Moon. God doesn't say we all have to be poor. What's important is that wealth or influence don't become things that stop us from hearing Him when God does talk to us.'

'Don't you think you're just being used? That they're using your journalistic skills for their own commercial ends?'

'We're *both* being used, Mr Moon. The difference is that I'm being used by God, and you're being used by the Maslow brothers.'

5

Buggerfuck

In 1933, the West Indian Learie Constantine, playing for Nelson, ran out the last Heslop Bridge batsman when the scores were tied. A single run would have given Heslop Bridge their only Lancashire League championship in one hundred and twelve years. Nelson's Trinidadian professional had given the batsman a ten-yard start before he made a move, then swooped to his right, picked up and thrown the ball in the same motion, and run the batsman out a split second later with a direct hit from more than forty yards that broke the single stump he'd had to aim at.

There was a framed 30 × 20 ins photograph, grainy with the enlargement, on the wall of the Heslop Bridge clubhouse which commemorated the incident. The photograph had been taken by a Heslop Bridge committee man standing by the boundary rope, who had positioned himself to capture Heslop Bridge's winning run, and what would have been the moment of their only championship. In the photograph, the Nelson wicket keeper was arching his head away to avoid being struck in the face by the splintered wicket. The batsman at the non-striker's end, Eric Chettle (founder of Chettle's Hardware on the high street), was no slouch for speed and had set off for the run without hesitation. The photograph caught him at full tilt with his bat stretched forward, reaching desperately for the safety of the crease. He was still two feet short of the line. His batting partner – the man who had turned the ball to square leg – was Leo Seed, the Heslop Bridge captain. In the photograph, Leo Seed was looking around to see what was happening. He was still looking across towards Learie Constantine, even though the ball had already been released, even though the wickets were already broken. In the distance, chalk-faced boys edging over the boundary rope had their arms raised, mistakenly believing Leo Seed's final single to be assured and the game won. The hat of one of the boys was in the air above him, thrown up in anticipation of the run's completion. The faces of the boys were beaming with jubilation. But on Leo Seed's anxiously incomplete expression, the reality of the situation was already evident.

Wilf Wardle hadn't been there to see it. Wilf wouldn't be born for another ten years. His father, though, had been there and never forgot it. He would beseech Wilf regularly to picture the impossibly perfect piece of fielding which, perhaps, only one cricketer in the history of the game had been capable of and which robbed Heslop Bridge of their single day of glory. Wilf's father was one of the boys in the photograph. He was the boy who had thrown his hat into the air in premature celebration of the victory. Wilf's father talked of the incident so regularly that Wilf sometimes felt as though he *had* been there that day.

Learie Constantine's run-out in 1933 was the thing the two of them talked about the day before the old man died in the hospice sixty years later. Expressing emotion had never come easily to Wilf's father. Wilf couldn't remember his father so much as holding his hand or putting an arm around his shoulder in all their years together. His father had worked for Heslop Bridge's slipper factory as a driver. He'd enjoyed the easy comradeship amongst the men at the start and the end of each shift, and the long and independent hours of driving in between. For as long as Wilf could remember, the two of them had lived alone. Wilf's mother had died of tuberculosis just after Wilf had started school, and the boy had grown accustomed to coming home from school to an empty house on Holker Street. He had grown accustomed to the absence of women, to arriving home from school to organize the housework for a father who was dishevelled by that day's solitary miles on the roads and whose speech was only ever the casual banter of passing colleagues.

At thirty-seven, Wilf's father had been involved in an accident in the factory's loading bay and had fractured two vertebrae in his back. After the accident, he was confined to a wheelchair and from then on Wilf had grown accustomed to his father *always* being in the house. It was inevitable that Wilf became his carer as well as his cook. Wilf's father told the welfare that they didn't need any help – that Wilf could look after him, that Wilf was a good lad. Going to work for Sid Eastham at the cricket club meant that Wilf could start early, nip home to sort out his father's lunch, and be home by mid-afternoon. Talking in the hospice about a remembered moment of sublime and bittersweet perfection on Heslop Bridge's tight little ground before the war, both of them (the middle-aged groundsman and the old man in the last days of his life) understood that they were really speaking about other things.

Wilf's one evening a week out of the house in the years that he had cared for his father was spent in the back room of Keith Cottee's builder's merchants. There were four of them – Wilf, Keith Cottee, Alan Bibby (who'd been in the same class as Wilf at school), and Jim McCready who was older than the other three and who, as Keith's business neighbour, ran the garage next door with his daughter-in-law, Joyce. The four of them took turns to collect the evening's take-away from the Taj Mahal on the high street; they played old jazz tapes on Keith's machine – Alan Bibby's trad jazz and Wilf's Duke Ellington and Oscar Peterson; they played cards and drank bottled beer, and discussed the sporting world and Sky's coverage of it, until the beers were drunk and the tapes all played and a hazy working-men's fatigue overtook them some time after midnight and they crept home separately, conscious of the public hush, through Heslop Bridge's streets.

You had to understand, Wilf sometimes liked to say on a Monday night after three or four bottles of beer (Belgian, American or French, depending on which one was on special offer at the Co-op Late Shop), that it was a trap old Learie had deliberately set. You had to understand, Wilf said, that Learie Constantine's reputation as the best fielder in the world was such that amateur batsmen weren't going to risk running a quick single if they hit the ball in his vicinity, especially with only one wicket left, and for the run that would win the Lancashire League title.

Wilf liked to look at the photograph displayed on the wall of the club-house. He would look at the distant speck that was his father's hat in the air, at Leo Seed's face turned to square leg, at the splintered wicket. At various points in his life, Wilf had stood on the spot where Learie Constantine had thrown down poor Eric Chettle's leg stump. He went there the day Lorna Catherall refused to walk home with him from school any more because he had to wear glasses; he went there the day he failed his eleven-plus, sneaking into the empty ground under the faulty turnstile on the bottom gate; the day Sid Eastham, the Heslop Bridge groundsman, took him on as his apprentice; the day the hospital doctor told him that his lorry-driver father wouldn't be able to walk (or drive) again. Whenever he was out on the field and was passing in front of the old wooden pavilion (which these days was used on match days as the spectators' cafe) he would stop and stand there for a moment and call the incident to mind. Sometimes, in a foolish moment, he would imagine gathering up such a ball himself and hurling it across the field and watching its remarkable collision with the single stump, and hearing the gasp of the crowd. Of course, *imagining* was all that Wilf could do. Wilf's glasses were jam-jar thick; his eyesight was so poor that he could barely have *seen* the wicket from forty yards, let alone hit it. Although his father had been a competent medium-pace bowler in his youth for Heslop Bridge's Second Eleven, Wilf himself had to be content as a boy with helping out in the scorebox, or with carrying the sawdust onto the field if the bowler's footmarks in the turf needed repairing, or with helping Sid Eastham to push the unwieldy sightscreen if a left-arm bowler came on during a match at the scoreboard end. That was the nearest Wilf ever came to emulating Learie Constantine.

When Wilf had first started his apprenticeship with Sid Eastham, the post of groundsman had been a full-time job, but dwindling club subscriptions and gradually falling match-day crowds over thirty years meant that his work had periodically been subject to cutbacks. By the time Oscar appeared on the scene, Wilf was down to two days a week at the cricket ground, with the remaining days being spent at the school and on the private gardening jobs he had built up around the town.

He was standing on the ground now – on his favourite spot where Learie Constantine had picked up and thrown – as the heavy night sky was slowly clearing beyond Holker Fell and a Billy Strayhorn/Duke Ellington tune played pleasingly in his head. A faint rain was falling. It was a month to the day since Jason Orr's assault on the school. Wilf, unshaven, bespectacled, blue-overalled, smoked a Benson and Hedges with satisfaction and let the Duke's immaculate orchestration run its course. There was an authority of sorts in Wilf Wardle – a dignity that came from being in a place he'd felt all along that he belonged and in wishing to be nowhere else. He was, at that moment, debating whether to have a bacon roll for breakfast. He saw Oscar appear through the bottom turnstile by the main road and begin making his way around the perimeter of the empty ground. Even with his poor eyesight, Wilf could recognize Oscar's deliberate and cumbersome walk. Wilf walked back off the field, past the club-house, to rendezvous with him in the workshed.

The Heslop Bridge club-house had been built to replace the wooden pavilion which, in the days of Learie Constantine and Leo Seed, had been where the players had changed. In the new club-house, the changing rooms were upstairs. Downstairs there was a bar and a large social room which hosted the Heslop Bridge Spring Fair every Easter, and the Holker Street School's termly family dance, and where Maureen Bibby ran her line dancing class every Monday while her husband was at his cards night at Keith Cottee's place. People who hired the social room for private functions collected the key from Wilf. Since the attack on the school, the social room in the club-house had also become the venue for the regular support group, for whom Wilf opened up and turned the alarm off and then passed the keys to Joyce McCready for her to lock up later on.

Wilf was fiddling with a lawn-mower plate when Oscar finally appeared in the doorway, clutching his plastic lunch-box to his chest.

'Wiff Wooder!' Oscar said slowly. His tongue didn't fully get around the 'l' sounds as he sought to pronounce 'Wilf Wardle'. His head cocked to one side, as if puzzling for a response.

Wilf looked up. He had a screwdriver in one hand and a metal plate in the other.

'Oscar Brigg!' Wilf said in response.

'Oscar Brigg,' Oscar said, nodding in confirmation that it was him.

'Oscar Brigg' and 'Wilf Wardle' were the only words that Oscar spoke, apart from an expletive he had mastered somewhere along the way which, as Wilf liked to point out, made life interesting for Oscar when he was shopping in the Co-op.

'What you got for dinner today, Oscar?' Wilf said.

Oscar put the lunchbox down and set out his sandwiches, pork pie, apple and Kit-Kat in a row on the bench to show Wilf.

'What's in your sandwiches?' Wilf asked. Oscar passed them over for inspection. Wilf peered through the cellophane at the neatly trimmed sandwiches with the crusts sliced off. 'Cheese and chutney? Not bad. Are these sandwiches for me, then?'

'Oscar Brigg,' Oscar said cautiously. There was an oddly lopsided expression on his face. Wilf smiled and passed back the sandwiches.

'Wiff Wooder!' Oscar said.

Wilf nodded, understanding that it was his turn. He ferreted in his rucksack on the floor and produced a vast, unevenly carved tuna sandwich from inside a bread wrapper. Oscar took it and inspected it.

'Oscar Brigg?' he said.

'No chance,' Wilf said. Wilf put his sandwich away.

Oscar rolled his trouser leg up. 'Oscar,' he said.

Wilf leaned over to inspect Oscar's choice of socks for the day. 'Mr Men, eh. You're Mr Happy today?'

Oscar nodded.

Wilf looked down at his own socks, a spiderman pair that Oscar had bought him the Christmas before last.

'Wiff Wooder,' Oscar said.

They rolled their trouser legs down.

'Bacon buttie and a brew before we make a start?' Wilf asked.

Oscar clenched his pale face in concentration for a moment, then he nodded. Wilf went on fiddling with the metal plate, then handed it and the screwdriver to Oscar and stood up to go in search of the matches to light the grill on the camping stove at the back of the workshed.

'See if you can get that screw out of the plate,' Wilf said, ' – it's stuck. I can't budge it.'

Wilf put the kettle on. Then he lit the grill and laid out the bacon on the grillpan. There was a clang behind him. Oscar, trying to lever out the screw, had dropped the metal plate onto the concrete floor.

'Buggerfuck,' Oscar said.

That was the other word that Oscar used.

It was Oscar who had found the parchment which had fallen on Heslop Bridge's cricket ground.

'Oscar!' he had said as he held it out for Wilf to take, four days after the tragedy at the school.

Wilf himself worked at the school with Oscar every Tuesday. He was employed by the headmaster to maintain the sports field and the planting beds and the wildlife pond and garden which he'd helped the teachers and children to create. On the day that Jason Orr had shot the nine children and orchestrated the explosion in the boilerhouse, Wilf ought to have been working but he had been ill from the previous night's curry. He hadn't witnessed the parchments falling onto the school's grounds, so the parchment that Oscar found out on the cricket field four days later and brought back to the workshed was the first one that Wilf had seen up close. The parchment had felt to Wilf like cracked skin. He had noted how dry and seemingly ancient the heavy paper was. He had looked at the unfamiliar foreign words that meant nothing to him, but that, in the way they were arranged precisely over twelve lines on the page with identical margins to the right and left, were evidently a verse of some kind. He had wondered what kind of words they were. He had wondered what kind of words would be enough to bring consolation to people who were in the process of burying their children.

Wilf had never been an overtly religious man. His only sense of God came from the gardens that he and Oscar maintained. Wilf had looked after the cricket ground since the 1960s, ever since Sid Eastham had invited him to leave the slipper factory at nineteen and become his apprentice;

and, as well as the work he did for the school, he maintained several of the big gardens up on the Holker road for the widows who couldn't manage them on their own.

Wilf's life had been spent outdoors. He saw the sense of balance that existed in his gardens. (He thought of them all as *his* gardens even though he only had a backyard behind his terraced house). He saw how things in nature fitted together, like a kind of natural ticking clock. He watched how the orchids he'd cultivated in Dora Hicken's greenhouse needed to mimic the precise appearance and the identical chemical pheromones of the female wasps that visited them in order to persuade the males to co-operate in the intricate process of cross-pollination. He was awed by the design that gave such miraculous vision to the kestrel that came down from Holker Fell and perched on the wires on the edge of the cricket field early in the mornings looking for mice. The natural world that he dealt with every day was so ordered, Wilf reasoned to himself, that *somebody* must have designed it. Someone must have been *in charge* of all this order to ensure that it all fitted together so perfectly.

For that reason, although the business of the parchments had surprised Wilf, it hadn't astonished him. There were things that you accepted, Wilf felt, that were simply impossible to fathom because they were there right in front of you in the way that he had accepted that his cousin in New Zealand could speak into a telephone and, on the other side of the world, he could hear her voice instantly.

Sometimes, Wilf reasoned, there must be temporary breaches in the order that God had established. Sometimes things would need adjusting – the way Wilf himself occasionally needed to adjust the thermostat in his greenhouses at Dora Hicken's four-acre garden for the orchids, or the way he might take his father's old watch to be repaired if the tiny cogs and wheels weren't rotating exactly as they needed to to drive the mechanism round at the right speed. And it was hard for Wilf to imagine a grosser breach of that order than Jason Orr's assault on the school, which had resulted in the deaths of nine children including Keith Cottee's little boy, and Lewis Chettle from the hardware shop on the high street, where Wilf regularly called in for odds and ends. No, the parchments – even needing translation from Hebrew and appearing around the town like that – hadn't surprised him anything like as much as Jason Orr's actions had.

Wilf had never *said* any of this. He had only thought it. Until Oscar came along, he had always worked alone. He was used only to thinking things rather than saying them. Looking after his father, he had lived a single man's life; since his father had died four years ago, the conversations he had about the world (save for the Monday evening card game with his friends) had primarily taken place inside his head. He fell asleep at night in front of the television, with the screen showing Sky's repeats of week-old football highlights, or some obscure snooker ranking tournament from Basildon. He ate microwave meals (Wilf believed that the microwave oven was the single greatest invention of the twentieth century). Twice a week he saved his morning paper for the evening trip to the launderette. Such a life was perhaps the reason he had taken easily to working with Oscar. As for women, there hadn't been any. It was just the way things had worked out. He got on with women well enough when he came across them. He had thought once or twice of asking out Joyce McCready, who he now liaised with over the keys for the support group meetings in the club-house.

But the technique of actually asking a woman out, and then contemplating all the things that might – or might not – follow on from this, his ignorance, the subtle and not-so-subtle rules and expectations that he, Wilf Wardle, a virgin at fifty-two, lacked all knowledge of, had deterred him gently, inexorably, whenever such a thought had occurred to him.

Oscar's employment with Wilf had started with a phone call, not long after Wilf's father had died. A woman had rung him, talking about supported employment. She mentioned Oscar, and asked if Wilf would give the man a work trial. Wilf asked where he was from. The woman called it Calderhall rather than any of the names the locals had always given it. She said Oscar didn't speak at all, but that he had worked in the grounds of the institution over a number of years. She said he wasn't dangerous or anything.

'Oh bugger,' Wilf had said, 'I could do with a bit of danger.'

Oscar turned out to be tall and thin, with long limbs and a pale face dominated by big, surprised eyes. Wilf had guessed him to be somewhere in his fifties. The woman was right – he didn't speak. He seemed, though, to understand instructions Wilf gave him, and was happy to be shown those that he didn't. He was slow to pick up routines, but Wilf noticed that if Oscar was asked to do the same things in the same way then eventually he got them right, and after that he *always* did them in the same way and never tried to cut corners. The woman had admitted at that point that there might be a couple of snags. She said that Oscar didn't like the dark – he even slept with the light on in his room. Wilf shrugged. Also, she added, as if waiting for Wilf to find something to object to, Oscar was claustrophobic; he was nervous of confined spaces. Wilf had looked around him in response to the observation, at the three acres of cricket ground, and the rise of Holker Fell in the distance, and the big sky running on towards Yorkshire.

'I'd the same problem myself in the slipper factory,' Wilf had said.

At first, the woman escorted Oscar to the cricket ground. Before long, he started to arrive on his own. Wilf himself taught Oscar the route to the school on the days when they were working there.

During their tea breaks, Wilf read his *Mirror* and smoked. One time, he noticed the way Oscar was watching him smoke. Wilf offered up the remainder of the cigarette. Oscar took it and drew on it, eyes closed. The exhalation was a kind of sigh. He would take a cigarette from Wilf at no other time of the day, but each lunchtime he would accept one and smoke it in long, slow, silent draws. Sometimes, while Oscar smoked his single cigarette, Wilf talked about his father, and about his lifetime's love of cricket. He told Oscar he felt lucky that his father and Sid Eastham between them had rescued him from spending his life in a factory he hated.

After a few months, Wilf made it his task to teach Oscar how to play Snap with a pack of cards from the club-house. They would play during their lunch break after they'd eaten. Oscar would silently slap his hand down onto the pile if he saw a matching pair; Wilf, his own cigarette gripped in the fingertips of one hand, would bring the other one down with a flourish and yell 'Snap!' loudly. Sometimes Wilf would pretend to cheat and would call 'Snap' when there were no matching cards. He would take them, but Oscar would silently decline to play another card until Wilf had returned the ones he had just taken back to the pile between them. Once, after Oscar had smacked his hand down to claim a 'Snap', Wilf picked the cards up himself.

'Aren't these my cards?' he said.

Oscar shook his head vehemently.

'Are you sure?'

Oscar shook his head again. Wilf paused, seeming to weigh up the matter, and pulled the cards up to his chest.

'*Oscar!*' Oscar suddenly said, in an outburst of complaint.

'Bugger me!' Wilf said, looking at him in surprise.

The woman who had first rung up, asking about a job for Oscar, and who called around periodically to see how he was doing, refused to believe that Oscar had spoken. She said Oscar couldn't talk. She said he'd *never* talked.

One day, the two of them were mending one of the bench seats that ran around the cricket ground. Wilf's screwdriver slipped and he caught his index finger and drew blood.

'Fuck bugger buggerfuck,' Wilf said, hopping around on the grass and shaking his damaged hand in the air. Later that summer, Wilf stumbled over a hammer he'd left on the ground and dropped the tea tray on which he was carrying their brews and a plate of biscuits. The mugs shattered and the tea slopped out and puddled on the wooden decking.

'Buggerfuck,' Oscar said, looking dispassionately at the wreckage.

'You're not kidding,' Wilf told him, surveying the debris.

Some weeks later, Wilf (who took three sugars) gave the wrong brew by mistake to Oscar (who didn't take sugar). Oscar took a gulp. He pulled his face and looked suspiciously at the tea.

'Wiff Wooder,' he said, pulling his face and holding Wilf's mug out for him to take.

Wilf looked, then grinned. 'You know something, Oscar,' he said, swapping the two teas around, ' – you talk too much.'

Occasionally there was bother. One of his clients, the wife of a local circuit court judge, refused to let Oscar work alongside Wilf in her garden. She said it would upset her two Pekinese to have someone like that around. She told Wilf that it was surely better that defectives were kept somewhere away from normal people, like they used to be. Wilf shrugged, packed up his equipment, drove off with Oscar, and never went back. Occasionally he caught some of the kids at the school shouting 'Spacker' or 'Cretin' across the yard at Oscar. It tended to be the same kids who vandalized the wooden benches at the cricket ground, the ones who gobbed out of the school bus on the heads of pedestrians. Wilf would say something back if the mood took him. He would apologize to Oscar. Oscar himself seemed nonplussed.

'Oscar Brigg, Wiff Wooder,' Oscar would say. It was as if this summary of the situation was sufficient protection for him against the inequities of the world.

They sat in the workshed, contemplating their separate worlds while the bacon cooked under the grill. Oscar had somehow managed to prise the bent screw out of the lawnmower plate and was now rolling it gently between his index finger and his thumb. Wilf, as had become his habit during their breaks, was fingering the texture of his and Oscar's parchment. The two of them had decided, for now, to retain the parchment for themselves. There were enough of them around the town for one not to make any difference, Wilf had reasoned. The ones from the school, which had been released by the police as immaterial to their criminal investigations, were in the custody of the support group, having been handed over by the headmaster.

'Oscar,' Oscar said, watching him.

'Yeah, I know,' Wilf said, 'you found it.'

Wilf had persuaded Oscar to show him exactly where on the cricket ground he had found the parchment on the morning it had appeared, four days after the massacre. Oscar had shown him. It was at deep mid-wicket in front of the old pavilion, on the precise spot where Learie Constantine had thrown the ball with impossible speed and accuracy sixty years ago to run out Eric Chettle.

Outside the workshed, it was almost light. Beyond the wall of the cricket ground, the day's traffic was starting to build. In the town, people passing acknowledged each other, or stopped to talk. Some shook hands. Since Jason Orr's attack (or since the parchments had fallen on Heslop Bridge, depending on how people chose to see it), the only reported crimes in the town had been a couple of traffic offences. A case of scotch stolen from the Co-op the day before the assault had been found returned, unopened, two days later in the rear loading bay of the supermarket. The bus shelter on the high street had not been vandalized for a month.

Wilf and Oscar sat on adjacent boxes eating their bacon rolls. The edge of Wilf's roll dribbled with brown sauce. On the day that Jason Orr had turned up at the school, Oscar had already arrived, expecting to meet up with Wilf who, unknown to him, was suffering from food poisoning inflicted by the previous evening's lamb balti. Wilf had subsequently tried to imagine the chaos of that morning – the siege, the panic, the explosion. He had asked Oscar some days later, on a morning such as this, when they had been supping tea, what it had been like on the day of Jason Orr's assault on the school. Oscar had been halfway through his daily cigarette at the time.

'Buggerfuck,' Oscar had said quietly.

6

Almost Debbie Reynolds

Joyce McCready had always liked Gershwin. She didn't *know* she liked Gershwin until she took up the oboe. Until then, she just knew that she liked the songs from a certain kind of film – the kind she had grown up watching as a girl, thinking wistfully of monotone New York skylines, and Central Park, and men dancing elegantly with their beaux on stage sets and sidewalks. Until then, she knew only that she had an affection for a certain kind of bittersweet tune remembered from those films: 'They Can't Take That Away From Me', 'The Man I Love', 'Nice Work If You Can Get It'. 'Our Love is Here to Stay'. This kind of tune, Joyce knew, could be a touchstone and a companion.

It had taken her a year's diligent practice, an hour each evening in the kitchen, to grasp the mundane rudiments of breathing and blowing and mouthing the reed of the instrument. After about a year, she found that she could blow her way patiently through 'Greensleeves' – without nuance but without muffing a note. At that point, her music teacher recommended a particular sheet music book from which Joyce was perhaps ready to pick out the melody lines of the songs, and Joyce saw that this was a

Gershwin song book and that the tunes were Gershwin tunes.

She had taken ballet lessons as a girl at the Betty Tring School of Dancing in Heslop Bridge. That was when she was Joyce Tattersall – with puppyfat. She wanted to be Debbie Reynolds, or Grace Kelly. She wanted her life to have a Gershwin soundtrack. But she grew weightier, realizing even before she failed to make the final line-up for Miss Betty Tring's end-of-term parents' concert – even before it was suggested that the Girl Guides might be more her thing – that she would never be Debbie Reynolds. By the time she started working at the slipper factory she was a size sixteen and accustomed to being overlooked. When Terry McCready from Stores led her into a darkened manager's office three-quarters of the way through the works' Christmas party, happy on Heineken and holiday pay and the prospect of a fortnight's leave, she was astonished, and then relieved to have been chosen for *something*.

She knew that, away from the factory, Terry McCready flew model aircraft for a hobby. It seemed, to Joyce, to be a promising hobby to have – guiding small objects hopefully into the blue sky and waiting for their safe return. When Terry said he'd marry her, she signed on at Weightwatchers and spent three months fasting down towards a size ten. She went through the marriage ceremony almost fitting the dress they'd bought, with black rings around her eyes and exhaustion in her face. She had recorded each pound's loss on the chart she had drawn up and had the feeling that she'd endured some astonishing route march. Terry observed that she wasn't a proper ten and there was still work to do to make sure she didn't end up a big lump again. When the Alan Marsland Trio closed their final set of the night at the reception in the Heslop Bridge Working Men's Club with their version of 'Our Love is Here to Stay', with some of the guests already drifting out onto the streets, Joyce was sitting underneath the white-sheeted top table, hidden from view, eating a Mars bar.

When her mother died, Joyce went to see a spiritualist. The idea had come from one of the team of girls working on Joyce's line at the slipper factory. The girls in the factory knew that Joyce read the horoscopes and, once – after a girls' night out, back at someone's house – they'd tried the Ouija board. The spiritualist turned out to be a woman Joyce had seen around the town who lived across from the Atlas Street hostel. The woman told Joyce a couple of things about her mother that Joyce had felt sure no one else but she had known. The woman asked her about her sister. Joyce said her sister had been the pretty one their father had doted on. Her sister, she said, was on her third marriage.

'Do you see much of her?' the woman asked.

'She's rich now,' Joyce said. 'She lives in Surrey. She's always unhappy about something when I ring her. Last time, she said the villa they have in Marbella had cockroaches.'

'You couldn't have children, love, could you?' the woman said after a while. Joyce shook her head. 'I wanted to adopt, but he said it wouldn't feel like it was his.'

At the end of the session, the spiritualist said, 'You're a good-looking woman, Joyce McCready, you shouldn't sell yourself short.'

'What do you mean?' Joyce asked.

'You know what I mean,' the woman said, ' – you're worth more than you think.'

Joyce asked the spiritualist whether she would ever meet anyone else.

'Will he be handsome, will he be rich?' the woman sang back to her in Doris Day tones. Joyce laughed.

'Do you want to find someone else?' the woman asked.

'Some time,' Joyce said, ' – I suppose. Yes.'

'That's a good start, then,' the woman said.

Through most of their marriage, Terry McCready had been the caretaker at the Holker Street Primary School. He secured the job at the school because the headmaster at that time, a man called Roy Carliss, flew his model aircraft on Sunday mornings alongside Terry at the memorial football fields in Heslop Bridge. Roy Carliss was well known around the town. He'd been at Holker Street for thirty years; he'd been telling the school secretary for eleven of those, each time they went to Windermere for the weekend, that he was going to leave his wife for her. Everybody's kids had gone to Holker Street. Everyone knew that Roy Carliss lied about things. Everyone knew he was booked out to non-existent conferences when there was a race meeting at Haydock Park or Chester. It was Terry McCready who placed the headmaster's bets at the bookies. They studied form together in the caretaker's storeroom before assembly. Some days, a teacher would have to fetch Roy Carliss so that he could lead the school in the Lord's Prayer and give out the day's merit badges while Terry finished completing the form guide on his own. It was Terry who kept the storeroom filled with model aircraft parts belonging to the pair of them, and curiously large over-orders of school stationery that went off in a white transit on a Friday at each month's end.

In bed, Joyce had to pretend to be Samantha Fox.

'At least your tits are the right size, if nothing else,' Terry told her. He brought things home for her to wear for sex. The absence of affection or intimacy puzzled Joyce. Terry told her he worked hard so he was entitled to his bit of fun.

'You're lucky anybody's in bed with you at all,' he told her, 'the state you've let yourself get into after all the good work we did.'

It was the changing face of school administration which ended Roy Carliss's reign: local management of schools, National Curriculum regulations, Ofsted inspections, performance league tables. The headmaster admitted defeat and was signed off with stress. Within a year he was retired on health grounds with a full pension. By that time, Terry McCready was already working evenings for Keith Doyle, driving the white transit. That was how Terry developed his taste for business speculation, and syndicate betting, and what he took to be the good life. That was how he met his seven-stone beauty from Warrington who was doing some part-time modelling for Keith Doyle. After he left, Joyce heard that he was living with the woman in her waterside apartment at the Albert Dock and was calling himself her agent.

A week after Terry left, Keith Doyle came around to the house to explain that Terry still owed him £3,000, on which he'd offered the house as security. He was nonplussed at Joyce's suggestion that he take Terry's collection of model Second World War aeroplanes and a two and a half foot flying replica Chinook helicopter that her husband had abandoned in the shed. He was more receptive, however, to the idea that Joyce could pay the money off working evenings for his business. Admin work, cleaning, packing – she said she didn't mind. Keith Doyle said he could do with someone on despatch.

Keith Doyle Enterprises was one of the modern, low-roofed units in what the council described as the Heslop

Bridge Development Park behind the railway line. Joyce's job – seven until ten, four evenings a week – was to wrap and despatch the orders coming in by mail. Sometimes the letters that accompanied the cheques or postal orders requested specific titles. Other orders would simply specify the *kind* of magazine they wanted, and Joyce would need to go searching along the storage racks for something that matched what the man was asking for: lessie bondage, golden rain, big tit sluts. In the office behind the glass, at the far end of the unit, two women answered the phones in booths with plywood partitions. One of the women had gone to school with Joyce; the other had worked for a while at the slipper mill before becoming pregnant. Joyce was surprised at how often the phones rang during the evening. One evening she went up to the office because the stationery cupboard was out of A4 envelopes. One of the girls was on the phone. Joyce could see over her shoulder that she had a crossword quiz book on the table in front of her. She held a biro in her free hand to fill in the clues. The second woman was drinking tea and smoking a cigarette.

'You want me to tell you how that makes me feel,' the woman who was answering the phone said. She was writing a word down in the crossword grid as she was talking. 'I'll tell you. I've just had to slip off my white lace bra so that I can play with my nipples some more while you talk to me. In fact, in a minute I think I'm gonna have to take my panties off too, cause I'm getting hotter by the minute at this end of the line, just thinking of you doing that for little old me.'

Joyce looked at the woman. She remembered her name – Maureen – from Mrs Jacob's home economics class. Maureen wore glasses. She had on an oversize pair of dungarees and a green cardigan. She had the phone wedged against her chin as she breathed and sighed into it.

'They're coming off now, big man,' Maureen said softly down the phone, 'and it's just for you. I just can't control myself any more.'

Joyce found the envelopes on a shelf and went back to the despatch desk. When she left at ten o'clock each evening, the two girls on the phones in the booths would still be there, taking the calls.

Four months into her employment at the unit, Keith Doyle explained that the interest on Joyce's debt was all but outstripping the money she was paying him from her wages in despatch.

'Is it my fault if my employer pays lousy wages?' she said.

'Life's such a bitch,' he told her. He asked her whether she fancied working on one of the phone lines since he needed to take on someone else for the calls and she had the right kind of voice for the work. The wages were a lot better on the phones, he said. She'd get the debt paid off much quicker that way. Joyce told him he could stick the phone up his jacksy. She went to her father-in-law who lent her his remaining chunk of the severance lump sum he'd worked thirty-five years for before his early retire-ment. In four months, Keith Doyle said, the debt had risen to £3,500. She covered the repayments to Jim McCready by working weekends for him at the petrol station he had taken on as a retirement business. He paid her eighty pounds a week. Compared to Keith Doyle, it seemed almost reasonable. In time, because she enjoyed the work, and because the slipper mill had new owners and a seemingly uncertain future yet again, and because Jim McCready had grown to rely on her to manage the business while he spent his time under the bonnets of old Rovers and Aston Martins in the workshop next door, she gave up the job in the slipper mill altogether and worked more hours at the garage, although her father-in-law never altered her wage, even after she eventually finished paying him back the money.

In Joyce's lounge, Jim McCready was asleep on the sofa. He had his dressing gown on. She had covered him with a blanket.

'Just five minutes, Joycey,' he'd said, as if to barter for any more would be a sign of weakness. He had moved into her house while they waited to get to the bottom of things with his impending hospital tests. The idea was that Joyce could look after him better under her roof. The weekly card school had transferred temporarily to her front lounge. Two nights ago, the other three men had trooped through her front door, mumbling thanks, sheepish in the unfamiliar environment until the second or third beer took the edge off things. Joyce, in the kitchen, listened, curious that they talked only about football. They pondered as they served beer and played their hands of cards and debated whether Alan Shearer had been the best striker since the war. Keith Cottee said that Shearer was the best he'd ever seen – not the most talented but the most effective, and with the best movement off the ball. Sometimes, Keith said, it had been like a man against boys down at Ewood Park. Wilf said that he'd always had a soft spot for Denis Law. Alan Bibby mentioned Johnny Haynes, then Bryan Douglas. He said he wished his son had seen Bryan Douglas play for Blackburn Rovers. Keith said his son had always been going on about today's players – Beckham and the like – as if they were *all* so much better than the ones who had gone before. Liam used to go on and on about David Beckham as if no one else before that had known how to cross a ball. Keith had said he wished he'd talked more to Liam about it. About things. You know . . . before . . . before what happened . . . at the school. The conversation had fallen away. Someone had risen to get more beers from the fridge, and the conversation had faltered. It had occurred to Joyce that this was the nearest the group of men had dared to get to talking of death.

While Jim slept on the sofa, Joyce started preparing tea using the vegetables Wilf Wardle had brought round when he'd delivered his get well card. She liked Wilf in particular amongst the card school participants because he seemed to be the one least bothered about winning, and because he employed the mentally handicapped man from the hostel. These seemed like good things in a world in which virtue was sparse and seemed vulnerable to all manner of corrosion.

While Wilf was at the door, he'd shown Joyce an article in his morning paper. 'Grieving Villagers Conned By Cruel Trickster?' the paper said. The source of the information, like that of several other reports in the press, was a commercial laboratory in Cambridge which had performed forensic tests on one of the parchments. He had handed her the carrier bag with the Mirror in it. 'There are three courgettes inside as well,' he had told her, 'from one of my gardens. The old man there always says to help myself, and they were ready for taking off.'

Joyce had examined the courgettes at the bottom of the bag. 'You'll be wanting a cup of tea, then, while you're here,' she'd said, more in hope than expectation that he would accept the offer.

'I can't stop.'

'Where are you going?'

'Dora Hicken's place,' he'd told her. Dora Hicken, he'd said, had finally been taken into a nursing home. It had been on the cards for a while. Dora's relatives had told Wilf they didn't want to continue paying him to see to the garden, but Wilf was still going up, unpaid, because he felt responsible for the place. If he didn't look after everything up there until something was sorted about the property, he was sure that no one else would.

Joyce turned to the horoscope page in the morning newspaper that Wilf had left with her. Sagittarius: 'Keep an eye out for the main chance – there may be an opportunity worth taking. But remember, there are people depending on you so be sure to think things through first before acting too hastily on impulse.' She sat wondering what opportunity, and how she might take it if it came along and seemed within reach. She wondered whether 'those depending on her' referred to Jim, who lay on her sofa dreaming, she supposed, of glistening engine parts and Alan Shearer's movement off the ball. She wondered how Dora Hicken's four acres were doing, and what kind of man it was that would do such a thing for nothing.

The petrol station was closed when Brendan pulled in. The pumps were unlit. There was no sigh of Jim McCready in his workshop. Brendan pulled the Volvo onto the forecourt and stopped the car to the side of the workshop doors. The service cabin was locked. The lights were out. Inside the workshop, the car was gone from the ramp; the inspection pit was closed; the tools had been tidied away from the benches.

He found Joyce in the back office, doing the books. She had on her customary black stretch leggings, and a cardigan draped over her shoulders.

'You're closed!'

'Are you just demonstrating that you're an investigator, B. Moon?'

Brendan shrugged.

'I've closed for the afternoon to give me chance to get the books in order. It's hard work running this place on your own.'

'What's up with your father-in-law? I notice he's not tinkering in the workshop today.'

'It'll probably be a bit before Jim's back to tinkering.'

'How is he?'

'He was struggling to manage on his own, so I've moved him into my place until he gets his strength back. He protested, of course. Said he'd only agree to come if I let him have his Monday night game of cards.'

'You got him back to the doctor's then?' Brendan said.

'I got the doctor to come out and see him. I told you what he was like, didn't I? She mimicked her father-in-law: "I don't like that doctor. I've already got my Gaviscon and my pills for the back pain. He's only going to tell me the same if I go again." But he'd lost a bit more weight and he wasn't eating. So when I said he could come and stop with me for a few days because he was feeling ropey I made it a condition that he'd see the doctor again. It turned out to be a locum who saw him, not his usual doctor. He's going to get him to hospital for blood tests as soon as there's a bed available.'

'You think they might get to the bottom of it now?'

'That's what we're hoping. It's going to do Jim's head in if he's got to sit around my front room for weeks before he can get back under his cars. And, in the meantime, I'm left running things here on my own. I don't suppose you've turned up on the off-chance of finding a bit of part-time till work?'

Brendan shook his head. 'I need directions.'

'What are you looking for?'

He showed her the address. She scoured the maps for sale on the rack behind the counter and took one out.

'I'll mark it for you if you want.'

'You've heard of it?'

She nodded. 'Everyone round here's heard of it. It's just not so easy to find. It's a bit off the beaten track.'

Madeline Geller's goading had confirmed to him that forensic information about the parchments wasn't going to be enough. Whatever he said wouldn't be sufficient to dissuade her; what he needed was an explanation for the origin of the Letters that would satisfy the community of Heslop Bridge, and persuade them to rethink their alliance with Fellowship TV. Only by losing their very public commission from the support group would Madeline Geller and her colleagues be sent scurrying for cover and the threat to the Maslows be curtailed.

The equation was simple enough. It started from Brendan's conviction that what he was dealing with was fraud. That was the point of equations – they were sober and simple. He remembered something from a management course he had been sent on by his first firm. The course had been run by a giddy, horse-faced woman, who Brendan supposed had never actually been involved in business, and a thinly bearded, seedy man he took to be a burned-out refugee from it. Between them, the two course leaders knew the crackpot theories of every management guru on the market, and had the patience of donkeys with all of them. On one occasion, Brendan recalled, they had expounded the difference between evaluation and assessment. Brendan couldn't remember any longer why the distinction was relevant, but he remembered the equation. *Evaluation plus decision equals assessment.* Brendan had liked that. He had enjoyed the way an apparent obfuscation had been organized and tidied up. Equations like that reached to the heart of the matter. They revealed the manifest simplicity of the world beneath all the distracting hullabaloo up on the surface.

Someone was responsible for the parchments. Eliminate everything that was not possible and what was left, no matter how improbable, must be the truth. That was the equation. And the one thing that seemed left to him, when everything else he had come up so far with had been discounted – if he discounted God – was Oscar Brigg.

He manœuvred the car off the forecourt and back onto the road, heading towards the slip road for the East Lancashire M65. The signs read Accrington, Blackburn, Preston, M6, South. At the turn-off a mile further on, signposted for Accrington and Whalley, he came off the motorway.

Whalley turned out to be an affluent Ribble Valley commuter settlement. It was smaller than Heslop Bridge but still almost a small town, nestled against the high steep side of Whalley Nab. The houses were stone-fronted. The window boxes were neat. The remains of a medieval abbey were tucked away down the river. The police station was a terraced house just off the main through-road. Brendan turned out of Whalley, following Joyce's directions at each turn. Within a few minutes on winding country roads he found what he was looking for.

There were no gates any more. They had been taken down. There were no walls, or even fences. There was simply a private road leading discreetly beyond a screen of carefully managed woodland and past manicured lawns. Most of the colony, Joyce had told him, was now unused, but by visiting he would at least get a feel of the place.

The buildings were a regimented series of two-storey dormitory barracks. The colony as a whole was bigger than the commuter settlement he had passed through down the road. It was a small town in its own right, hidden in the middle of a valley in northern England.

In Oscar Brigg's time it had been a town of 2,000 inhabitants, Joyce had told Brendan. She knew something about it, she said, because her father-in-law had worked at Calderhall before he'd taken early retirement and a pension. He'd worked there for thirty years, as foreman on the maintenance crew, before he had used his lump sum to buy the lease on the petrol station. He himself had come across Oscar Brigg in the colony. If Brendan wanted to know anything about Calderhall, Joyce had said, he should talk to Jim. She guessed her father-in-law would be grateful for the company. She said it was driving Jim nuts not being in an overall, bent over an engine.

Brendan peered into one of the deserted red-brick barracks. It was dark inside. The long dormitories were stripped to the floorboards. Across the compound it was very quiet. From the colony's vast central building a brick-built bell tower rose another eighty feet in the air from one buttress. The bell had long since been removed. It was a silent, secret town. Brendan tried to imagine people like Oscar Brigg spending their whole lives in this place, hidden from the world. He tried to imagine what kind of lives they would have been, and how the outside world would seem to a man like Oscar Brigg. A single loud bang from beyond the perimeter of the compound – a car backfiring on the road, or a farmer's gun in a field – punctured the silence and made Brendan start. A hundred black crows rose screeching from the high trees all around him and took to the air. As the flutter of panic in him subsided, Brendan realized that his mobile was going off. The call was from his London office. The message was for him to contact someone. There was no phone number to ring, just a name and an address. It was a Salford address. He double-checked the name. Fr Wynn. The address was the old gym on the Cheetham Hill road. Brendan's only thought was that it must be a mistake. Surely, by now, twenty years after he'd last set eyes on him, the old priest must be dead.

7

Defence and Counter

In the intervening years, it had become a place he dreamed about. In the intervening years, Fr Wynn had, to Brendan, become the last great man. He was the yardstick by which the failings of all other men could be judged, the measure by which the others in Brendan's mind had fallen short.

It came almost as a surprise, driving in off the East Lancs road, for Brendan to find the neighbourhood still there, some of it at least recognizable, with domestic life still going on, and lines of Manchester traffic still running through it. In reality, though, things had changed. Brendan had known that much from the repercussions for his own profession. He knew that there were postcodes in parts of the city which rendered properties uninsurable.

In the eighties, punters had travelled the length of the country to come to Manchester, and when they arrived they bought Speed and Ecstasy to use in the all-night clubs which had mushroomed to cater for the acid house boom. Ecstasy, it turned out, was worth more to the city's underworld than heroin. It was meteoric, but it couldn't have lasted. Before long, the drug barons had started to lose control. The eventual police crackdown had resulted in offending clubs being shut down. Closed circuit television sprang up all over the city. Gangland bosses were pinned down under constant surveillance and regular stop searches.

That was when the gangs had turned back to heroin and cocaine; that was when they started searching for younger recruits to run for them as a way of bypassing the police surveillance. Equipping the kids with weapons was a tactic to ensure that *their* runners could compete effectively against those of rival outfits for a shrinking share of the lucrative market. As the kids grew up in the Nineties, they started to break into the business in their own right. Already veterans of the scene, they had fewer qualms than their predecessors about carrying guns in the struggle for control of their business in the city's down-at-heel neighbourhoods.

Bursts of demolition and the collapse of a property development consortium had created a dozen acres of derelict land behind the gym. Over several years, the levelled land had been colonized by rough convolvulus and couch grass growing between concrete foundation slabs. Ragwort flourished between the fractured stone, and here and there on the open ground an occasional wild poppy strained for survival, a dot of scarlet in a jungle of coarser and more vigorous life. Around the pockets of rubble remaining from the demolition, children had fashioned muddy bike tracks – graceful, arching figures of eight written in the dirt.

Brendan parked at the side of a four-storey building cornering the derelict plot. Bedsheets were hung at the windows. There was an old fridge outside in the basement yard. He locked the car and walked back around the corner onto the main road where the traffic was heading towards the city centre.

There was a smell of urine in the hallway, and racist

graffiti on the walls of the building he entered. At the top of the stairs, there were scorch marks where a bin or a pile of newspapers had been set on fire. On the floor, the lino had frayed to an assortment of ill-fitting pieces. Brendan stood by the big doors on the landing, gaining his bearings, inhaling the gym's ancient smells of liniment and sweat, and in that moment he was eight years old again, carrying the duffel bag in which he'd brought his boxing trunks and towel through the winter-dark tea-times down from Providence Street. A group of youths were slumped against one wall. Several smaller boys were out on the floor of the gym, shadow-boxing, working the punch bags. Their grunts rang across the room above the percussion of their soft-shoe feet, and momentarily Brendan Moon was one of them, arriving for the juniors night at Fr Wynn's gym. Momentarily, the errand on which he was engaged was no more complex than the resumption of his work on the basics of defence and counter. Jab, move and cover-up was always the priest's mantra. Make it hard for your opponent to find you. Brendan had taken his mentor's lesson to heart. And with the sight of the old ring, and the punch bags in their familiar place, being worked by two solemn, round-faced Pakistani boys in grey sweats, he felt a distinct momentary confusion about why he – Brendan Moon of Providence Street, whose right hook when it came (Fr Wynn said) always left him exposed, whose father managed the hospital loan store – should be standing in the gym's doorway in a man's suit, with a man's louring memories in his head, and a man's sharp stubble on his face.

The old priest wasn't dead. No one knew, though, how old he was any more. No one was even sure whether he was still a real priest any more. His arrival in the city as a boyish cruiserweight of a curate came at a time when fighting was the mannish preserve of the boxing gyms and the docks and the pubs. That was a time when the Manchester hoods, who'd made good on the ration black markets, had worn camelhair coats and driven Jags, and bought rounds in their local pubs for the regular Friday-night drinkers.

Fr Wynn still wore a cassock, as he'd done when he first arrived in the city. It swished about his feet as he strode around the remains of his former Salford parish with the walking stick that he now used. Like his longevity, and the fallen scaffolding of his face, the medieval cassock awarded him a kind of invulnerability. Around him in these streets, fifteen minutes from where the city's commercial heart had been lavishly regenerated in steel and glass after the '96 IRA bomb blast, teenagers conducted skirmishes for a share of the city's drugs trade on the land behind the gym and on the nearby housing estates on mountain bikes with machetes and Ingram Mac Tens, while a crabby Leinster priest – huge and ancient enough to have cuffed their parents over the head for swearing – still walked amongst them, an untouchable and impatient spirit.

The priest himself had stayed on, even though it had been years since he'd had his own church to run. The diocese had acknowledged the changing demographics of the city and the falling away of attendances at services by reorganizing its parishes. As part of the restructure, it had consented to the sale of the land and the demolition of the church which Fr Wynn had served for forty years. If the truth were told, the diocese weren't sorry to see him go. He was too unorthodox. He fought too rapturously for the poor. Now he spent his time in the boxing gym above the former Co-op off the Cheetham Hill road. It was the priest himself who had founded the gym, in the days when runny-nosed boys came to him wanting to be Potter's Bar's Johnny Wright, or Dick McTaggart, and when Fr Wynn taught his charges to move and shimmy like the Hungarian maestro, Lazlo Papp. Kids still came into the gym. Seldom, though, did they come in alone. They came in groups – not, as a rule, to box but to pass time, mocking, conspiring, eyeing those outside their own set warily across the floor, hanging out away from the cold of the street and the prying eyes of the city's uniformed Dibble.

In the absence of a church to run, Fr Wynn had involved himself in a more mundane kind of salvation. He had given the room at the rear of the gym, and half shares in the kitchenette, to an education and counselling programme he had helped to set up to deal with the neighbourhood's burgeoning drug problems. The programme ran daily to the accompaniment of the rhythms of sparring and the dull strike of bags from the few boys who still came to box. The service mediated in disputes. It gave out contraceptive advice. It referred members of the rivalrous groups and the sullen girls attached to them to legal aid solicitors, debt advisers, housing benefit, or the local GUM Clinic for counselling and HIV testing. Jean Carr, the woman who ran the programme with Fr Wynn's help, did so with the finances for the project always on the verge of running out. Between her sessions, the priest's voice would rise to a snap in the hall, protesting about a lazy guard of hands or a shoddy movement of feet.

'Did you know, Brendan,' Fr Wynn said as he looked around the office for tea bags, 'that outside Ulster, there are more routine armed patrols in this part of the city than anywhere else in Britain?' He said it as though the fact that so many of the villains targeted by the patrols were children made the whole thing ridiculous. He was searching in the drawers of the desk when a woman entered the room.

'The tea bags have gone again, Jean,' he said.

Jean Carr was short and wide at the hips. She was dressed in corduroys and a man's jumper, with a man's short hair. Brendan found it impossible to gauge her age. Sixty, he guessed, though some of the lines on her face might only have been tiredness. She seemed not to notice Brendan.

'They're in the bottom of the filing cabinet where you moved them,' she said. She was rummaging through a pile of papers on the top of the desk that she evidently shared with the priest. 'You put them there so you could reach them more easily.'

'I didn't move them anywhere,' he protested.

She didn't answer. The priest, indignant, moved across to an ancient gun-metal filing cabinet to prove their absence. He bent down with difficulty to the bottom drawer. A moment later he rose with a handful of tea bags fished from the bottom of a plastic catering pack.

'I've found them,' he said, placated. To no one in particular, the priest added, '– I don't know what I'd do without my Jean.'

Jean ignored the remark.

'Did I tell you this is Brendan, Jean?'

She pulled out the report she had been seeking from the chaos of paperwork in the filing tray. 'I guessed,' she said. She gave Brendan a sidelong glance.

'I used to teach him, many years ago.'

She flicked through the pages of the report. 'I know. You told me.' She seemed determined to be unimpressed at Brendan's arrival.

'I'm brewing up for us. You want a cup of tea?'

She shook her head. Fr Wynn stood up and manœuvred himself past the desk, with the tea bags in one hand and his stick in the other, heading for the kitchen. In his youth, the priest had rowed for Leinster. There had been a fleeting chance at selection for the Olympic Games, lost in the maelstrom of war on the European mainland. He had boxed at the Irish ABA Finals in Cork while he was still a schoolboy. At the seminary, he had climbed peaks solo in the Boggeragh Mountains, and held the First Fifteen's forward eight together as a rampaging flanker. Now, there was arthritis in his hips, and his knees were ancient and ruined. His bulk, once his strength, had become his liability.

With the priest gone from the room, his colleague finally turned around towards Brendan to examine him.

'Do you know what he wanted me for when he rang me up?' Brendan asked to ease the momentary tension he felt at being inspected.

'He wants your help.'

'With what?'

'Let him tell you.'

Brendan shrugged. 'I'll do what I can, I suppose.'

'Just remember,' she said, 'he's not a person who's ever needed to ask anybody for help before.' She looked at him a moment longer, appraising the man who had been sent for, then left the room.

Left on his own, Brendan looked around the walls of the office. As a boy, he had seldom been allowed inside the priest's inner sanctum, though he had a clear recollection of walking past the room and seeing it lined with boxing photographs. He had wondered frequently as a child what feats would have been required for his own portrait to be hung on those walls. The subjects were caught in a range of stilted poses. Brendan recognized some of them, including Frankie Clough, smiling foolishly for the camera, with a Northern ABA medal around his neck on a ribbon. Beside the boxing photographs, a posse of strong, pale young men in woollen, crew-necked jerseys grinned from a sepia print. Underneath the photograph, in longhand, was written 'Leinster Eight, 1940'. A small clutch of medals hung from three nails punched roughly into the chimney breast. On the far side of the room, above a two-bar electric fire, a large crucifix secured to the wall with bolts showed Jesus's Sacred Heart weeping blood, and the crown of thorns on his head. A black and white photograph hung to one side of the crucifix. Brendan peered at it for a while, trying to decipher the image. It showed what seemed to him to be a praying figure, perhaps the Virgin Mary, illuminated grainily against a night sky surrounded by the lancet arches of a medieval church roof. The only softening touch in the room was an emptied milk bottle on the fireplace next to the priest's medals in which two small red poppies were propped in water. His gaze passed on, to more of the boxers – white-chested, tight-jawed, determined, hopeful, young. Always young.

'Did Jean give you a hard time?'

Brendan turned around. Fr Wynn was standing in the doorway with two teas, his walking stick hooked over one arm.

'Not really.'

'She's protective,' the priest said in his cracked, bass voice. 'She likes to look after me because I'm old and she thinks that this sometimes makes me a helpless child.' He put the two mugs on the desk and edged around into his chair.

'I imagine she works hard,' Brendan said. He said it because he imagined the priest thought so. Brendan supposed that Jean and her street-level project had succeeded in changing nothing. He imagined it was mocked in semi-public by the slouched youths gathered in the recesses of the gym each day.

'She's not always had an easy time of it,' Fr Wynn said. 'Her son died in the end. It was drugs mostly. It made her braver than she'd been until that point. There wasn't anything else to fear after that, but it was a long road. She feels strongly about the work that gets done in this place. She feels, like I do, that everyone else has given up on the boys who come here. We're all they have left, Brendan. Here, have your brew.'

The priest lifted up one of the mugs for Brendan. It was chipped at the top. The red, white and blue logo on the side was of the defunct Manchester Olympic bid which a different, glossier part of the city had once pursued with messianic zeal. The priest settled himself back in his chair in stages behind the desk.

'I suppose,' Fr Wynn said, when he had organized himself, 'that you thought I'd be dead by now.'

Brendan smiled in acknowledgement. The two men drank tea and remembered things from thirty years ago.

'I didn't ever want to miss school,' Brendan remembered part-way through their recollections. 'Even if I was sick, I didn't want to stop off. And the gym – I was the same with the gym. I used to run all the way from home to get here when it was a gym night.'

Reluctantly he stopped there. For a second, he had wanted to say something else. For a second, Brendan had wanted to say, I ran down here in the evenings because of you; because once I believed that you – Fr Wynn – were the arbiter of the world. And I thought that one day – when God decided it was time – he would make you into a saint. I always wanted to run here because in the end, even when I grew out of that notion, I saw at least that you were the man my father wasn't.

'I recall you even bringing your boxing shorts with you one time when you had broken your arm and had a plaster cast on it.'

'I remember that,' Brendan replied, '– I'd fallen off the top of the slide in the park. I remember trying to persuade you that I could still spar in the ring with one arm.'

'And I remember sending you home.'

'I used to box shadows walking home afterwards along the canal bank.'

'It wouldn't be so safe to do that now,' the priest added. 'A boy was raped and left for dead on that stretch of the canal not so long ago. Just last winter. A terrible thing, Brendan. How people can be driven to do such things it's hard to know. A lot of it is the drugs, I would say. We even have children now who deal them in the playground. It's quite routine to find it.'

'I don't suppose I knew what drugs were until I left Manchester.'

'I listen to the conversations of boys out there in the gym now, and it frightens me how much the children know. But it frightens me how much they don't know, too – about having fun, about how to *live*. They're hardened. And I'm not talking about boxing. A youngster can box like a tiger and still be a child. You were like that. No, I mean at such a young age they've lost the capacity to wonder. They miss so much like that. There's time enough in this world to be a grown-up without having to start while you're still in short trousers. A bit of innocence never did anyone any harm.'

'You think there's still room for innocence?'

'Surely. Surely I do, Brendan. I think that for me, the Gospels themselves are all about retaining a sense of innocence, a sense of wonder about the world and its possibilities. How else do we maintain hope for the future?'

'Don't you think wonder is a bit of a luxury these days, Father?'

'No, I do not, Brendan.'

'Maybe a priest gets to take a more simplistic view of things than the rest of us.'

'Are you saying I'm not living in the real world, Brendan? Are you saying I'm out with the fairies? Is that what you're saying? You think it's a luxury being a man of God?'

'I just think a calling to be a priest must make some things easier. The way you *see* things. I mean, from your point of view, God speaks to you. That's how it's meant to happen, isn't it? Isn't it going to be harder for everyone else? From what I see, people are confused enough about things without being encouraged to romance more. Wasn't there a survey done in America that said more people believed in alien visits than in evolution? The danger with innocence, Father, is when it's really just lack of knowledge.'

The old priest turned towards the photograph Brendan had been examining to one side of the crucifix. 'Do you know what that is, Brendan Moon?'

'I guessed it was a likeness of Our Lady. A depiction of her praying in a medieval church.'

'Yes, it's the Blessed Virgin Mary. But it isn't a likeness. It's a photograph. The Virgin Mary began appearing on the roof of the Coptic Church in a suburb of Cairo early in 1968. She spent the next three years appearing there intermittently to the congregation.'

'You don't think there's any chance it might not have been for real?'

'There was no doubt about it. More than a million people were said to have witnessed the appearances over the course of the three years. That is not something that you or I can explain away. The photograph up there is one of those that were taken of Our Lady during one of her appearances in the church. You see, Brendan, it isn't just priests who are given the reassurance. The reassurance is there for anyone who wants it.'

'You mean like the halberd of St Servius you used to tell us about in confirmation class, falling out of the sky? Like the Letters from God that fell on Heslop Bridge?'

'Such things seem meant for reassurance, wouldn't you agree?'

'From God?'

'Certainly from God. I know that in this knowing age, people are happy to cast doubt on such things. But those who perceive the truth of these things will not be put off.'

'But why Heslop Bridge, for instance, Father? Why not other tragedies?'

'God didn't send his Son amongst us for a particular generation, Brendan, or for a single people. He did it for everyone. It seems reasonable to suppose that any interventions He makes are done to give hope to everyone who has been crying out in the wilderness and has needed to hear God's voice.'

'You wouldn't argue that it meant the recipients were more deserving, more in need, than anyone else say with those parchments?'

'The tragedy for those people was great, but no one is going to argue that others haven't suffered as much.

And then, of course, we can't fall into the trap of thinking we can work all this out for ourselves. We can't. We're not meant to.'

'Don't we need to know the answers, Father? How can people be reassured if things don't seem to make sense?'

'I suppose that was what people said in the wake of the Resurrection. I suppose there were those in Palestine who were demanding answers 2,000 years ago, sceptics demanding proof. And then there were those who just had faith in the truth of what had happened. And who do you suppose were the more blessed and comforted of the two? I'll tell you. The ones who had faith. The ones who allowed their faith, through it, to be reaffirmed. I don't understand electricity, Brendan, but when I flick that switch over there on the wall, the light bulb comes on. I don't always need to understand something to believe in it.'

'But there is an explanation that can be given to account for electricity.'

'And there are explanations for everything that happens on Earth – reasons for things being how they are.'

'But you're saying we can't divine all of them, only some of them?'

'Yes.'

'So you'd argue there were reasons why Heslop Bridge, for example, might get chosen? Reasons why the bereaved families there were sent parchments?'

'Yes.'

'And we can guess at some or all of God's reasoning but not be *sure* that we know the whole of it?'

'Yes.'

'Father, why would God send parchments to seven families and have the rest scattered around the town?'

'Would it not make sense, Brendan, that the bereaved families each had a parchment of their own?'

'It would, Father. Except that there were nine bereaved families.'

'Nine?'

'Yes.'

'Are you sure?'

Brendan nodded. 'I'm sure.'

'You seem to know something about these Letters, Brendan?'

'My employers are involved. I've been doing some work for them in Lancashire over the last few weeks. In fact, I wanted to ask if you knew anyone with a knowledge of Hebrew texts well enough to have a look at one of them for me.'

'Do you have access to these Letters?'

'Yes.'

'Perhaps I do. Do you remember Nicholas Pacynko? Maybe not. He would be a little older than you. He would have boxed here before your time. He teaches religious studies at the university. He might be able to help you.'

'You see,' Brendan said, 'what puzzles me about those parchments is that, if it were true, why do you think, in a small town where he knew it would cause consternation, God would deliberately choose *not* to bequeath Letters to two of the families?'

'Perhaps two of the parchments are still waiting to be discovered?'

'Are you telling me that things despatched by God can get mislaid?'

'You sound disbelieving.'

'I am.'

'But surely you can see that you'll never disprove *all* of

God's interventions. There'll always be *some* that you can't explain. Like the Virgin Mary at Cairo; like a thousand others that many of us believe God has instigated; like the Resurrection itself.'

'I'm only concerned with the ones I'm assigned to investigate, Father.'

'The rest can be left on the shelf for others to ponder?'

'They're good stories, Father – all of them sitting there on the shelf.'

'You are a professional doubter, Brendan.'

'And you are a professional believer.'

'And neither of us can see the whole picture. After all, are you able to say it wasn't a miracle that I tracked you down at just the moment I needed you? Who is to say what is a miracle and what isn't? Does the laboratory which investigated your parchment know enough about DNA to say that what makes us what we are as human beings isn't in itself miraculous? Or that the origins of the Big Bang that started the universe was not an act commissioned by God? Can you answer me that?'

'You're preaching again. It's what you believe in – it's your trade. But we're not in class any more, Father. We're in your gym – and there's piss in the hallway, and the kids are dealing in the schools.'

The priest sat back in his chair. 'Yes. It's funny how the young always think they know it all. It's only as you get older that you see how, in truth, we really do know less and less.'

'I'm not young, father. I'm thirty-eight years old, and if I remember rightly, I'm here because it was you who needed the help, not me.'

'Thirty-eight is just beginning. I suppose, in some ways,

seventy-eight is just beginning. And yes, it was me who asked you.'

'How did you find me?'

'A man came to visit me here. Kevin remembered you from school. He said you and he were in the same class.'

'Kevin Eatough?'

'He remembered the name of the insurance company you were working for.'

'We swapped Christmas cards for years, me and Kevin. We lost touch about the time I moved to Kent.'

'So there I was needing an insider in the industry, and a week later there was Kevin on my doorstep come to talk to me and remembering you.'

'You want insurance sorting out for the gym – is that it?'

'That's part of it.'

'You don't have insurance?'

'We used to have. We had any number of break-ins. One of them cleaned us out of the drug project's computer and software. We've had a lot of vandalism, too. We had to claim – we couldn't have managed the repairs otherwise. In the end, though, what the insurance company were proposing as premiums became preposterous. We just couldn't afford them. So we let the insurance lapse.'

'What about other insurance companies?'

'We tried them. Jean must have rung every one in the Yellow Pages. No one will touch us.'

'Couldn't you sell this place and get somewhere more suitable?'

'We've thought of that, but it isn't as though this place has any saleable value. It's in the wrong area to be worth anything and it needs too much work doing on it. No one would buy it. I know, I've tried.'

'So you want to reinsure?'

'We need insurance.'

'Have you found enough money now to be able to afford the premiums?'

'Brendan, will you just push the door shut behind you.'

Brendan leaned back and pushed it shut.

'I've had a proposition put to me,' the priest said.

'From who?'

'From a businessman.'

'A businessman?'

'In the drugs business, Brendan. Someone who grew up using the gym. Someone who feels he owes a debt to me.'

'What sort of proposition?'

'He knows, as I know, that this building is decrepit and falling apart around our ears. He knows we can't defend ourselves against the vandalism and that, before too long, there'll be nothing left. The businessman has said he is willing to help. He will advance me the money for the insurance. The amount would be repaid afterwards, with a small amount of interest added.'

'Afterwards? After what?'

'He would arrange for the gym to catch fire one night.'

'Arson?'

'For a good reason, Brendan. The insurance money would enable us to lease another building for the project, and for the gym. There's a place we've seen half a mile away that would be ideal. Better security, not falling apart. And the businessman would be paid his money back.'

'The criminal.'

The priest shrugged. 'Now who is it taking a simple view of the world? I've known this man since he was three, Brendan. I trust him. He says it can be done.'

'It gets done every day.'

'He said that.'

'You'd be breaking the law, Father.'

'I'd be saving the work that goes on here. The Council say they won't rehouse us. We have no money. We need your help, Brendan. I need your help. I need to ensure that we'd get our money from an insurance company. You'd know how to help me, wouldn't you? You can prevent fifty years of work going down the drain.'

'You know the consequences if you were caught, Father?'

'I'd go to Hell? I thought you might want to tell me that was just a story.'

'You'd go to prison.'

'No one sends priests my age to prison, Brendan. Not for this.'

'What about your reputation in the eyes of the community?'

'What about my reputation in the eyes of God?'

'I don't know much about God, Father.'

'But you know about insurance investigations – about what they'd look for, about how to make a fire look accidental? What to avoid? How to make sure an insurance company would agree to pay out?'

Brendan nodded.

'And you'd tell me. You'd write something down, or tell me. And vet the small print in the policy we were being offered, to make sure the insurance claim would be valid afterwards.'

He assumed that it was Jean Carr who had coaxed the priest out beyond his depth into these murky waters. Soon, with or without Brendan's help, Brendan knew the priest would be floundering. He dealt with these people. He knew more about this hard-edged place than the priest ever could. You couldn't do deals with these people, Brendan knew, and come out unscathed. Even if you somehow got away with it, you couldn't mix with them and remain unsullied.

'Can I ask you something, Father?'

'Of course.'

'How do you cope with this?'

'With what?'

'With *this*! With all of this. The break-ins. The smell of piss every time you walk up those stairs. The teenage hardcases outside with their hair shaved up their skulls who think they're Al Capone but can't write their names. The girls hanging around them who are going to be mothers while they're still children. How do you maintain hope that things will get better? How do you cope with circumstances that reduce you to breaking the law just to survive?'

The priest thought about the question for a while. 'The land behind the gym,' he said eventually, 'is the boundary between the turfs of two of the principal local gangs. Not gangs, really. Groups of kids, whose elder brothers first brought them in here before they started infant school when they thought this was a glamorous place. They still come in here because they know me. They know they'll get help if they need it. These are the same kids who are running heroin packets out to nice estates whose families, five years ago, thought they were safe from that kind of thing.'

'That helps you to carry on?'

'I carry on because I know that, if God is anywhere, he must surely be in a place like this. After all, where else *could* he be? God has a plan, Brendan. The alternative is too unthinkable even for me. He must have a plan. And this, all of it – despite what you are thinking – must somehow be part of it. I have no need to go looking elsewhere. This is where I'm meant to be.'

'I envy you,' Brendan said.

'I thought it was you who had the good suit and the car. How can you envy me?'

Brendan shrugged. 'Just your certainty. I envy your certainty.'

'Who says I have certainty? I have *faith*. That's not the same thing. Don't put me on a pedestal and assume I don't have doubts like the rest of you. I have my moments of weakness too.' He went quiet for a moment. 'Can I tell you something?' he said eventually.

'Sure.'

'When Jean's son died, the night he died, we slept together, Jean and I. I broke my vows. I don't know how it started. I think it was just needing the warmth of another human body. It only happened that once. We've never spoken of it since. So don't think because I have a faith that it's all easy and sorted. Because it isn't.'

'But you know what it is you're looking for.'

'I suppose so. I suppose I do. And what about you? What is it that you're looking for, Brendan?'

Brendan drank his tea. 'I don't know. What should I be looking for? To tell you the truth, Father, I stopped looking. You do the kind of job I do and one of the things that happens is you stop looking. I was involved in a case a few years ago. Some fraud. It turned out to be big-time fraud. I spent three months on it. Then one morning I came out of my comfortable house, in a village where three of the houses have thatched roofs and where there's even a village pond with ducks, and the car in my garage had been beaten with baseball bats in the night. Pummelled, and I hadn't heard a thing. There was a note on the windscreen. It said "Next time it's your son."'

'What did you do?'

'As quietly as I could, I let the case drop. That's what I did. I didn't think twice. Never told a soul. Because I knew what I wanted. I knew where I was going and why. That's why I let them walk away. You ask me now, Father, all this time later, and I say I don't know what I'm looking out for. Not God, that's for sure. I like to keep things simpler than that. At the moment, I'm just looking for a solution to your insurance problem.'

Brendan looked about him, at the photographs on the wall, the bleeding Christ crucified, the Virgin Mary on the roof of the Coptic Church in Cairo. 'All this time later,' he said, as if astonished at the sudden realisation, 'and you're still here.'

'Getting old in the same place has its advantages. People know where to find you. That's how Kevin Eatough found me.'

'Kevin once kicked my ball into the lake in the corporation park. I fell out with him for a week over it.'

'Is that so?'

'Afterwards, I thought it was God punishing me because he knew I'd broken my promise to give up eating toffees for Lent.'

'Kevin Eatough as God's Instrument?'

'I suppose.'

'I'm not sure that's exactly how things work. But, like we said, who's to know for sure.'

'What did Kevin want?'

'Hm?'

'When he came to the gym to see you. What did he want?'

'He wanted to talk about his son.'

'He has a son?'

'He does,' the priest said. 'It was Kevin's son who was assaulted down on the canal last winter.'

8

The Testament

The doctor in the hospital had been bearded, with strong hands. They were fisherman's hands, Brendan remembered thinking. They resembled the hands of the fishermen he and Jack had watched in the narrow village harbour they had found a couple of days previously in the hired car, while Carol had stayed back at the hotel to sunbathe in her usual spot by the pool. They were, Brendan had supposed, the inherited hands of the man's ancestors, the hands of a hundred generations of Greek fishermen, except that quite suddenly one generation had thrown up a medical houseman in the Kerkira Hospital whose task at that moment was to explain formally to the British couple that the life had passed out of their son.

Brendan had watched the doctor's hands all the way through the meeting. The man had been talking, in his passably good English, about the arrangements that could be made to fly the body home from Corfu. The room had been shaded away from the day's heat out in the streets. There had been the hum of a fan somewhere, and a faint sense of nurses moving coolly past in the corridor outside, and Greek words somewhere in the building, running like water.

Brendan had known then that he would never again think about the geography of fishermen's hands without being reminded of Jack. He knew then – as Carol had spoken with the doctor, and as he himself sat watching those coarse, apologetic hands resting on the hospital coat – that he would never again encounter a professional wearing a white coat, never enter a hospital, without it meaning that his son was dead.

Time passed. Carol left. Things changed. But at the age of thirty-eight, standing in the reception hall of the Accrington Victoria Hospital, with a black drizzle floating off the evening moors, Brendan knew – as he knew each time he had cause to be around doctors – that he would be compelled to look at the hands of each one of them on his way through to Jim McCready's ward. It was not a matter of choice. He would look at the bony English hands of each doctor and he would remember the fisherman's hands in the Kerkira Hospital. And when he looked, he would be moved to wonder each time whether *these* hands, unlike those of the fisherman, might have saved Jack – might, in some unconscious rearrangement of the past, save him still. It was the same instinct which compelled him to scrutinize the changeling face of every small boy who passed him in the street. It was instinct. It was not possible *not* to look, or, momentarily, to hope. Each time it was the same inexorable, expectant search for the face of his son. Medical people hurried past him along the corridors of the hospital with anxiety and expectation in their faces, and Brendan had an urge to whisper to them as they went by: I know a secret – that you are powerless against this tide of injury and chaos; that so much of what you do, in the end, is futile; that this is pantomime. Go home instead and check on your loved ones – your strong men, and your bright warm children, your safe lives. Right now, before it is too late.

Jim McCready had been in the hospital for five days, and they were still carrying out tests. The bed next to his had the curtains drawn around it. Behind the curtains were the sounds of a bed-bath being administered, and grunts of protest from an old man. Joyce had left the ward in search of a vending machine for coffee on the next floor. Brendan had driven her over from Heslop Bridge. The lift had saved her the trouble of catching the usual two evening buses.

'Isn't there someone who could give you a lift now and then?' Brendan had asked on the way over.

'Wilf Wardle offers sometimes to bring me over from Heslop Bridge,' Joyce had told him, 'but I keep telling him I can manage.'

'Wouldn't it be easier to accept the lift than keep making the journey on two buses each way?'

'I wouldn't want to feel obliged,' she had said. 'Jim's my responsibility.'

'What did Wilf say when you told him that?'

'He said "OK". I like it when people know when to give up with me.'

'What about Jim's son?'

'Terry? He's been once, apparently. Jim had a row with him, and he scuttled off after twenty minutes.'

Jim McCready was sitting up in bed. His skin was tinged with yellow from jaundice. He had lost some more weight since being admitted to the hospital. The illness had made him more dependant, and willing to talk. He and Brendan sat listening to the growing battle of wills beyond the curtain encircling the next bed while they waited for Joyce to return.

The nurse persisted in her attempts to bed-bath the man who, with increasing peevishness, was trying to obstruct her. Eventually, she admitted defeat and called through the curtain for assistance from a colleague.

'He's a bugger, that one,' Jim McCready said to Brendan. 'It takes him an hour and a half to button his dressing gown and put his slippers on after breakfast, but he can beat us all to the *Countdown Conundrum* every afternoon on the telly. Used to be a schoolteacher. Now he thinks the nurses keep coming to rob him, so he spends his time complaining to the hospital management and dictating letters of protest to the Health Authority. I encourage him.'

A second nurse arrived and disappeared inside the curtain. Brendan could hear the man muttering and the nurses remonstrating with him. Then they heard a woman's scream. The first nurse appeared, cradling one hand. There was blood on the fleshy part of her palm where the man had bitten her. Another nurse and then a doctor appeared. Eventually Brendan could hear the man weeping quietly. After another few minutes, the curtain was pulled back. The bed had been remade. The man was lying down. His face was white and tired. His hair was dishevelled. His expression was vague.

'All the entertainment's free in here, you know,' Jim McCready said. He leaned conspiratorially over towards Brendan. 'You want to know something, though?'

Brendan nodded. 'What?'

'This place is *full* – ' (he paused for effect and looked round conspiratorially) 'of sick people.'

'Is that right?' Brendan said.

'Crammed to the rafters. It's a wonder I don't catch something with these sick people all over the place.'

Joyce returned to the bedside with two plastic cups.

'So, did you tell your visitor anything useful while I've been gone?'

'We've been watching the punch-up next door,' Jim McCready explained. 'Blood was drawn,' he added happily.

'I thought you were going to talk to him about Calderhall.'

'Give us a chance, woman. What did you get from the machine?'

'Coffee. Why?'

'Stick to the hot chocolate, or the soup.'

'You're an expert?'

'The coffee gives you the runs.'

'You're a wind-up merchant, Jim McCready.'

'Maggie told me.'

'Who's Maggie?'

'One of the nurses. She's top tottie is Maggie.'

'I beg your pardon?'

'That's what the lad in the corner with the broken leg calls her. We're both big boob men, me and Darren over there, and we agreed that Maggie is definitely top tottie.'

'Well, if the coffee makes me ill, at least it'll give me a rest from coming to visit you for a few nights, won't it? I dare say Maggie will see to you while I'm away.'

'Yeah, well, I wouldn't want you coming to visit me if you were sick.'

'I know,' Joyce said, smiling at him, 'you might catch something.'

Jim shifted himself against his array of pillows and looked across at Brendan. 'So what is it that you want to know?'

'Sorry?'

'About Calderhall. That's what you came for, isn't it?'

'I'm not really sure what I want to know,' Brendan admitted. 'Just a bit of background. What it was like? Can you tell me how long you worked there?'

'Until 1984. It all began to change then. That was when I got early retirement. They were making a lot of people redundant – winding the place down. They'd moved a lot of the patients out, even the low grades, so they didn't need the same level of maintenance work around the colony as before. That was when I paid my bond to the oil company for the petrol station lease. Eighteen thousand I paid. That was most of my lump sum from the Health Authority.'

'And before that, you'd worked at Calderhall for how long?'

'Pretty much all my working life – from nineteen. I did my apprenticeship while I was there, in heating systems. Went to nightschool at the technical college for it once a week.'

'Did you like the work?'

'Not at first. No one liked it at first, but you got used to it.'

'What did you get used to?'

'Well, the defectives who were kept inside,' Jim said, ' – and the people who did the keeping in. Sometimes, it was hard to know who was worse. There were some mean buggers running that place, I'm telling you. They used to laugh at me, some of the staff, when I was young, because I got upset at some of the things I saw – some of the things they did, especially to the low grades. They used to say, "Remember, Jim, these aren't like you and me. These aren't people."'

'What are low grades?'

'The inmates who weren't any use to the staff. High grades were the ones who could be put to work – in the laundry and around the grounds, that kind of thing.'

'Did you know Oscar Brigg inside the colony?'

Jim McCready nodded. 'You mean Oscar who helps Wilf out nowadays? Yes, I saw him in there.'

'How did you first meet him?'

'I unrolled him from a mattress.'

'In a bed?'

'In a field.'

'A field?'

'Did you know that he used to sing?'

'Who, Oscar Brigg?'

'Yes. Not in English. In some gobbledegook language of his own that he made up. He'd not be quite a man by then. What is he – a year or two younger than me? He'd be seventeen or eighteen then. Sometimes, apparently, he sang. In the laundry, and in the dormitory. The staff didn't like him singing. So one day a couple of them made Oscar drag one of the heavy mattresses out into the field behind the dormitory, and they whacked him a good few times and rolled your man up in it and left him there, beaten up and suffocating. When I found him, he was nearly dead with exposure. *That* was when I first met him.'

'What happened to the men who assaulted him?' Brendan said.

'What happened? What do you mean "What happened?" Nothing happened.'

'Was there an investigation?'

Jim McCready shook his head. 'You don't understand,' he said.

'What don't I understand?'

'There were no investigations. There wasn't *anything* once someone had been sent there. They stopped being people after they'd been sent there. The soldier who'd been demobbed in

1945 who supposedly had a fit on Nelson railway station when he was travelling home and was admitted – he stopped being a man once he was locked up in there. I knew him in the sixties and seventies. He was an old man by then, with a face that was scarred from the beatings he'd taken over the years. The lad who was taken in for stealing a bicycle – he stopped being a person. The old woman whose mother had sent her there at fifteen because she'd had sex before the war with a black man. They all stopped being people once they were inside.'

'How long were people confined in there?'

'Forever. That's what was meant to happen. If you were sent there, you didn't do a few years and then get out if you'd behaved yourself. If you were in, it meant that you were feeble-minded, or a moral defective, and that was that. There weren't any appeals. That was your home for life. Patients just grew old and died there.'

'Weren't there any rules?'

'Not really. Not that I saw. Except for the ones that the families of staff who ran the place made up. It was like the mafia. You'd have a group of people from the same extended family running one particular block, and not having to answer to anybody. A lot of them hadn't any qualifications for what they were doing. Once they'd done five years in the colony they were *given* something that said they were qualified, but they weren't. When one retired, they just arranged for someone else in the family to take over. They could do anything. They were just drunk on power. Outside the colony they were nobodies. Just little people. But, inside, they were like gods. Whatever they said went.'

'Did you complain?' Brendan said.

'I was a boy when I started there. I had a job to keep.

Later on, I had a family and a mortgage. Like I said, you got used to it. It became normal.'

'Did anyone ever complain?'

'Sometimes someone said something,' Jim McCready said. 'It didn't do any good, though. The names of trouble-makers got forwarded from ward to ward, so that the experience of working in the colony became too menacing to bear for anyone who was outside the circle. I remember one group of staff kept an alcohol still on the go for years, brewing the stuff in a toilet block that was kept permanently off limits to the inmates. All of us on Maintenance had instructions to keep away from it. They even had the colony's administrator running a private printing business with them, using the colony's money to finance its running costs.'

'No one ever made a fuss?'

Jim McCready shrugged. 'There were a few good people,' he said, ' – a few that somehow managed to survive there and who tried to do good with the inmates. But what could one person here and there do against a whole tribe of folk who'd lorded it over the place for thirty or forty years?'

'What about Oscar Brigg? What happened to him after the time you found him rolled in the mattress?'

'I took him back to the dormitory. The staff just laughed. I don't know what happened after that, really. I saw him around the colony sometimes. Not often. Sometimes I'd go years without seeing him. I don't know what they did to him. He was always deathly pale whenever I did see him, like he was kept inside a lot. A few times his face was a mess, like he'd been hit. One time he was limping when I saw him – that was when he was a lot older – maybe in his thirties. I remember he was walking across the compound with a group of other patients and some of the uniformed staff. I remember, he had no shoes on. Someone told me around that time that he still sang sometimes, and the staff still hit him for it.'

Brendan stayed at the hospital while Joyce helped to feed her father-in-law, cutting the meat on his plate and dabbing his chin with a tissue if, as sometimes happened, he misjudged the distance between the fork and his mouth. The two men discussed cars. Jim talked about a Triumph Spitfire he'd once souped up in the garage and taken out onto the West Pennine Moors roads. He said that on one stretch he'd managed a hundred and twenty. 'That was before they put those bloody speed cameras everywhere. No sense of fun, some folk.'

Afterwards, Brendan drove Joyce back to Heslop Bridge.

'They don't want to treat the jaundice until they've finished all the other tests,' she said. 'That's what they've said to me.'

'Does he always get tired that quickly?'

Jim had fallen asleep before they had left.

'His energy's coming and going a bit at the moment,' Joyce said. 'He doesn't always last as long as he did tonight. Having you turn up perked him up a bit. He liked being able to talk about his cars. It's no good him talking to me about them – I don't understand, so he gets mad at me. But it's as if there's only so much energy to go around these days. He was always a strong man. Fleshy. You can see the bones in his chest now. I keep wondering whether that's why he's speaking slower. It's like even his jaw is getting heavy for him.'

'About working in Calderhall . . .'

'I've never heard Jim talk about it much before – other than in passing. It's as if he's decided it's time to talk about it now. I do know that there's a couple of families in Heslop

Bridge who used to work at the colony who he wouldn't ever have anything to do with, even after he finished working there. He'll cross the road to avoid them. But I never found out much about it. He's never been a big talker about anything other than cars, has Jim. It's a *man* thing, as I see it. Give a man the choice between talking – I mean really *talking* – and almost anything else and he'll usually go for the anything else. Don't you think, *B. Moon?'*

Brendan nodded. 'Probably.'

He dropped Joyce off outside her house. She said she had double practice to look forward to before bed. She'd missed a couple of nights already this week because of rushing to visit Jim in the hospital, and she was in danger of forgetting what an oboe looked like. She was meant to be working on an upbeat version of 'It Ain't Necessarily So'. Her music teacher had told her that at the moment it sounded more like 'Seventy-Six Trombones'.

'So at least that's an improvement,' she said happily, 'at least it sounds like *something.'*

Back at the hotel, Brendan wrote up his notes. Jim McCready had given him the name of someone to contact in the Archive Section at Calderhall. Who knows, he had said, maybe Oscar Brigg's file might have surfaced again. He also told Brendan that he had once met a man who had gone to visit Oscar Brigg. The man was standing outside the gates of the colony very early one morning, as Jim McCready was arriving to start his shift. It was 1968 – Jim was adamant that he could remember the year precisely because of a football match he'd been to the night before which had stuck in his memory. The man was carrying a small valise, as if he had travelled a long way and might have stopped overnight in the village down the road, and he said that Oscar Brigg's father was dead. It was winter, and there was snow on the ground. The man had taken his hat off to speak to him. He had an accent. Jim McCready said, as far as he knew, this had been the only visit Oscar Brigg had received in the decades he had spent in the colony.

Nicholas Pacynko was urbane, relaxed, amused. He had taught Religious Studies at the university for twenty years. He had been known to Fr Wynn ever since he, like Brendan, had learned to box in the old priest's Salford gym. His study was an explosion of books surrounding a desk and a couple of expensive-looking Georgian wing-backed armchairs.

'You have to understand,' he said, 'that I was the smallest boy in the school. There was nothing to me at all. All my life, I've always been nine stones, fully clothed. If you were skinny and small and Jewish as well, you were additionally cursed. If, on top of that, you were clever and liked books, you just had no chance.'

'It mattered that you were Jewish?'

'Before the Pakistanis and Indians started arriving, the Jews took most of the stick in Manchester for being different. It was my parents' idea to have me learn how to box. That's why they sent me to Fr Wynn's gym. There I was – poor skinny little Salford kike being taught how to defend himself by an Irish Catholic priest. I will say this, at least, for the Catholic Church – they breed an effective class of boxing coach.'

'You didn't enjoy boxing?'

'Most weeks I got beaten black and blue in the ring. I was a sitting target for the local lads. My family were sure it was doing me good, toughening me up. I carried on going at my

parents' insistence until I was fifteen. I suppose it tells you
what kind of world they expected me to have to face. You
know what the irony of all this is – that I'm fifty-six years old
and I've never thrown a punch in my life. Of course, by the
time you get to be a university professor, there isn't much
call for defending yourself in the street. Then again, the
burden of being Jewish isn't what it used to be.'

'Your parents had it tougher than you?'

'Yes.'

'Are they still alive?'

'My father is. As it happened, it was my father who
helped me to resolve the riddle of that Hebrew text you gave
me.'

'Your father?'

'Well, you know you were interested in the language of
the verse? You were asking if there was any significance in
it – as a Christian text?'

'Yes.'

'Well, it's interesting. It's obviously written in Hebrew,
but then you didn't need me to tell you that.'

'And Hebrew is the language of the Bible?'

'Well, yes and no, and that's what makes your *Christian*
verse interesting. The *Old* Testament books were all written
originally in Hebrew, but the New Testament Gospels were
different. Hebrew wouldn't have been any good to the early
Christians. You have to remember that Hebrew, by then, had
become less and less familiar as a spoken language to the
ordinary people in Palestine. Well before the emergence of
Jesus, public readings of the scriptures in the synagogues
had to include an oral paraphrase in the Aramaic vernacu-
lar.'

'But there *is* Hebrew scripture which has survived, isn't

there? The Dead Sea Scrolls are written in Hebrew, aren't they?'

'They are. But those books – Isaiah, Deuteronomy – they're written in the ancient form of Hebrew, the kind which uses no vowels or word breaks. It wasn't until the Massoretes started to standardize the process that written Hebrew changed.'

'Who are the Massoretes?'

'They were the Judaic scholars who undertook the task of editing and standardizing Hebrew texts around 500 AD. Until then, all written Hebrew was a consonantal text. It consisted, as I say, only of consonants. The Massoretic text added vowel points and separated the individual words out in order to ensure proper pronunciation.'

'Why would that make things interesting for me?' Brendan asked.

'The text you gave me,' Nicholas Pacynko went on, 'was written in the Massoretic text. When the books of the Old Testament were being written, and even when the New Testament Gospels were first being compiled – possibly in Aramaic, probably in Greek – the Massoretic text was unknown. I'd missed the point myself at first. I'd been looking simply for inconsistencies in the language, but there aren't any. What you gave me was a beautifully written prose poem. What I hadn't wondered, until I stepped back from it, was why a Christian God would have chosen to communicate in a version of the Hebrew language which was developed specifically to support Judaism in its struggle for authority against the new Christianity.

'I showed my father the verse you gave me. He was brought up as an Orthodox Jew. He's read the Talmud every day of his adult life. His observation after he'd read it seems as succinct as I could have wished myself. He said that if this was meant to be a manuscript that came from God, then it was a Jewish and not a Christian God.'

The village of Sillot was six miles away from Heslop Bridge. It was a former slate-quarrying settlement, built on a ridge of moorland and facing Holker Fell across a narrow farming valley. Oscar Brigg's brother lived down an unmade farm track. There was a 'For Sale' sign at the road, and the track itself dropped down a severe gradient between two walls enclosing grazing land. It was only wide enough for a single vehicle and Brendan, who had missed the turning twice, struggled to get the Volvo down it.

Even at first sight, Brendan realized that this couldn't have been the man who had visited Oscar, hatless, in the winter of 1968. At that time, Karl Brigg would have been in his twenties. The man Jim McCready had spoken to outside the colony was at least a generation older, with thinning hair and an accent.

Karl Brigg had a paunch and a stubborn shaving rash. His suit was stressed and shiny with age, and he wore an anorak over the top. There was a wagon parked up on the hard standing area in front of his house. He was fiddling with the ropes which secured a tarpaulin on the back of the wagon.

'In winter, nothing gets down that track,' Karl Brigg told Brendan with satisfaction. 'Even the mail gets left at the top of the road.' He seemed proud of the fact.

There was another 'For Sale' sign in front of the house, advertising both the house and the barn that was attached to it which was in the process of renovation. Trenches and pipes ran around the barn in a sea of excavated mud.

Brendan was led through the work-in-progress, stepping around the puddles and mud towards the house.

'It was the farmhouse, originally,' Karl Brigg said as he led Brendan through the porch and into the hall. 'There's still a bit of land goes with it but we lease that out for grazing.'

'You're selling?' Brendan said, indicating the sign.

'Maybe.'

'Maybe?'

'We'll have to see how things go,' Karl Brigg said. He seemed cagily uncommitted to the prospect. 'I'm going to get changed, I've a man coming. You can wait in the kitchen if you like.' He indicated a doorway and walked off, leaving Brendan standing in the hall.

The kitchen was dark. It was beamed and fitted in heavy wood. Brendan switched the light on by the door as he went in. There was a red Aga stove on the far side, and a vast wooden table in the middle of the room, surrounded by four ancient padded Regency dining chairs. There was a notice board on the wall to one side of the Aga, with a series of bills, seemingly unattended to, pinned haphazardly to it. The one at the top was an invoice to BabyTech Ltd, Director: Karl J. Brigg. On the invoice, in red pen, was written 'Bastard. Not to be paid. KB'. None of the other bills had been paid either from what Brendan could see. On one of the work surfaces was an office filing tray. The bottom two shelves were jammed with correspondence. The top one held several editions of a newsletter – *The Lantern* – from a local religious organization. Brendan picked one up. 'Friends,' each one began, 'We are the righteous few.' The name 'K. Brigg', and the address, 'Higher Brookhouse Farm', were handwritten in the top corner of each one. A series of paperback books were jammed in between the filing tray and the fridge freezer. Brendan read the titles. *Seven Habits of Highly Effective People. Awaken the Giant Within. Getting to YES.* There was another book left out on the kitchen table next to a pile of unopened mail. He picked it up. *Believing Yourself to the Top* was written by an American, Brent P. Theisman. Passages throughout the book were underscored with a double line in red biro. There was a bookmark embossed with 'Lantern Christian Brotherhood' marking a page. Brendan opened the book at that page and read the underlined section.

'You ARE a giant. Your destiny is in your control. The time to seek that destiny is NOW, by ridding your mind of all those unwanted obstacles to success.'

As he read, Brendan realized he could hear a voice somewhere in the house. Upstairs, Karl Brigg was involved in a conversation on the phone. The man's voice rose loud enough for Brendan to listen. It seemed to be a disagreement about money. Brendan wandered back over to the filing trays. He took out a handful of the correspondence from the bottom tray and sifted through it. One of the letters was a County Court judgment, pronouncing that a £3,000 debt incurred fourteen months previously by BabyTech to a supplier, plus court costs, should be repaid at £220 a month. There was a letter from Companies House informing Mr Brigg that he was in breach of a protocol by failing to provide the information detailed on the attached document. At the bottom of the pile were half a dozen colour brochures for a private nursing home. The front cover of the brochures said, 'Beech House: A Christian Home for the Elderly'. Its proprietor was listed as 'K. Brigg'.

When Karl Brigg came down, he had changed into

dungarees and wellingtons. As he walked into the kitchen he switched off the light Brendan had put on. The two men sat around the table in the kitchen's newly restored gloom.

'You don't have any sway with the council, do you?' Karl Brigg asked.

Brendan shook his head.

'Pity. I've spent twelve months being mucked around by them. It would have been handy if you'd been from the council.'

'Having some trouble?'

'All I want to do is get permission to expand the factory another forty feet on the land at the back. But can I get them to give it? You'd think town halls would be falling over themselves to encourage the likes of me to create some more jobs for people.'

'Business is going well then?'

'I work hard. I built that business up from nothing. We make baby mattresses. Now there's a tough market, but I still export 60 per cent of what I make. That sounds like success to me. Does that sound like success to you?'

'You have other businesses as well?'

'I have a lot of experience in business. I'm well respected for it. "Wealth creation is the engine of civilization". Brent P. Theisman. You know the book?'

'I don't.'

'You should read it. I'll lend it to you. You might learn something. What business are you in again?'

'Insurance,' Brendan said.

'Oh yes. One of the leeches, eh. It's true, though, isn't it? What do your lot contribute to this country compared to your average manufacturing business? No competition, is there?'

They heard the front door bang out in the hallway, and

footsteps. A moment later a woman appeared in the door-way.

'Before you start,' Karl Brigg said, 'he's not here viewing the house, so don't be saying you're being kept in the dark again. He's come about my brother.'

'Why?'

'Search me. Ask him yourself.'

The woman looked over at Brendan. Then she turned and left the room and they heard her going upstairs.

'Your wife?' Brendan asked.

'Women, eh!' Karl Brigg replied. 'You can't live with 'em . . .' He grinned uncomfortably. 'She gets things out of proportion. That's what they do, isn't it – get things out of proportion.'

'Can I ask you about your brother?' Brendan said.

'Has he passed away? Is that why you're here?'

'Oscar's still alive.'

'Yeah? Still alive! Good. Good. I'm glad he's still alive. How is he?'

'He's fine. When was the last time you saw him, Mr Brigg?'

'Me? Not for . . . You have to understand, Oscar was in an institution. He gets looked after. He's been looked after all his life.'

'I know that. I was just curious.'

'The last time I saw him? I went to see him in Calderhall. They were closing the place down. They contacted me as next of kin.'

'Yes, it said so in the file that's reappeared.'

'I didn't even know he was in there until then. That was how I found out where he'd been brought up. That was when I saw him. That's the only time I've seen him since we were boys.'

'That was what year?'

'I don't know. Eighty-six, eighty-seven.'

'It wasn't you who went to see him in the 1960s then?'

'Me? No. Like I said, I didn't know where Oscar was until the people there contacted me.'

'You don't know who it might have been – the man who went to see Oscar in the colony after your father died?'

'Not a clue. The old bastard never had any friends, so nobody would have gone anywhere at *his* bidding.'

'Your father?'

'I didn't even go to his funeral. He committed suicide, you know. That's how he died. In 1968. What sort of ending is that for someone who spent his life putting me down as a failure?'

'He put you down?'

'When you're the brother of an imbecile, there's double the pressure on you to shine. Oscar couldn't do anything – he couldn't read or write. He could never have taken care of himself. There's a photograph I have of him somewhere – you'll see what I mean.' He went out of the room and came back a few moments later with a biscuit tin full of photographs which he emptied onto the kitchen table. He sifted through them until he found what he was looking for.

'See, that's him in the picture, with my father.'

He handed it to Brendan. The boy in the picture had a clumsy face and was grinning wildly at the camera, excitement spilling from him at the idea of being photographed.

'He went to the village school like the rest of us,' Karl Brigg said, 'but he didn't do any of the schooling. He was just given tasks to do, fetching things or tidying up, but he couldn't do anything useful. One time, he went rooting in the box with my father's heirlooms and got himself dressed up in a shawl and one of those little hats – a skullcap, and went dancing down the street in them. It was after that my father decided to send him to the home.'

Brendan leant across the table to pass the photograph back.

'Keep it,' Karl Brigg said.

'You don't want it?'

'What would I want it for? You take it.'

Brendan inspected the photograph again. 'How old was your brother when he was sent away?'

'Ten. He was a year older than me. I don't suppose it was long after the photograph was taken. I didn't know where he'd been sent. My mother didn't know either. My father wouldn't tell her. He said it was a place where they'd look after Oscar better than we could. He was like that, my father – wanting to be the big boss all the time, thinking he always knew best. He came to England before the war and met my mother, and all he wanted was for me to become a proper Englishman – university, and then medicine or the law. He pushed and pushed to get me into the grammar school but when I got there I never worked hard enough to satisfy him. I was happy enough fooling around with the lads, and I finished up going to work on a stall at Clitheroe market. That wasn't good enough for my father, of course, but it was the best education anyone could have got, starting out in the business world. Something I once got told by a fellow stallholder was more use than everything my father yapped on at me about all those years: there's nothing more satisfying to a man of the world, this guy said, than being in search of a dollar in business. What do you think of that? Isn't that true? Nothing so satisfying. That's what made me. That's how I got where I am. That's how come I was

President of the local Chamber of Trade three years ago. People hold me in respect. But not that bastard. Best thing he ever did was to off himself.'

Brendan was manœuvring the Volvo gingerly around to point it back up the hill when Karl Brigg's wife came out of the house, clutching a box. She carried it across to a small Fiat which had been parked next to Brendan's car.

'Need a hand?' Brendan asked.

'No,' the woman said, ' – thank you.' She smiled. Brendan saw that there was a bruise on the side of her face.

'You're selling?' he asked, nodding towards the house.

'Yes. You really didn't come to look around then?'

Brendan shook his head.

'It's hard to know with Karl. I've had to learn over the years that he's something of a stranger to the truth. I don't suppose he told you why it's for sale?'

'No, he didn't.'

'We're in debt.'

'I see.'

'I'm sorry about all the mud,' the woman said. 'It's a building site. He promised it would be finished a year ago, and look at it.'

'It doesn't look very finished.'

'Nothing ever is. He never changes. One time he bought a snooker hall without even telling me. That was after he'd promised me yet again that he wouldn't get us into any more debt. I only found out when I discovered he'd mortgaged this place to pay for it to be reroofed and there was a problem with the bank. We're still paying for the snooker hall twelve years after we sold it at a loss. That's without mentioning the visits we've had from the bailiffs over the years for different things. What did he tell you about his brother when you asked?'

Brendan explained what Karl Brigg had told him.

'He missed something out,' she said once she had climbed into her car. 'He forgot to say that the only reason he went to Calderhall was that someone told him he could get money – benefits – paid to him if he agreed to look after his brother. He thought it might be a good wheeze to stick him in the nursing home we ran at that time and pocket the money.'

'So what happened?'

'He went to see what his brother was like after all those years, and he couldn't cope with what he found. He got more than he bargained for. Still, that happens to a lot of us.'

She looked back at the house, and then at Brendan. She was crying.

'What about the bruise?' Brendan asked.

'It doesn't matter any more,' she said, touching her cheek, ' – I'm leaving him soon.'

9

Letters from God

Joyce pulled the cakes out of the oven and set them down on the cooling rack. She wiped her hands on the apron she wore over her flowered pinafore dress. Her face was florid from the kitchen's warmth and her feet, swollen from the heat and from standing, were squeezed tight inside her court shoes. She carried the cakes across the kitchen, stepping around a stack of white boxes in the middle of the room. The opening bars of 'A Foggy Day' were playing in her head. As she conjured the tune, she found herself working out the fingering for the notes, pressing the tips of her fingers lightly against the wires of the rack. Through in the lounge, Jim was asleep. He had been discharged to Joyce's house after two weeks in the hospital. Following his return, Joyce had marked each of the subsequent days off on the calendar on the wall beside the fridge.

She tested the parkin she had baked earlier, and looked for the knife to slice it into portions. The round of baking was in preparation for that evening's meeting of the support group. She was getting it ready in good time in order to give Jim his tea before she went. She liked to arrive early at the club-house. Each time, she liked to have the cakes laid out on the cricket club's oval serving plates before any of the others arrived; she liked to get the two big kettles going on the gas in the kitchen, and rinse out the army of teapots, and she liked to be there to help Wilf Wardle set out the chairs.

She had baked two slabs of parkin and a tray of gingerbread cookies. As she cut up the parkin it occurred to her that some of the slices were perhaps cut too thin. Parkin was, after all, best cut thick. She knew why, though. It was because she needed the accident of leftover cake at the end of the meeting. Wilf, who opened up the building for the support group to use, was not himself involved in the proceedings which followed. He was happy simply to hand over the keys to Joyce once the room was readied and the chairs were set out; he was not at ease with meetings and agendas. But if there was cake left over, he and Oscar could sometimes be tempted in to sit with her and finish it off with a cup of tea when the meeting was concluded and everybody else had gone.

Wilf preferred to set his own pace and rhythm than have it set for him by others and, as Joyce had long known, he was happier doing this outdoors than in. Each week when she arrived at the cricket club with her baking, Wilf was riding the tractor, with Oscar Brigg sitting motionless alongside him, working his way sedately up and down the ground in the summer's evening sunshine, the grass-cutting blades whirring behind him as he trimmed the outfield in readiness for the weekend fixtures. He was content simply to be cutting summer grass. Joyce liked it that this was enough for Wilf Wardle on summer evenings – to be patiently working his way up and down the Heslop bridge outfield, and seeing the brackish lines of Holker Fell each time he turned at the far boundary rope to face the town, and lining up the blades for the next swathe of grass. To think about such things was to keep the demons of her own domestic life at bay.

When Brendan stepped into Joyce's hallway an hour later, he saw the piles of small boxes stacked six high through into the kitchen, and the racks on the working surface set out with buns and cakes whose smells still filled the house. Through in the lounge the gas fire was turned up full. Brendan felt the heat in his face as he entered the room. Jim McCready was on the settee. His back was wedged almost upright by a cluster of pillows. There was a blanket over him. His breathing was fast and shallow, and his hair was tousled. There was a waxy sheen to his skin from the jaundice. On the sideboard, next to the radio which was playing quietly, bottles of pills were lined up in sequence. Next to them was a cardboard tray, stamped with the name of the hospital trust, containing a dozen multi-vitamin drinks in oblong plastic cartons. Brendan sat down in the armchair on the far side of the settee. Joyce followed him into the room and squatted on one of the standchairs flanking the drop-leaf table at the back of the room on which more of the white boxes were stacked.

'I've not seen you for a while,' she said.

'I've been busy. So have you by the look of things.'

'I make twenty pounds for each gross I pack,' she said, explaining the boxes. 'I have to relabel each bandage and put it in a plastic sleeve.'

'How long does that take?' Brendan asked.

'It depends.'

'On what?'

'On how much Jim's awake, and on how much I can be fagged to keep at it. Eight or nine hours for a gross.'

'That doesn't seem like much.'

'You make it sound like I've a lot of options. I'm supposed to sort out my own National Insurance and stuff, because I'm meant to be self-employed. Keith Doyle only subcontracts to people who do the homeworking for him, but you get to the stage where you just think "Sod it!" Anyway, my horoscope at the weekend said I was going to be lucky with money this week, so I'm guessing no one will find out for a bit that I'm not paying tax on it.'

'What about the petrol station?'

'They came to see me from the oil company while Jim was in hospital – two men in good suits. Men in suits are never good news. They'd cottoned on to Jim's little deal of letting out the workshop next door without telling them. Someone must have shopped him. The men said they'd been watching him for a while – not that it was doing any harm to anyone. It's not like Jim was swindling thousands out of them. I think, as far as they were concerned, it was just a good excuse to squeeze him out without having to offer compensation for terminating the lease early. They're going to revamp the site – put a carwash and a mini-market in. I told them that under the circumstances they might as well take it off my hands there and then. I just gave them the keys and walked out.'

'What did they say?'

'Nothing – it's what they wanted anyway, wasn't it? I don't suppose it's the end of the world. It's not as if I could have kept it going for much longer on my own. At least with this,' – she gestured at the boxes – 'I can get a bit of work done in the house while he's sleeping and then see to him when he needs it.'

'Are you managing?'

'I have to. He doesn't want Terry around, not that Terry

was likely to offer, and they say I can have a home help if I start struggling to get him to the loo on my own – that kind of thing. But at least this way, I can cope – for now.'

'Is there any sign of him being on the mend?'

They both glanced across at the settee, at the upright, sleeping figure.

'They said he's got nodules on his pancreas.'

'Nodules?'

'They said it's affecting his liver already. You know what they said, B. Moon? They said he might have six weeks left if he's lucky. They said you can't manage without a pancreas. How can he only have six weeks? I asked them – you've only just *found* it. Shouldn't he have two years or something? Isn't that what you're supposed to get with cancer? They said he might not even get *that* long. They said it's spreading and there's nothing at this stage they can do. That's why they said he could come home for the last few weeks. They said there wouldn't be any pain with the morphine.'

'Does he know?' Brendan said.

'He won't talk about it.'

'About dying?

'About the "C" word. The nearest we got was when he was busy telling me how he was going to be out and about in the car again by the autumn. I had to say to him, "You know what this illness means, Jim?" He wouldn't have it at first. I swear, we nearly had an argument about it. But then, after a while, I could see him starting to fill up. He put his head into my arm, and I could feel him shaking, but he wouldn't *say* anything. I keep thinking that if he'd been diagnosed sooner, maybe he wouldn't be having to go through all this – maybe it would have been different.'

'I doubt it.'

'That's what the hospital said. But for all those months, that bastard was prescribing Gaviscon for a stomach upset, and paracetamol for back pains. All those months I kept bullying Jim to go again when he kept getting the pains, and all the bugger kept telling him was to take more Gaviscon. They reckon you can't survive without a pancreas, but it shouldn't be like this.'

'I don't suppose it should.'

'They said only something remarkable could save him now – a miracle. Do you think I should pray for a miracle, B. Moon?'

Brendan didn't answer. Joyce put the palm of her hand over her eyes and smoothed it slowly down over her face, as if trying to wipe the fatigue away.

'Anyway – tea?' she said finally.

'Tea would be good.'

After a moment's thought she stood up and went into the kitchen. Brendan watched the fitfully sleeping figure of Jim McCready. After a while, he reached into his jacket pocket and took out the photograph Karl Brigg had given him at the farmhouse – of Karl's brother Oscar, and the boys' father. He examined it as he had done a dozen times since it had been given to him, reflecting on the fate of the boy and the mystery of the man.

Nicholas Pacynko, too, had studied it curiously when Brendan had shown it to him on his return visit to the university. He had gone back a second time in order to be introduced to the academic's father. Pacynko had rung to tell Brendan about a Jewish writer – Jacob Baum – his father had known of in pre-war Germany. Baum, he said, had come of age just as the Nazis were taking power, but in the aftermath of the Nuremberg Laws his work, like that of other Jewish artists, was not allowed to be published. However, a collection of poems he had written in Hebrew were later rumoured to have been printed, illegally, in Baum's home city of Frankfurt. The poems had been Baum's attempt to reconcile the idea of a loving personal God with the suffering the poet was witnessing amongst Germany's Jewry. According to Josef Pacynko, their clandestine publication had been under the title *Letters from God*.

'When I was called to the tribunal,' Josef Pacynko had explained to Brendan, 'they sat me down – the officials in charge of running such things – and they gave me three choices. Maybe they did the same for the man you are so interested in who came to England.' He had held up three fingers to demonstrate. 'They said to me: farming, or mining, or textiles. You choose one of them, they said. So I chose textiles, and they sent me here to Manchester to work in a mill, which was work that I knew, so afterwards I stayed. And a lifetime later, I am still here.'

'Did you know Jacob Baum – the poet?' Brendan asked.

'I met him once when I was only a boy. I went with my father and brother on the train from Darmstadt – we were about one hour's journey from Frankfurt – when he was giving a reading in the city. Before Jewish artists had been silenced, Jacob Baum was already known in the region for his writing. My father had a copy of his short stories and I remember there was a picture of the author on the cover, of the man my father said was a hero. That was why he took my brother and I on the train to Frankfurt to hear Jacob Baum read.'

'Was that very long before you left Germany?'

'About one or two years – 1937, I would say.'

'Did other members of your family survive the war?'

The old man examined Brendan's face, then shook his head. 'This,' – he gestured towards Nicholas Pacynko – 'is my family.'

'Have you ever been back?'

'Some things in life it is best not to return to.'

'Let me pass you this, Dad.'

Nicholas Pacynko was offering his father the photograph he had been studying. The elder Pacynko took it and propped it up on his lap while he fished for his spectacle case. Pushing on his reading glasses, he examined the photograph for a long time.

'You recognize the man in the picture?'

'Yes,' Josef Pacynko said, nodding slowly. He had turned the photograph around towards his son and Brendan, his finger pointing at the man Karl Brigg had identified as his and Oscar's father. 'A little older, but yes. Jacob Baum. That is him. That is the poet. He died in Frankfurt in 1938. I attended his funeral.'

Brendan heard the chink of crockery. Joyce came back into the lounge carrying a tray. He slipped the photograph back in his pocket. Joyce set the tray down and the threads of their conversation picked up again backwards and forwards over the sleeping Jim McCready.

'Jim only talks about getting better,' she said as she poured the tea. 'He talks about getting stronger. It helps him to get through the day. I don't know, underneath it all, whether he's really just scared, but we have to talk all the time about how much good the vitamin drinks are doing him. We talk about how well he's doing in managing to walk to the loo on his own, and about how he's managing to avoid using up all his morphine allowance – as if it's a sodding competition. As if it *matters*.'

Brendan took the cup she offered him and took a sip of the tea. Jim's lungs pushed and pulled at the air in the middle of the room between them.

'I read a report in the paper the other week,' she said, 'from America. It said a tornado had veered away from a small town. Afterwards, someone who'd been taking photographs of the funfair the night before the tornado was due noticed that on the developed film he could see the outline of Jesus amongst the reflection of all the lights.'

Brendan smiled ruefully.

'It makes you wonder, doesn't it?'

'Does it?'

'It does when I hear things like that. And then you hear about people getting better sometimes,' she said, ' – the illness suddenly going away, even when it seemed hopeless. Do you think I should pray for Jim?'

'If it'll help you.'

'Do you think it might help Jim?'

He was aware of her watching him again, looking for comfort, waiting for an answer. 'No,' he said.

'You don't think I should pray?'

'I mean, I don't think it will help Jim. There are no miracles – not the way you mean. There will always be people who'll claim them, but it's not the same. There'll always be someone somewhere saying that a pomegranate he opened had the seeds inside arranged to spell the word "Allah"; or someone who says he left a suitcase open in his bankrupt factory and that God filled it with money for him; or those, like the woman I came across from a church in

Bethnal Green, who insist on telling all the other passengers whenever she flies that she knows the plane won't crash because she hasn't finished the work God has chosen for her. Every Sunday, if you believe all that stuff, people are in church having the demons that have caused their deafness or blindness or cerebral palsy cast out of them; and AIDS is an Old Testament-style plague sent by God to wipe out gays; and Elvis didn't die – he ascended into Heaven and he's coming back to save the whole world, Joyce, and he'll be strumming a guitar while he does it. And what happened in Heslop Bridge. It was just . . . the parchments were written by a man. That was all. They're just verses written by a man. I think they may have been written by a Jewish man.'

'A man?'

'A writer, called Jacob Baum.'

'You don't *know* that.'

'He's been dead a long time, but I'm sure they were his verses.'

Joyce stayed silent for a while, looking first at him and then at her father-in-law.

'How do you know?' she said finally, ' – are you sure?'

Brendan nodded his head.

'What are you going to do?'

'I'm going to put it in my report.'

'And say what?'

'And say that, after the first ones were blown out of the school in the backdraft of the explosion, the others were placed strategically around the town.'

'Can you prove it?'

'Most of it. Bits are still guesswork, but I've spent the last few weeks trying to piece it together.'

'You're saying someone *put* them there – in all the places they were found afterwards?'

'Yes.'

'But you know that Karen Cottee and the others are planning to go through the courts if the Maslow company won't concede that the parchments are genuine.'

'They are genuine; they're just not miraculous.'

'It doesn't matter which way round you put it; they're still set on going to court. Even if you said all that to them, I don't think it would make much difference. Madeline Geller told them before she left how much money they would get from the Maslows if they won. People are saying that the owners of the slipper mill are looking to pull out, so now the support group are talking about using the Maslows' money to turn *that* into a peace centre in memory of the children.'

'They couldn't afford to take on the Maslows in court. These are men with more pounds than there are grains of sand on a beach.'

'So why don't you just persuade the Maslows to donate some money to the support group?'

'Because they don't have to – because it's their money. Because that's not how the world works, Joyce.'

'Fellowship TV have said they'll help.'

'Fellowship TV are a hard-nosed business who can see a marketing opportunity.'

'Madeline Geller said if Fellowship TV could have all the parchments, her organization would pay the court costs for the support group to fight for the money.'

'And what are they going to do with the parchments? Put them on display in big glass cabinets in America and charge families from Hicksville, Pennsylvania, thirty dollars each to see the holy relics, and have them buy souvenir brochures, and then stop off at the McDonald's Drive-Thru on the way out when they're done?'

'At least there'd be a chance of having the peace centre here if they won.'

'Do you want to see more of those people you're getting now coming to gawp at the school with their mouths open and their cameras clicking? Do you want to see people in wheelchairs being lifted onto the tarmac on the school drive begging to be cured so they can walk again?'

'What's wrong with people coming to the town if they think that something wonderful might have happened here? It's better than only remembering it for what Jason Orr did.'

'Do you know how many years something like this would drag on in court, Joyce? And for what? They'd never get the money. They'd never win, and the Maslows would make them look like idiots.'

On the settee, Jim McCready shifted his weight. He opened and then closed his eyes. For a while they were startled into silence.

Eventually, when Joyce spoke, her voice had lowered. 'Do you know who put the parchments in all those places?'

'I can't prove it yet, but I think so.'

'Well, God help whoever did it.'

'I'm not saying it was malicious. What if they'd only done it to help?'

Joyce shook her head. 'I listen to people talking in the support group every week. I go around to some of their houses to help with the sitting service. I think some of them have only survived all this because of the parchments, because of what they meant – what they *thought* those verses meant.'

'I just came here to find out the truth, Joyce,' Brendan said.

181

'No matter what?'

'And now I've found it, you can't expect me to lie about it.'

'I'll tell you what, then, B. Moon – if you do prove that someone carried all this out as a hoax, I hope you're going to give whoever it was some warning, because they won't be able to stay here. They'll have to leave the town. They'll have to leave the country. Can you imagine losing a child, B. Moon? Can you imagine having to be one of those parents in Heslop Bridge and there *not* being those verses for them to hang on to? Can you imagine what would happen if people found that it was someone living in the town who had tricked them? There'll be a lynch mob. If someone like Gary Greenalgh goes after him, he'll be lucky to get out of Heslop Bridge alive.'

Brendan sat forward on the edge of his seat. He looked at the floor for a while. 'It was Oscar Brigg,' he said finally.

It hadn't been so difficult once he knew what he was looking for. Nicholas Pacynko had given him leads that he had followed up, and twice he had visited the Jewish Museum in Manchester, who had put him in touch with a number of specialist organizations abroad.

The father of Karl and Oscar Brigg had arrived in England at the port of Harwich in February 1938. The Public Records Office were able to confirm that much to Brendan. Jacob Baum had sailed from the Hook of Holland, carrying a German passport. The name inside the passport was 'Otto Baum'; it was his brother's name. There was evidence that, for the next twelve months until the outbreak of war, a series of pleas were lodged by Baum with the authorities for his family – parents, grandfather and sister – to be granted the visas which would have allowed them to join him in England. Each of his requests was made as 'Otto' and not 'Jacob' in order, Brendan supposed, not to awaken the suspicions of the British authorities about his own documentation.

Jacob Baum's internment during the war, which lasted a year, began with his arrest in Manchester on 12 May 1940. The Jewish Museum in the city helped Brendan to identify him as one of the 1200 enemy aliens who were transported to Canada in the early summer of 1940 on the SS *Etrick*.

Just as the war was ending, Baum had married an English girl. The marriage certificate showed him to have been fourteen years older than his bride – thirty-four to her twenty. By that time he had been employed as the teacher at the village school where Marion was helping out. Sillot's two-classroom school had only sixteen pupils. Marion attended to the infants and Mr Baum taught the nine juniors. He had been taken on by the Education Authority following a letter of recommendation provided by the Anglo-Jewish Association and a reference from an employer in Didsbury for whom he had worked before his internment as a private tutor to the family's children.

The Holocaust Research Centre in San Francisco was able to confirm that Jacob Baum's family had been amongst the 10,000 Jews of Polish extraction expelled from Germany in August 1938, a few months after Jacob himself had been helped by them to leave Germany for England. The Baums, like others in Frankfurt, had been assembled in the city's Concert Hall and then driven in trucks to Neubenschen on the Polish border before they were led the two kilometres at gunpoint from the trains to the border. Waiting to cross to Zbaszyn on the Polish side, anyone with money exceeding ten marks had it confiscated. The Baums appeared to have travelled on from Zbaszyn to Lodz where they had relatives. The Zydowski Institute in Warsaw confirmed that they had taken lodgings on Kosciuszko Alley close to the synagogue, and that they had perished there during the second year of the ghetto under the increasingly insane stewardship of Chaim Rumkowski.

In addition to the marriage certificate, Brendan also retrieved copies of the two birth certificates for Oscar and Karl. On the eve of his marriage, Jacob had changed his surname from Baum to Brigg, but on each of these certificates and on everything else which followed in England – as Jacob grew increasingly estranged from Karl, as he committed his idiot first son to the institution intended to shelter him from the outside world, as his teaching career unfolded and his marriage faltered – he continued to use his brother's Christian name.

The extant portion of the file on Oscar Brigg, which was finally uncovered by the Archive Department at Calderhall, was three inches thick. Attempts at escape, and the use of sedatives, were first noted two months after admittance to the paediatric unit at Calderhall. Classification on transfer from the children's ward was high grade. Self-harm, to the hands, was recorded on a number of occasions. There was mention of an operation to remove glass splinters from beneath the left knuckle. Paraldehyde was first administered in 1962. Solitary confinement in the side room was noted regularly for 'wilfulness' and 'disobedience'. Escapes were made over the high fence of the Calderhall compound in 1958, 1961, 1968 and 1973. Each time, he was recaptured in the local countryside within twenty-four hours. Periods of confinement resulted in each case. There were two separate admissions to the hospital block, in 1965 and 1967, as a result of 'restraint and control by application of a towel tourniquet to the neck, resulting in a loss of consciousness'. In 1968, there was treatment recorded for 'scalding to the chest and right forearm'. In 1981, it was noted that paraldehyde was still being prescribed, and there was mention of a pre-frontal leucotomy having been performed at some previous stage of incarceration.

Finally, the police report on Jacob Baum's death (the death certificate listed him as Otto Brigg) recorded suicide by gunshot.

As he approached the gym on the Cheetham Hill road, Brendan could see up ahead where the exterior had been blackened by fire, just as Nicholas Pacynko had described.

Part of the building's roof appeared to have collapsed, and the pavement had been cordoned off to pedestrians until a final decision was taken to demolish the remaining shell. The cordoned area spilled out into the road to protect the scaffolding erected around the front of the old priest's gym, and it was this that necessitated the temporary traffic lights that were interrupting the progress of the passing lines of cars.

Brendan waited in the long line of afternoon traffic for the signal to change to green. He could see the skip set out in the road where rubble from the building had been deposited. The entrance porch, from which the wooden stairs had formerly led to the upstairs boxing gymnasium, was boarded up. No one was gathered at the scene. He could see people walking past, oblivious, unconcerned.

According to Nicholas Pacynko, Fr Wynn had taken to sleeping in the gym, and to advertising the fact in an effort to secure the premises. He had believed that his presence would be enough to deter vandals, but he had been wrong. His body was found in the tiny office which had been the centre of his world for half a century. The other side of the door had been barricaded and the gym set alight using petrol.

It seemed like the façade of any of the other derelict buildings littering the neighbourhood. It was a place that might have been abandoned and left to stand for years. There was nothing there to indicate that a week ago this was a living social centre, nothing to say it was the place where generations of neighbourhood boys had spent their formative years, or to mark the spot where Fr Anthony Aloysius Wynn had spent a lifetime trying to better the world around him, using only the raw ingredients he had to hand. There was nothing there to say that Brendan Moon himself had spent the bulk of his own childhood in that place, in the comforting shadow of the vast Irish priest who taught him the value of defence and counter. Jab, move and cover up. Don't make yourself a sitting target. Nothing there to say that he – Brendan Moon, of Providence Street, Salford – had been formed and moulded in that soiled and dampish and liniment-smelling place which once had stood at the top of the stairs leading from that porch, but which now existed only as a memory.

It was the sound of a door softly closing. Like the day he had spent in the Kerkira Hospital, and the one on which his father had cleared his belongings from the upstairs lodgings he was renting in Abbott Street and slipped away, this one served to confirm that, in the end, Brendan had failed those he had loved. Up ahead, the lights changed to green. The traffic in front of him nudged away. He slipped the car into first gear and moved closer towards the remains of the gym at a funeral pace. The lights changed to amber again. On instinct, Brendan signalled left to avoid queueing through another round of lights. He parked the car a little way down the road, intending to walk around the corner to the gym from there.

For a while, he sat motionless in the car. The only sounds were the ticking of the engine as it cooled and the traffic shuffling past on the main road behind him. He took out his phone and checked for messages. There were none. He pressed buttons to reach the memory where his store of numbers were kept and idly scrolled through them. There were dozens. After a while, he realized that almost all of them were related to his job. He found Joyce McCready's number, inserted on the night he had gone to talk to her father-in-law in the hospital – when Jim McCready was still having tests and was still full of misplaced optimism that he'd be driving around the hills and fiddling with his engines before the autumn. He found Fr Wynn's number, left for him when the priest had contacted his firm, asking for his help. He continued to flick forward. He came to an entry for 'Connie' and stopped. There was no surname. Then he remembered it was the old woman he had spoken to after he had driven home from the Heslop Bridge memorial service. He flicked forward through several more numbers, then went back. Connie. He recognized the area dialling code as Ashford. He'd typed it in after he'd spoken to her that night. He still remembered the notes he'd made in Jack's storybook: *Bagpuss, rectory, schoolteacher*.

He started to dial the number, then cancelled it. He dialled again. It rang and rang. When, eventually, it was answered, he recognized the voice as the old woman's.

'I'm sorry to bother you.'

'It's no bother,' she said, ' – who am I talking to?'

'Is it Connie?'

'Do we know each other?'

'Not really. We spoke once before – on the phone. I rang you, by mistake.'

'Did you?'

'You might remember – Sam Shepherd. I said was an architect. I said I built bridges, abroad.'

'Yes?' She sounded unsure.

'I said I was looking for someone. Marmaduke.'

'Marmaduke? I don't think I know anyone . . .'

'I rang quite late.'

'Marmaduke? Oh, that's right, I think I do remember.'

'I'm sorry about that.'

'So what can I do for you, Mr Shepherd? Are you ringing to tell me that you've found your friend?'

'No, not that.'

'You've lost somebody else, perhaps?'

'I rang you to apologize.'

'What on earth for? Anyone can get a telephone number wrong.'

'No, it wasn't like that.'

'Wasn't it?'

'It's what I do . . . it's what I used to do.'

'What is?'

'Make phone calls.'

'What sort of phone calls?'

'To people I don't know, to talk. Sometimes I need to talk. I'm only ringing back to explain.'

'You can explain if you like but honestly, it doesn't matter. Are you all right?'

'I wanted to explain, and to say something else.'

'What was that?' She sounded suspicious.

'I wanted to tell you that I don't build bridges.'

'Don't you?'

'And my name isn't Sam Shepherd.'

There was a pause.

'Why are you telling me this?'

'I told you – I just wanted to explain that Sam Shepherd wasn't my name.'

'What is your name?'

He didn't answer.

'Hello?'

She waited for him to say something. 'Hello? Are you still there?'

'I don't know if he shouted for me as he was falling.'

'I'm sorry?'

'I couldn't hear. I was under the water.'

'Who was?'

A breath had caught inside him and bubbled just below his throat.

'You spend your life watching over someone,' he said, 'and all you're left with, when you let down your guard – when you stop watching over them for a moment – is to wonder if they cried out for you.'

'Who?'

'Jack.'

He was aware of the heaviness of his body.

'Who is Jack?'

His head was aching. 'My son,' he said.

He could feel the weight of everything in his face. He could hear her breathing at the other end of the line. *Don't put the phone down. Please don't put it down yet.*

'Jack was your son?'

He felt the rush of relief that she was still there and had answered.

'Yes.'

The pressure of the breath was still caught high up in his chest.

'He was nine.'

He dared not breathe out for fear of choking.

'What happened?'

'He had an accident.' His voice was forced. 'Four years ago.'

'And afterwards, you made phone calls?'

'We were on holiday,' he said. 'He fell.' He closed his eyes. In the darkness, Jack was falling again, and Brendan was falling with him. They were tumbling together through blue water, and the old priest was falling too. Brendan's ears were full of the hissing pressure of water billowing around his head.

He opened his eyes. He was back in the car and he could feel the features of his face being pulled taut. 'I was under the water. I don't even know if he cried out.'

'Is that what you wanted to tell me?'

'We flew him home. When we buried him, I wore the wrong shoes to the funeral. The service was seven minutes late starting.'

Things held for another moment, until he felt the first sob rip out of him from somewhere far below.

'Help me, Connie.' He felt the tears come, squeezed out in spasms, and he dropped the phone and covered his broken-open face with his hands.

At the end of the block, by the four-storey property on the corner, where the fridge still stood in the cellar yard and Oxfam sheets were still tacked up at the windows, he turned off the main road and walked to the edge of the dozen derelict acres immediately behind the former gym. He stood looking at what was there now. In the two days since the priest's death, the land – colonized and subdued for a decade by couch grass and convolvulus, by bike tracks and mud and syringes – had become a field of poppies.

10

Reaching the Hearts of Men

Jacob Baum's family had moved to Frankfurt before the First World War. Hannah would have been seven that year; it was the summer before Otto was born; Jacob would follow two years later. Their father was the accountant for a Polish weaving mill, until the offer of a job through a cousin who worked for the Rothschild banking organization. In Frankfurt, they settled beyond the Untermain bridge in a third-floor apartment in the Jewish district.

Otto grew into a noisy and energetic child who dealt only in practicalities. In class he was frequently chastised for failing to pay attention, for not taking life seriously enough, for presenting such poor schoolwork. He was often in trouble for fighting in the neighbourhood, mostly when other boys teased him by making fun of Hannah.

Hannah, the eldest of the three Baum children, didn't go out to work even though, by the time Jacob started school, she was old enough. There was something wrong with Hannah. She was too trusting. She spoke to anybody in the street, even strangers, as if they were friends. People said that Hannah had been born slow, but Jacob's mother just called her *special*. As a boy, Jacob knew that it was a particular kind of specialness, though, because their mother worried about Hannah being too friendly with some of the men in the district, and she had needed Dr Solomon to perform an operation because she wouldn't have been able to look after the baby. As for Jacob, the youngest, he was the bright and gifted child his mother had yearned for. He was also the frailest – an intense and shy boy who found people difficult but study easy.

At eleven, Jacob contracted a severe bout of pneumonia. He was treated by Dr Solomon for several weeks and was nursed slowly back to health in the apartment by his mother and by Hannah. He spent a year convalescing at home, happily devouring books, making up stories for Hannah with which he would keep her entertained each afternoon while their mother napped. The illness left Jacob smaller and less robust than other boys his age, and his mother elected after that not to send him back to school but to have him educated privately by a tutor, a Hungarian called Isabella.

In the end, Jacob fell a little in love with Isabella in a distant, dreamy, adolescent way. As for Isabella, she was quick to spot the boy's gift with words and to encourage it. She read him Goethe and Dante; she took him to the theatre; she introduced him to her well-read friends, and oversaw his own first attempts at writing stories.

His brother, meanwhile, was out wandering the streets beyond the Jewish shtetl, occasionally falling into bloody fights with sullen German boys in the narrowing streets on the edge of the Romerberg, or hanging around Meikle's tailor's shop on the ground floor of the Baums' apartment block. Inside the shop, Otto flattered and coaxed the women who called on Meikle for their custom. Otto was a good talker who made it his task casually to persuade the daughters, who cooed at him from behind their mothers' skirts, that before too long he'd have a house down on the Untermainkai by the river, beside the Rothschilds and the rich gentiles of the city. Meikle himself had a good eye for business and before long Otto was employed to look after the shop when the old man went on his errands around the city, and he was eventually taken on by Meikle as his apprentice.

As for Jacob, his stammer had made him more comfortable in the company of older people than with boys of his own age, and Isabella observed her protégé's envious glances at Otto's worldly triumphs.

'You mustn't bother yourself about your brother's success with girls,' she told him, ' – the time will come, Jacob, when you will find a good girl for yourself. It is your life that will reach the heights while your brother is climbing no higher than some woman's Mount of Venus. Otto doesn't see things as you do. Your experience as an artist goes deeper than his. Your understanding of the world is more thorough – your destiny is higher.'

Jacob's first collection of stories was published in 1935. The tales were based on middle-class Jewish characters he had met through Isabella, and charted the impact on their domestic lives of the rise of the Nazis in Berlin. By 1936, the collection had also been published in France and Sweden, and they won him a good deal of praise if very little money. His stories were lauded as 'gentle and heart-rending', and Jacob was praised for his 'simple and spellbinding prose' and for 'an ability to convey the heartbreak of an entire community in the subtlest detail of ordinary Jewish lives'.

'You know, little brother, you're going to be even more famous than me!' Otto had told him, embracing him in a bearhug, on the day the first foreign review reached the Baum household.

'And what is it, exactly, that you are going to be famous for, Otto?'

'Something,' Otto had said happily, 'something will occur to me. Meantime, I am famous for being brother to the most promising writer in the country.'

By the end of that year, with Jews in Germany already banned from teaching, from working in hospitals and universities and from the civil service, publication of books by Jewish authors was forbidden. Jacob's only subsequent work would be the clandestine publication of his Hebrew poems a year before he was helped by his family to escape the country. The future he had dreamed of was over before it had barely begun.

When he left Germany, Jacob did not take a copy of his poems with him. Instead, they were rewritten from memory during his long internment by the British authorities. On his arrest in England he was allowed to take only one small case. He packed a single shirt and the wooden box with which he had fled Germany, containing his folded tallith, his skullcap, candlesticks and Bible. Then, along with a dozen Mancunian Jews – some loudly indignant, some nervously accepting their fate – he was bussed across the East Lancs Road to Liverpool and billeted, along with other German and Austrian passport-holders, in a section of streets cordoned off from the rest of a housing estate by barbed wire, and patrolled by uniformed soldiers. The soldiers guarding them were civil, and apologetic about the lack of information about when the detainees might be released. Those being held passed their time bartering for cigarettes and writing letters.

At the start of July 1940, they were transported back to Liverpool by bus. The expectation was that they were being moved as preparation for their release. Instead, they were taken to the Prince's Landing Stage and loaded onto the SS *Etrick*, a 15,000-ton freighter. The following day, the ship set sail into the Atlantic with its cargo of Jewish German pass-port-holders and several hundred Wehrmacht prisoners of war. Ten days later, it entered the Gulf of St Lawrence. Jacob Baum and the other detainees – all newly classified as enemy aliens – were fitted with prisoner of war uniforms and held for a week in a fenced compound of huts on the outskirts of Quebec. After that, they were moved to their permanent detention centre in Canada in a huge abandoned railway shed cut into the forest on the Canadian Pacific Railway between Quebec and Montreal.

It was there, through the long and solitary Canadian winter, in a railway shed 300 yards long with an adjoining exercise compound, that Jacob spent his days and nights rewriting his Letters from God. He had already earned a reputation amongst his fellow detainees for being a self-sufficient loner, and he showed no one else what he was working on. By the time the visiting official from the Home Office reclassified him in the summer of 1941, he had re-drafted each of the verses which he had originally written in Frankfurt for Meikle the tailor.

People had expected Meikle to live forever. No one in the community expected a death like that – not in Frankfurt. Even in 1936, so long after the changes, even after the increasing number of demonstrations against the Jewish community and the riots, it came as a shock. People had supposed at that point that the worst was behind them. They expected things to get better. That was what Meikle had said – that things would get better, that the crisis would blow over. It had happened before, Meikle said, and no doubt it would happen again. It was the traditional curse of being Jewish. A few yobs, a few anti-Jewish slogans in the streets – he himself had seen it many times in his own life-time. It was the fate of Jews to be outsiders, Meikle said; people would soon tire of the fool in Berlin, once it was clear that all he had to offer the Germans was permission to daub the Star of David on a few shop windows. It would pass.

It seemed as if half the Jewish population of Frankfurt attended the funeral. Who in their community did not know Meikle? Otto and Jacob helped to carry the coffin. Jacob's father and grandfather walked behind. Jacob delivered a eulogy. As the local writer, he had been asked to compose something to mark Meikle's passing. He had imagined what God might say to such a gathering of people in light of the old man's death. With the untried, unsullied faith of youth, he had tried to imagine how God might reassure his people that the contract of faith between God and Man should not be broken by such a sudden, unexpected, apparently mean-ingless event.

Within six months, a collection of verses on the same theme, composed by Jacob in Hebrew, was privately published. The title of the pamphlet was *Letters from God*. The work was dedicated by Jacob to Meikle the tailor. The publisher secretly sold a thousand copies around the city and through an underground network of Jewish contacts as far away as Koblenz and Wiesbaden.

By then, the exodus of Jews from Germany was at its

height. Seventy thousand Jews who had been able to obtain visas had already left the country. Those who remained found themselves in a state in which they were no longer citizens. In Frankfurt, the Baums themselves could no longer go to the theatre, or eat in the city's restaurants, or mix openly with Aryans on the streets. Otto's own work, now that he had taken over the running of Meikle's business, seemed safe enough. As for Jacob, barred from teaching in the city's schools and denied the opportunity to sell his books openly, he made a living tutoring and giving readings within the Jewish district. By then, the two brothers were also working together for the Lux Group. The organization consisted of a tight-knit circle of Jewish professionals in Frankfurt with whom Jacob had first become involved in the mid-1930s through his publisher, Max Gotweiss. Excluded from their individual professions as most of them now were, the members of the group made it their task to document the treatment of Jews in the region. They took their name from one of their members, the film producer Stefan Lux, who had taken his own protest about the treatment of Jews to the assembly rooms of the League of Nations in Geneva. Here, in July 1936, he had delivered a letter intended for the British Cabinet Minister, Anthony Eden, and then had produced a gun and killed himself in the press gallery, surrounded by journalists, as a protest against the escalating persecution.

'I do not find any other way to reach the hearts of men,' Stefan Lux had written in his open letter to the British Minister, 'when such persecutions have failed to pierce the inhuman indifferences of the world.'

Jacob and Otto had argued about Lux's actions in the aftermath of his death. For Jacob, the act was one of noble self-sacrifice. 'It's a gesture that will surely alert the whole world to our dilemma,' he told his brother. 'Is that kind of sacrifice not commendable?'

Otto was not convinced. 'He would have been better blowing up the Nazis in the Reichstag than blowing off his own head,' he always insisted, ' – it was just a waste of a good Jew.'

At Otto Baum's suggestion, the Lux Group eventually based itself in the back room of Meikle's shop. It was also Otto who persuaded the group to do more than simply collate information about mistreatment of Jews in Germany, but actively to pass on that information to the British and American press through a contact he had made with R. T. Smallbones, the British Consul-General in Frankfurt.

Most of the dozen-strong members of the group were graduates, teachers, artists – intense and thoughtful intellectuals. In contrast, Otto was muscular, straightforward, practical. He was uninterested in theory or argument, or in self-sacrifice, unconcerned about the niceties of procedures. He was motivated solely by the desire for revenge against those who had cornered Meikle in the Romerberg, on his way back across the city one day, and dragged him for half a mile through the streets, beating him with sticks and then bludgeoning him to death in a shop doorway and hanging him from a lamp-post while the police and a small crowd had looked on approvingly.

It became clear to Brendan that Jacob told none of this to the girl he would come to court in England. He made no attempt to translate the verses into English, or to have them published in England. When he married Marion in the early months of 1945 and moved into the farmhouse, he put the

box containing the verses and his prayer items in a cupboard in the room they designated as his study.

Before she married him it seemed likely that Marion knew
only that he was a German national of Polish parents, that he
was a teacher, that he was nothing like her father who she
lived with and whose twin pillars of faith were the farming
prices and the hellfire sermons of the Methodist preacher
who came to Sillot once a month. She knew also, perhaps,
that there were depths to this newly arrived man that were
exotic and out of reach.

They were bleak and self-denying days. The Wehrmacht,
Marion knew, might come parachuting into the fields outside the village at any day. The business of winning the war
had reduced most things to the kind of brutish practicalities
and simple, bumptious slogans so loved by her father. And
yet suddenly, alongside her in the school, there was a man to
marvel at, a refugee who accepted the privations of war but
whose accent and patience and loneliness made the simplest
of his sentences into a kind of poetry for her.

They knew in the village that he had been interned early
in the war, then released. They knew that for the remainder
of the conflict he was required to visit the police station in
Heslop Bridge six miles away from Sillot each Saturday.
They gossiped about him in the Post Office, and one of the
parent helpers, Jean Wilton, made a play for him when the
Harvest festival stalls were being packed away. Jean
Wilton's husband was somewhere in North Africa. She had
already had several of the Canadian infantrymen up in the
fields (once she'd had two of them together), but it was
pretty, blonde Marion who won the foreigner.

In the evenings he read to her – poets she hadn't heard of
in languages she didn't know. He read with an authority

and a restraint that thrilled her. Marion had taught the infant class in the little school since the autumn of 1940 when Miss Widdop had retired but, although she taught, she *knew* nothing; she had been nowhere. In that last summer of the war, she was wooed by his talk of foreign cities with wide rivers.

Afterwards, years afterwards, not when she was having her affair but much later – when her husband had died and she had come to feel misplaced, as though the wrong things had somehow happened to her, as though she had slipped carelessly into someone else's life – Marion would try to recall how she had first thought of him, how it had *felt* for her life to be opening out in the hands of Jacob Baum. She would try to remember how he had seemed to her in those early days together in the Sillot schoolhouse – contained and considered, secret, full of wisdom mysteriously won, not saying anything about so many of the things it was apparent that he knew, being grateful for her small domestic attentions, being reliant on her knowledge of Harvest festival and Advent and Lent, seeming at night – lying beside her – to be an angel from an unfamiliar lost Paradise. She recalled the fishing trips he had taken her on in the days of their courtship, while far away the war was still being fought and nobody knew for sure which side was going to win and whether they would all be slaughtered. Sometimes – almost impossibly, thinking back – they had camped out overnight after a day's fishing and slept under a blanket wrapped up in each other while the River Hodder flowed steadily past them outside in the dark. The fish they had caught hung from the branch of a tree outside the tent where Jacob had tied them and they flashed silver in the moonlight. She had liked to smell the morning rising up in the woods all around them. She felt breathless and young. She felt she was being explored for the first time. She felt as though her life was finally beginning.

'You mean his passport says he's called Otto Baum?' Roy Sowerby asked.

Marion nodded. She was lying with her head in his lap in the darkness of the empty cinema. He was smoking and looking up at the ceiling. She knew she would have to be back on the bus home soon – Karl would be finishing school, then her husband would arrive home for his tea.

'So why'd he change it?'

'He thought it would be better for me and the boys if we all had an English surname. He wasn't even called Otto in Germany. His real name is Jacob – he travelled from Germany on his brother's passport.'

'Why didn't he use his own?'

'I think it was easier for him to get out of the country that way. The war was coming. He said his brother had died by then.'

'Were they trying to arrest him?'

'I don't know.'

'Bloody hell, he might have been a bank robber.'

'Don't be stupid, Roy.'

'I'm not. What d'you mean, don't be stupid?'

They sat in silence for a while after that. Marion lay still, thinking. Roy was just smoking and staring at the ceiling.

In the evenings, Marion would be with her husband but she would be thinking of Roy. In a strange sort of way, she knew, Roy was more attractive to her when he wasn't with her than when he was. In some ways, Roy was a lesser man than her husband. Roy didn't try to understand her.

He could say things that were crude and boorish, and sometimes he didn't seem to care what Marion herself felt. They never discussed their future together. He never once asked her about leaving her husband, or about getting married, and for that reason Marion knew that eventually the affair would end. At times, when she was with him during the day, when Karl was at school and her husband was teaching, it was all she could muster to *like* Roy. Yet back at home in Sillot, in the evenings with Karl and her husband, she longed for Roy, because he was all the things that her husband lacked and because he made her feel real and necessary.

They always met during the day. Roy Sowerby was the projectionist at the Heslop Bridge Empire, and more often than not they arranged to meet inside the empty cinema after Marion had travelled down from Sillot on the bus. The cinema didn't open its doors for the first presentation during the week until 5.30 p.m., and Roy Sowerby would leave the side door unlocked for Marion. Their meetings were sometimes hurried and always secret. They never sought to meet further afield than Heslop Bridge in order to have a meal together. They had never eaten together – not even had a cup of tea, even though there was a storeroom at the back of the projection room where he kept a kettle and a stove. They had never slept in a bed together. They made love in the projection room, occasionally in the seats of the stalls, and once, memorably, on the stage above the pit where in the days of silent movies the piano had once been positioned.

'Have you had sex with other women in here?' she asked him.

'Don't be soft,' he said. He lit up a cigarette.

She didn't believe him about the women. She wasn't sure if it mattered.

'I ought to go,' she said.

'Why?'

'The bus back to Sillot is in an hour. I need to be home for Karl.'

'So stay half an hour.'

'No. I'm going.' She stood up from her seat in the stalls.

'What if I put the reel in and show you that scene at the airport again – the one you like.'

She thought. 'Why would you do that?'

He didn't answer her but pulled himself up from his seat. *Casablanca* had been showing at the Heslop Bridge Empire for two weeks. Marion had seen it twice already as a paying customer in the evening. Each time she had been on her own. In addition, Roy Sowerby had run the film several times for her in private during the afternoons. Roy went up into the projection room. After a few minutes the film began running.

'This isn't the right bit,' Marion shouted up from the empty stalls of the cinema, ' – it's further on.'

Roy did something with the reel on the projector which speeded the film up so that it would reach her favourite part more quickly – the bit where the two lovers were at the fog-bound airport preparing for their separation. Speeding the film up made the characters on the screen move rapidly and with ridiculous jerky movements, as if they were characters in an old Buster Keaton or Charlie Chaplin comedy. Marion could hear Roy starting to laugh at the figures scurrying around comically on the screen, but she didn't join in.

Finally she said, 'It's coming up now.'

Roy was still laughing.

'You can slow it down now,' she said.

But he didn't slow it down. He kept it running too fast.

'Roy! Slow it down.'

He carried on laughing. Ingrid Bergman and Humphrey Bogart were scurrying like hamsters and then yip-yapping away in front of the aeroplane hangar. She shouted at him to stop but he wouldn't. Roy was laughing so much that she heard him fall off his chair up in the projection room. She stood up and put her coat on and walked out of the auditorium towards the exit door.

She was halfway down the street, heading for the bus stop, when he caught up with her. Not caring who might see, he grabbed her and turned her around.

'Don't go,' he said, ' – I'm sorry.'

'No, you're not.'

'You have to come back,' he said.

'No, I don't. I've had enough of you, Roy. That's it. Go and find yourself another married woman for sex.'

There was a sudden childish panic in his face as he realized he might have gone too far. 'I never had sex with anyone else there,' he said.

Marion could see the rhythm of his pulse in the blue veins on the backs of his rough hands. She realized he was holding her hand in the street in the middle of Heslop Bridge, where the villagers from Sillot sometimes came to make withdrawals from the bank or to shop, and that it was the middle of the day. She realized that he thought she was walking out on him for good, that he didn't know what came next, that he didn't know enough about life to see what might happen after such an argument.

'I'll come on Thursday,' Marion said quietly.

'I'm sorry,' he said, panicked.

She tried to pull her hand away, but he held onto it. 'Someone might see us,' she told him, but for a moment he didn't care.

From the study in the farmhouse, Jacob wrote letters addressed to members of his family in Germany and Poland and, until 1952, to Isabella at her address in Frankfurt, but no replies ever came back.

As the years went by, his life focused increasingly on his teaching. He was a good teacher. He cared about the children. His manner in the classroom was formal and strict, but he understood the requirements of teaching in a place like Sillot. He understood that some of the children had been up since five o'clock doing chores or caring for siblings, that some were sewn into their clothes, that some had lives of quiet, sustained and uncomplaining abuse at the hands of their parents or in the beds of their fathers, in a village in which six or seven people from seemingly unrelated families boasted one blue eye and one green one. The challenge of passing knowledge to pupils in these circumstances breathed life into Jacob each morning. Teaching literature and mathematics to children who, in the course of a lifetime, would travel no more than three or four streets from where they set out, and who in all probability would spend their lives in service to the slate quarry, steeled him and held him together. Only when the schoolday was over and he was walking back through the village and up the hill, past the quarry which had given birth to Sillot, did the life in him seemed to slacken.

He saw women gathered in the street, talking and looking across at him when he passed on the other side. If Jacob tipped his hat to them, they acknowledged him but in that restrained and self-conscious way which said that they were tolerating his presence; that they were watching him for doing things differently, for electing never to drink in the village pub, for planting the wrong plants in his garden, for having an accent which even at its softest was clipped and organized and manufactured from a more fluid set of words in his head, for the fact that his eldest son had been born an imbecile and sent away.

Perhaps it seemed like a curse. There were enough old wives' tales in villages like Sillot about what gave rise to feeblemindedness to make this seem a possibility. It was only Jacob himself who knew that the curse was his – that the family flaw which had produced his sister Hannah's disability had been passed on to his own son. By the time they realized that something was wrong with Oscar, Marion was already expecting again. Her first reaction had been to say that she didn't want to see the pregnancy through – that there was a woman in the village who could attend to the matter – and she was persuaded to have the child only gradually by Jacob. And so, a year and a half after Oscar's birth, she gave birth to a normal child, her second son, Karl.

Perhaps it was the relief of having a normal son that made her closer to Karl – that made Karl *her* child. As for Oscar, it was Jacob who took the prime responsibility for organizing his days, as though in Oscar's disability he saw a reflection of his own stunted and diminished self. He took it upon himself to be the protector of his elder son, and so it was that Oscar, who had the schoolteacher's features but none of his intelligence in those trusting eyes, became Jacob's companion about the village. Where Jacob had previously gone walking on the moors alone, now he took the child with him. As they tramped across Holker Fell, they sang the Yiddish folk songs which Grandfather Emmanuel had taught to Jacob. When Jacob spent his evenings marking the children's classwork or setting the next day's work, Oscar sat with him at the table in the upstairs study, watching his father work, or playing with the wooden picture squares Jacob had bought for him in Heslop Bridge. When Marion grew fraught at the boy's failure to conform – when he crashed around the house, when he threw tantrums born of frustration at not being able to say clearly enough what he wanted, when he woke the sleeping Karl, or broke things, or wet the bed night after night – it was Jacob who pleaded mitigation and took the boy off with him to give Marion and Karl respite for a few hours. Jacob himself set just one rule for Oscar in the house – that he was on no account to go into his father's study without Jacob being there.

'No go in thi'?' Oscar would say in the smooth, pebble-shaped words that were his currency.

'No. There are things of mine in there that are important.'

'Whoah in?'

'School things. Things for learning.'

'No on my owe?' Oscar would repeat carefully.

'That's right,' Jacob would say.

'No wid-auw you?'

'Not without me.'

'No.'

And so they would repeat the same careful conversation whenever the two of them entered the study together so that Oscar would always remember not to go in there on his own.

When Karl was old enough for school, Jacob took both of the boys with him each morning. Oscar learned to shape an

'O' with his pencil when the class were practising their names, but his writing went no further than this, and he could read nothing. Jacob occupied him during the school day with chores around the classroom, or with his building blocks, while he taught the other children their lessons. In the main, the children accepted Oscar's presence in the class. The only disturbances came when, as he sometimes did, Oscar filled his pants and a ripple of suppressed and giddy laughter would start to ride around the room until Jacob realized and escorted the shame-faced and tearful Oscar out to the latrines in the yard and cleaned him up.

Oscar's one talent within the classroom was for rhythm. He would drum the top of his desk in time with any piece of music Jacob played to them on the wind-up gramophone he sometimes brought from the house; or Oscar, in a quiet place of his own, would tap with his pencil to private music inside his head with a regular and insistent rhythm. At the Christmas musical performance and the end of year concert, Oscar would provide the rhythm for the children's songs on a two-drum kit Jacob had found for him in a Heslop Bridge junk shop, and the women of the village would applaud him and pity his poor mother, and Jacob, stiffening himself against their pity, would smile encouragement at the boy from the side of the stage.

So it was that Jacob steered the boy through childhood to his ninth year, until the day he returned from an errand out of town to find Oscar, up ahead of him in the street, wearing the skullcap he had unearthed in his father's study, and dancing for the entertainment of a group of village boys gathered around him. They were all Jacob's students at the Sillot school. Karl, who should have been taking care of his brother, was amongst them. When the boys parted for a moment, Jacob saw that the tallith was tied around Oscar's shoulders – the prayer shawl's cream-coloured material was muddied with boot prints as though at one point it had been dropped and stood on. Oscar's trousers were around his ankles. Everyone could see that he was wearing a nappy. The village boys were laughing, egging him on, pressing him to keep on dancing. Oscar was twirling and jigging for them in the prayer shawl and the skullcap, with his wet nappy hanging between his legs and with one of Jacob's candlesticks brandished as a walking stick. They hadn't yet seen the schoolteacher coming up the hill towards them. One of the boys snatched the brass candlestick from Oscar. He held it up like a sword. He pulled a face and the other boys laughed. Oscar grasped for it but the boy kept it out of his reach. Oscar's face clouded.

'No,' he shouted, 'owe lady's stick. Me the owe lady stick.'

The boys passed the candlestick to each other, keeping it away from Oscar who was becoming increasingly frantic. Then it was dropped. It fell into the mud. Oscar dived to retrieve it but one of the boys' boots stepped on top of it to prevent Oscar from lifting it. They were all laughing at Oscar who was kneeling in the mud, shouting for the boy to lift his boot. He was braying like a donkey. There were tears in his eyes. He looked around at them all, pleading for help. Then he saw his father. The other boys followed his gaze and observed the schoolteacher approaching. They edged back, away from Oscar who picked up the candlestick. Instantly the distress was lifted from his face. As Karl and the other village boys melted away, Oscar began to move towards his father down the street, still using the candlestick as a walking stick.

'I'm *lady*,' he was saying. 'Loow! Loow! I'm owe lady dancing!'

Jacob saw that people in their houses were watching. He struck his son a single blow across the face with an open palm. Its force knocked Oscar to the ground. It was the first time the boy had ever been hit. Jacob walked on, towards the house. Behind him, Oscar's towelling nappy had slid to his knees again and he was struggling to catch up. He was crying.

'Not go in on owe,' he was shouting out to his father as Jacob walked on ahead of him. 'In wid Kar, go in wid Kar.'

Jacob didn't answer.

'Go in wid brudde,' Oscar pleaded, ' – not go in on owe. In wid brudde!'

But Jacob couldn't speak. HIs anger which had spilled out at Oscar was as much for Karl, who should have been protecting his brother from this, and for the villagers, who had watched the pantomime from behind their twitching curtains and chosen not to intervene. In Jacob's mind it was as though he had returned to the streets of Frankfurt and had been forced to watch the septuagenarian Meikle being dragged through the streets for entertainment. In the end, though, his real grief was in being forced to conclude that this was not, nor ever could be, a world for someone like Oscar, who was different from the rest. Jacob had to accept that, no matter how hard he tried, he could never keep a close enough watch over his son to prevent a repetition of the humiliation Oscar had endured in the street. That was the night he told Marion that he was going to send Oscar away, to be looked after in a place where the boy would no longer be exposed to such risks.

*

'Jacob?'

Sometimes she lay beside him in the bed, still talking to him after he had fallen asleep. Her father's slow and encroaching illness (he had developed Parkinson's disease in his fifties) had made Marion a light sleeper. Jacob went to bed bleary with fatigue and slipped quickly into sleep each night. He was drained, she supposed, from the effort of overcoming his public shyness to control and tutor the Sillot schoolroom. If ever *he* couldn't sleep, he went to work in his study and fell asleep at his desk. So when either of the boys woke during the night, or when the owls who colonized their dilapidated barn were active, or the wind was blowing through the fields, it was Marion who was more easily roused.

After Oscar went away, it became harder. She awoke more easily, sometimes in panic. In the noises of the wind up there around the house, she imagined that she heard Oscar's voice crying for her. She would lie in the darkness, wanting Jacob to wake and put his arms around her and comfort her. Sometimes, though, if he woke too quickly, he would speak in a different language and that would frighten her because he would never tell her what he had been saying.

'Jacob?'

He would not tell her where Oscar had been sent. It had been his decision alone – as if only he was entitled to decide Oscar's fate, as if Marion herself lacked some necessary experience to play a part in the matter. He would say, after-wards, only that Oscar had gone to a safer place, somewhere he would be looked after, where the boy would not have to be an outsider all his life, or run the risk of being mocked for the handicap that would always mark him out as different. And he repeated, whenever she petitioned him, that *this* (he meant Sillot, he meant streets and towns and people and the shortcomings of men) was not a world for the likes of Oscar.

'You still have Karl,' he said to her eventually one night, as if Jacob *didn't* have Karl, as if Oscar wasn't her child too. He was drugged with sleep when he said it, but it was no matter. In the end it was the sentence that would permit her to seek the consolation of Roy Sowerby. She realized that what she had taken in Jacob to be strength was only an inability to confide and trust in her, in anyone. In the end, she understood that she would never truly be allowed to become a part of him.

But not yet. Not yet.

'Jacob?'

Sometimes he stirred, making small rasping noises with his breathing, as if he was trying to find his way to the surface from a place deep underground. It occurred to her that she didn't know what he dreamed about.

'Jacob, do you love me?'

Sometimes, there would be some small high-pitched animal shriek outside in the darkness, some tiny gobbet of distress, then a lull again. Sometimes it was just the trees blowing, unseen.

'Jacob, tell me we'll be all right.'

But Jacob was asleep, unable to find a way clear from his fitful dreams. It was then that she put her hands together in the silence and started to pray, in the way her mother had taught her to as a little girl.

'Our Father, who art in Heaven,' she said. Her eyes were closed as she said the words.

They had found Otto's body in the river. He had been beaten

before being thrown in the water, and the injuries made it hard for Jacob to recognize his brother.

The family had been sitting around the table in the apartment. It was Otto who noticed the truck pull up in the street outside and the men get out. They heard the sound of boots on the stairs, and counted the number of floors they were climbing.

'Lock the door.'

'They will have seen the light outside.'

'Maybe they're looking for someone else.'

'And maybe they're looking for you boys – lock the door.'

They heard the battering of a fist or a stick on the door.

'Just sit still.'

'Open the door.'

'And let them in?'

'They'll break it down otherwise – they know someone's in, they'll have seen the light.'

'No! Jacob, Otto – go and hide in the bedroom. You can get out onto the roof from the balcony.'

'They could be looking for someone else – *open the door*!'

The door smashed open. There were six of them, some with clubs or sticks. They looked around the room, taking in the place.

'Which one is Jacob Baum?'

There was silence in the room.

'The writer, Jacob Baum. Which of you is Baum? The rest of you are not wanted. Or we can take you all if Baum does not come forward for questioning.'

That was what he dreamed about sometimes. He dreamed he was looking again into the eyes of the flushed and drunken inquisitor who was asking for Jacob Baum. He dreamed about the silence prevailing in the family apartment in those few seconds. He dreamed about the fear which at that moment had made him want to vomit and filled his head with giddy air, and the fleeting moment of self-preservation that forbade his body to move. Sometimes he dreamed that he heard the scrape of a chair and the sound of another man in the silence standing up, of Otto standing up and saying to them casually, 'I'm Jacob Baum, have you read my books then, boys?'

He dreamed of the touch on his shoulder as his brother walked past him. He dreamed of the way his own body stayed rigid with fear, and the way his head swam, as his brother moved sedately across the room towards the men by the door. And he dreamed for the rest of his life of the dawning realization, perhaps an hour later – with his parents out in the streets organizing a search in the neighbourhood for Otto – sitting alone in the room by then, that he had shit in his pants and that it had gone dark outside.

Jacob parked the car on a side street around the corner from the guest house. He knew from his previous stays that new arrivals weren't meant to check in until four o'clock, so he went over the road to the café and ordered a coffee and a small cake and sat watching people coming and going.

When he had first started visiting the Lake District twenty years ago, he had hoped it was a place he would be able to bring his family to. Marion herself showed no interest in walking in the mountains, but for a while he pictured himself leading his grown boys onto the fells. He would stand alone at the edge of some gulley, or on one of the ridges above Borrowdale and he would imagine saying, 'Look, boys, look at that view. Isn't that the most beautiful thing? Don't you

215

feel you are on top of the world up here, above all the troubles of the world?'

But it hadn't happened like that, because Karl had consistently declined Jacob's entreaties to go with him, and because of the way things had worked out with Oscar, Jacob had only ever gone alone.

Early that morning, back in Lancashire, he had driven to Calderhall. He had stood outside the main gates for a long time, not sure what to do. In the end he had stumbled across a man – Jim McCready – arriving for his early morning shift. It was Jim McCready he had entrusted with the parcel, with a plea for it to be passed on to Oscar. There had been something about Jim McCready's face that encouraged Jacob to trust him with the errand. Jim McCready himself had been a little suspicious of the pale, austere stranger waiting at the crack of dawn by the main gates. Jacob had explained that the parcel had been sent by Oscar's father. Oscar's father was dead, Jacob had said. This (the delivery of the parcel) was an errand his father had commissioned before his death. And then he was gone. Lacking courage to the end, it had occurred to him as he moved away. The day's first promise of light had been creeping into the fields, as if such an errand might be the beginning of something and not the end.

When he was found, the only unusual thing, according to the short report Brendan found in the 2 December 1968 *Keswick Advertiser*, was the reference to the book. It was folded down on its spine, according to the woman who ran the guest house, as if Mr Brigg had been reading it and had left it unfinished. It was a foreign book with a stamped second-hand price on the back. It was written by a man called Jacob Baum. It wasn't as if Mr Brigg had been an oddity or anything, she said. He was a very polite, softly spoken man. He had stayed at the hotel previously, though always alone. The book was still on the bed when she went in. She hadn't touched it because it was spattered with blood. He was a decent man, she said – he had seemed like a decent man. A quiet man. He must have felt he had failed in his life, or that his life had failed him. He had packed his things neatly in the suitcase. On the dressing table, she said, Mr Brigg had left enough money to pay his bill.

Brendan stood in front of Karl Brigg's farmhouse, looking down at the valley. It was a view, he imagined, that Jacob Baum must have grown to love in his twenty-three years there. The former farmhouse had been old even when the newly married couple had settled there in 1945. It had been Marion's home in Sillot, of course, before that – the one she had shared with her father. By the time Karl Brigg took it on after his mother's death, it would have been a well-maintained building, reroofed, with the timbers replaced and the garden extended. But in 1945, Brendan supposed, it must have appeared to Jacob as though nothing had been done to the property for generations. It wasn't difficult for him to picture Jacob Baum – a man in his mid-thirties, seeking to construct a new life for himself – wandering around the place with its air of ramshackle melancholy, its damp brick-work choked by ivy, its floors creaking in the low-ceilinged rooms, the wooden frames of its ancient sash windows soft and rotting.

The long and narrow cultivated garden area would, at the time – according to Jacob Brigg – have been dense with shrubbery, soft underfoot even in high summer, and dark under the canopy of two ancient elms, standing guard over the sagging and dilapidated boundary fence. In the spring, Karl Brigg told Brendan, each room of the house smelled of moss and he and Oscar would go hunting for frogs in the cellar. In summer, the place would be thick with dust, and with spiders that colonized the high cornices. From September, most of the rooms back then were too draughty to sit in without a fire being lit. But Jacob would have loved the house, Brendan felt sure. He knew enough about the man by now to know that much. This is *my* house, he would have thought, rolling the sumptuous notion round in his head. The house would surely have given Jacob a sense of belonging, allowing him to feel part of the procession of local life in a way that little else did. It surely made him feel English.

For all of his life in Sillot, Jacob was destined to be an outsider. Much of it, Brendan supposed, was connected with the man's profession. The village teacher, residing in an inward-looking community like Sillot in the northern hills, was, at that time, part of the community but still separate from it. For all that the formality of his manner, and his public shyness, and the unspoken events of his past accentuated it, it was his job first and foremost which set him apart from the village. He would have been acknowledged by everyone else when they passed him in the street as *Mr Brigg*; when they talked about him, they would have referred to him as 'The Schoolteacher'.

'He was Jewish, wasn't he?' Brendan said.

Karl Brigg nodded. 'My mother told me after he died. I didn't know while he was alive. He never talked about it. I don't suppose I ever asked. You know what kids are like.'

'Were you brought up Christian?'

'I was brought up *English*. That's what was important to the old bastard. That's why he changed his name to Brigg. He wanted our name to *sound* English.'

Brendan lifted the array of photographs from the tin Karl Brigg had brought out again at Brendan's request. He had seemed keen to invite Brendan in this time, happy at the chance to talk.

'You know she's gone,' he said.

'Your wife?'

'You spend a lifetime working for the benefit of someone – and then they just walk out.'

'Why did she leave?' Brendan asked.

'How should I know? If she thinks she's getting half the business and a share of this place . . . if that's what she was thinking when she left . . . she can sod off. Where's the loyalty in just getting up and going like that? Why should anyone have to put up with that?'

He went quiet. Brendan carried on working his way through the photographs.

'Who is this one?' he said, holding one up for Karl Brigg to see.

'My father. He's the one sitting down. My mother found that photograph in my father's things after he died.'

'And the other man in the picture?'

'She said it was his brother.'

Brendan looked at the two pale young men in formal suits. 'Do you know anything about the brother?'

'Never met him. He died in Germany before the war, my mother said. That's all I know.'

Brendan shuffled through the remaining photographs – of Oscar and Karl as young boys, of Marion, of the farmhouse as it had changed through the years, from the first snapshot taken by Jacob himself in 1946, with Marion standing fresh-faced on the porch, to its present appearance.

'Will you carry on with the sale?'

Karl Brigg looked across at him, puzzled.

'Of the house,' Brendan added, ' – with your wife having left.'

'My life's over now, isn't it?' Karl Brigg said, 'she's fucking ruined it.'

11

It Ain't Necessarily So

September. The smooth lawns of the houses up above the town are hidden from the road. There is an innocence to this early hour. The morning hangs like a pause, and the stillness promises sunshine later in the day. Beyond the crown of the hill, the bypass is hectic with early-day commerce and the rude and persistent business of men hurrying to do deals, but the big houses in their acres above the town seem immune to all that, each property's land moist with autumn and set above the woods where herons have settled on the river.

Into this land comes Wilf Wardle. His Lada Estate is fourteen years old and pitted with rust. Duke Ellington's 'Newport Up' is bouncing out of the radio. Duke Ellington is second on Wilf Wardle's list of all-time heroes, behind Learie Constantine, and in the back of the Lada it seems an interesting fantasy that the Duke himself is stretched out on the back seat. It comes from Wilf living on his own all those years, of having only himself for company, that such things are imaginable. The Duke, it seems to Wilf, has that between-concerts, between-cities lethargy on him: shiny shoes, top coat, heavy bags under his eyes and the slumbers of a child beneath the pork-pie hat tilted over his brow,

wishing the *cat* at the wheel was gentler over the ruts, and so
Wilf – appreciative of the Duke's daytime torpor and enjoying the notion – eases back on the accelerator. He continues
to steer his way one-handed up the unmade road, the empty
box trailer behind the car bouncing on the ruts, his right
arm tapping rhythm against the car's side through the
wound-down window. Wilf knows the ruts and divots well.
This land is his land too – his land *first*, Wilf would say.
Inside the car, Wilf's front-seat passenger, too, taps a steady
rhythm to the music of the cassette, until Wilf brings the
Lada to a halt in front of a set of wrought-iron gates. The
sign fixed to the nearside gatepost announces 'The Croft'.
The 'For Sale' notice, which has been up all summer, now
has 'Sold Subject to Contract' fixed over the top.

'One gate each?' Wilf asks.

Oscar Brigg looks around at Wilf, then opens the passenger side door and shuffles out of his seat. Wilf stops the
cassette and follows Oscar out of the car, leaving the engine
running. Both of them wear suits and black ties in readiness
for the funeral. Oscar unhooks the metal hasp and the two
men push open the two gates.

'Do you want to walk up to the house, Oscar?' Wilf asks.
It is a walk Oscar likes, past the long line of shrubs and borders Wilf has cultivated over the years. Oscar nods. Wilf
climbs back into the car and edges the Lada between the
gate posts. He stops ten yards beyond them. Behind him,
Oscar lets the gate fall back in place on its unsubtle hinge. It
gives a clear ring, a mid-range and satisfying clang. Dora's
gates, Wilf thinks, always seem to ring louder in the thin
autumn air than they do through the summer's heavy,
thicker days.

Wilf drives slowly on, past the two terraced lawns he

created during the long hot summer months of 1976, past the flower borders, up to the house which has been deserted since June when Dora Hicken finally moved out into the nursing home. He parks up at the side, facing the greenhouse. He sits there for a while with the engine ticking, then pushes the cassette back in to allow the Duke and his orchestra to play on to the frenetic conclusion of the track. When the music finishes, he turns the engine off. In the sudden silence he can hear birdsong in the morning trees. He looks around behind him, half curious. The back seat of the Lada is empty. He smiles. The Duke, perhaps, has made some sudden and surreptitious exit.

He has tended this garden since 1974 when Dora's barrister husband died and she asked Wilf to take over the responsibility of managing the four acres.

'It's not much to shout about, is it?' Wilf told her, looking around the place the day after she had approached him.

'He wasn't much of a gardener, was Jack,' she explained, ' – more of a golfer, really. That's why it's a bit of a wilderness out there.'

'So what do you want doing to it?'

'Anything you like,' Dora said. 'My brother has a place in Spain I use quite a lot. I'm back and forth, especially in the winter, so I'm happy to leave the planning up to you.'

And so she did. For twenty-six years, Wilf spent five or six hours a week on the garden. Whenever Dora was due to go away, she would leave a tea-towel draped over the kitchen taps as a signal for Wilf to check that the house was in order by using the spare key she had given him. Every month, he submitted the bill for his time and materials, written down on a torn-out margin of his *Daily Mirror* which he always left for her on the work bench in the outhouse, along with any requests he had for new projects he wanted to pursue for the garden: the terraced lawns in 1976, the greenhouse in 1979, the fruit trees, the back fencing, the first experiments with the orchids. Usually, he found his money on the bench the following week. The money was left in a white envelope, together with Dora's permission for the new projects. She always gave her permission. She never asked to see a bill. He once overcharged her by £3. 12 for a set of bedding plants by adding up the cost wrongly. The following week, when Dora put out his money, he left the £3. 12.

Down in the woods, the crows caw in the tall trees. Wilf breathes in the morning air. His boots crunch on the gravel drive as he shifts his weight. During the summer months his work outdoors gives him a peasant's tan on his crumpled face. These days, though, he is starting to feel a stiffness in his knees in the first hour of work, and his temperamental back needs to be coaxed gently into motion each morning with a set of exercises the osteopath has recommended.

Oscar comes into view, walking steadily up the drive.

'Shift a leg,' Wilf encourages, ' – we can't go to a funeral towing a trailer.'

While Oscar is unhooking the trailer, Wilf, out of habit, inspects the house. All the familiar ornaments of Dora's that he has grown accustomed to seeing on her windowsills are now gone. The curtains at the windows are drawn. Wilf completes his circuit of the house. He stops, turns, and eyes the path ahead of him. He takes a deep breath.

'Are you ready?'

Oscar looks around. Wilf composes himself, then suddenly breaks into a lumbering run over the gravel. He takes six strides, building up a modicum of speed, feeling the protest in his knee as he does so. At the edge of the blue azalea bush he takes off. He lands several feet away on the same leg he has taken off from, then stretches out with the other leg, swinging his arms forward for momentum, the way his PE teacher had taught him half a century ago, before the final jump. He lands heavily, swaying to hold his balance to prevent himself falling and dirtying the suit. He looks back quizzically to examine the distance he has covered. It is some way short (as it always is these days) of the record he set on a hot June afternoon at Dora's in 1977, while Dora sat with friends on her patio around the back, listening to the Wimbledon tennis commentaries on Radio 2 with her customary glass of Pimms.

Wilf shakes his head in mock-sorrow at the below par effort. Oscar watches him. Wilf stands there for a while on his landing spot, enjoying the moment.

'You fancy having a go today?'

Oscar looks down at the unfamiliar suit he has been pressed into wearing, then shakes his head. 'Wiff Wooder,' he says.

'I don't blame you – it's a mug's game at our age.'

When the trailer has been detached, they wheel it to one side of the path and leave it there ready for their return after lunch. Wilf backs the Lada down the drive and turns it around by the gates, and they head into Heslop Bridge. On the way down, he turns over the tape. The melancholy opening bars of the Duke's 'Chelsea Bridge' begin to play.

> 'Death is nothing at all,' Keith Cottee reads,
> 'I have only slipped away into the next room.
> I am I and you are you.
> Whatever we were to each other – that we are still.'

Keith Cottee is reading Henry Scott Holland's poem at the microphone behind Jim McCready's coffin. On the front row, facing him, Wilf Wardle and Oscar Brigg sit side by side in their dark suits. Next to Wilf is Joyce McCready in a black smock which reaches to her ankles. Beside her at the end of the bench is the oboe she has brought from home. The church is filled with people from Heslop Bridge who knew Jim, or who know Joyce. Brendan can see Lewis Chettle's parents from the hardware shop, Sam Cottee's father, several of the teachers from the school, and Alan Bibby – the other remaining member of Jim McCready's card school.

It is Joyce who has asked Keith Cottee to read the poem. She does not trust herself to read it out loud, and Terry is not here to ask. He has sent flowers, and a note to Joyce saying he and Tammy can't make it back to England for his father's funeral. As the reading proceeds, Brendan is drawn to watch Oscar Brigg's face. It reveals nothing of what he is thinking. It isn't used as a means of expressing emotion. Its smooth, still features give nothing away.

> *'Call me by my own familiar name,*
> *Speak to me in the easy way which you always used.*
> *Put no difference in your tone;*
> *Wear no false air of solemnity or sorrow.'*

In recent days, Brendan has twice visited the Atlas Street hostel. Within his own room, Oscar Brigg seemed to occupy only a very small space. Perhaps that was because of the way, as Brendan observed, Oscar made no surplus movements. It occurred to Brendan that the room in the hostel was the first space in Oscar's adult life that belonged to him, and was itself much more than the space he was afforded in his long solitary spells in the dormitory's sideroom at Calderhall. Perhaps there were parts of his room, Brendan pondered, that Oscar had yet to commandeer; how far must half a dozen steps from the bed to the landing have seemed when, for three quarters of his life, he could only have imagined such a journey.

'Laugh as we always laughed together,
At the little jokes we enjoyed together.
Play, smile, think of me, pray for me,
Let my name be ever the household word that it always was;
Let it be spoken without effort,
Without a ghost of a shadow on it.'

Brendan has been told by Wilf what Oscar's torso looks like – the extent of the scarring, and the burn marks – but, like the uncommitted nature of his face, Oscar seems instinctively to disguise the nature and extent of the physical damage, carrying his body stiffly, consciously, as if it were something foreign he has been left in charge of.

It is Oscar's eyes that are the most obviously remarkable thing about him. He has large green eyes in deep hollows. In his own room at the hostel he had watched Brendan unflinchingly, but at times of his own choosing; at other times, he had fallen back into himself.

'What is death but a negligible accident?
Why should I be out of mind
Because I am out of sight?'

As Keith Cottee continues to read, Wilf leans across and whispers something to Oscar, smiling. Brendan watches

Oscar nod seriously in response. All Oscar's movements, Brendan realizes, are deliberate and considered. The strait-jacket is one of his own making, as if he is wary of attracting attention to himself, as if the most effective way of survival in the end had been to become invisible.

> *'I am waiting for you for an interval,*
> *Somewhere very near,*
> *Just around the corner.'*

Nicholas Pacynko has written to Brendan about the poppies. Jean Carr, the woman Fr Wynn had appointed to run the youth drug project from the gym's premises, had been picked up by a local police patrol at two o'clock in the morning, planting more of the damned things on her hands and knees on the land behind the gym. She had protested that they were nothing to do with her – that the poppies were from *God*, that she wasn't drunk, that the policemen were pigs.

Fellowship TV seem less interested in acquiring the Heslop Bridge parchments since the letter Brendan sent, marked 'private and confidential', reached Madeline Geller. She is, Brendan understands, currently in the former Yugoslavia where two Serb widows in the southern town of Bujanovac claim to have been spoken to on several occasions by a statue of the crucified Christ in the local church. Since the last manifestation, one of the women has been in a coma; the other has made a string of television appearances claiming that the two of them have been given a series of prophecies and instructions to be revealed to the world over a prescribed number of months.

*

'Nothing is past; nothing is lost.
One brief moment and all will be as it was before.'

After the poem, Joyce rises and moves to the front, carrying her oboe. The church is hushed. Joyce coughs. She nods to her audience and gestures to the oboe.

'Forgive me,' she says, 'this is just something I wanted to do. I wouldn't do it normally in public, you understand, but I feel I'm amongst friends.' There are smiles around the church. 'If anyone doesn't recognize the tune,' she adds, 'I'll tell you what it is afterwards.'

She plays 'It Ain't Necessarily So'. The notes sound rich and smooth inside the cool church. To Brendan's ear she plays an occasional false note but what do these matter – she has honoured her father-in-law in a way that she considers fitting. Afterwards, she will tell Brendan that she missed the *D flat* twice. Brendan will say that it didn't sound anything like 'Seventy-Six Trombones'. She will thank him and kiss his cheek.

There had been no miracle for Jim McCready. Joyce prayed, but no one responded to her prayers, Brendan understands, because there is no one to hear them. We are on our own and we watch over each other. There is no one to conjure poppies for would-be dead saints; no one to catch falling children; no one to wipe the slate clean of pancreatic cancer. Instead, there are women, distraught with grief, who push bedding plants into rubbled earth in the dead of night to mark a good man's passing. There are small bears pinned by the ear to shiny black headstones smothered at the base by forget-me-not and sunshine-yellow carnations. There are women who ease their once seemingly immortal men through the last long hours in narrow hospital beds. There are sips of water; old emnities being permitted to lapse; debts reconciled; pangs of irredeemably lost opportunity; affection, unspoken and inadequately nurtured, prevailing in the last moments; hands held in the unconscionable night; glimpses of elusive love, unconditional and fleeting; vigorous and well-lived lives stilled and finished in a heartbeat.

Then nothing. Except for those who are left behind to press on and who must remember to eat a little something for strength, and load the washing machine back at the house, and ring the surgery to organize the death certificate, and add soap powder to the supermarket list for the weekend, or the kids will have nothing to wear after Sunday, and see the ordinariness of the day roll on, and hear the aching jollity of the DJ on the radio, and remember to take nothing for granted ever again because this commodity – this ability to breathe steadily and take in blue sky on clear mornings, to recall the details of Alexander's march into Asia, and Manchester City's greatest season, and your son's favourite flavour of ice cream (mint choc chip), the route of the walk you took with your first love, the kiss of warm, foreign sun after a foggy English season, the vermilion brilliance of simple geraniums in pots on dusty patios on summer days, this fragile mystery of life itself in which we are each other's Heaven and Hell – is the wonder to rejoice in.

Oscar knew the location of each family's house. This wouldn't have mystified Wilf who told Brendan that, once taught, Oscar could remember the layout of every garden they had worked in and never forget the whereabouts of a plant pot or a tool they had put down. Oscar had delivered his father's verses one at a time, in a series of journeys he made from the hostel under cover of darkness – one for each grieving household with the exception of the Sewells and the Swanns, whose families had worked at Calderhall and who Oscar knew too well to venture near. After that, finding himself unwilling or unable to stop, he chose to leave other parchments in locations that were special to him – in the field where horses ran; in the cold stone parish church of Holy Souls where Oscar and Wilf always dropped off flowers from Dora Hicken's place each week, and where the two men sometimes sat for a short prayer in the front pew; on the outfield spot on the cricket ground from where, Wilf liked to tell people, Learie Constantine threw the ball to run out the last Heslop Bridge batsman in 1933.

Jim McCready had made sure that the package of verses entrusted to him at the gates to Calderhall on that morning in 1968 were passed to Oscar, who kept them hidden in his room. He couldn't read them but he understood the power they held, and the secrecy they inspired. He knew it was right to hide them from the authorities at Calderhall and later from the hostel staff, just as his father had hidden them from his mother and from Karl. When he did transfer them, it was for safety because two of the other residents in the hostel had their rooms broken into. He moved them to the school where they seemed secure in their store at the far end of the boilerhouse, where only he and Wilf ever went. On the day Jason Orr walked into the school and pandemonium broke out, Oscar had hurried to rescue the parchments, but in his panic to escape the siege he dropped them. He scrabbled to pick up as many as he dared but left some behind before fleeing to hide in the relative safety of the changing huts. Jason Orr's explosion blew off the door to the boilerhouse store and three-quarters of its roof. The backdraft blew out everything loose, including those parchments which Oscar hadn't managed to gather up in his rush to flee the building. In the weeks that followed, as Heslop Bridge grieved for its lost children, pale-faced, stiff-gaited Oscar Brigg – incarcerated since he was ten years old on the grounds that he lacked some essential humanness and deserved nothing better – was the attending angel, scurrying around Heslop Bridge in the dead of night to apply the balm of his father's Hebrew verses of condolence.

'Thanks for turning up this morning, B. Moon.'

Brendan and Joyce McCready, keepers of a shared secret, stand side by side.

'I know he'd have appreciated it.'

The funeral buffet in the cricket club has concluded. Since then, Joyce has changed from her funeral black into a favoured pair of slacks and a cardigan. They are standing on the back lawn of Dora Hicken's place. The sun has finally broken through the high September cloud. They have been helping Wilf and Oscar to load up equipment from the outhouse onto the trailer. For now, Wilf and Oscar are on a short break, enjoying a cigarette.

'Of all the gardens he and Oscar have tended,' Joyce says, 'this was Wilf's favourite. I can't remember how many years he's been seeing to this place for Dora. He *talks* about it like it's his own, that's for sure. For a man with a six foot by six foot flagged yard, this place has been like heaven for him. Mind you, I don't think in all the years he's been employed by Dora he's made a penny profit out of her. I think he worked here just for the love of it.'

'Does the new owner not want to keep him on as the gardener?'

'Wilf didn't tell you about meeting him up here?'

'No.'

'Keith Doyle has bought the place off Dora. He's the man I do the packing for. He offered me a job once answering one of his phone lines – talking sex to strangers – but I told him where to go. It shows there's a lot of money in it, though, for him to be able to buy this place. One day last week, when Wilf and Oscar were up here, Keith Doyle appeared from inside the house. They watched him stand on the edge of the goldfish pond, peeing into it. He'd been drinking.'

'What happened?'

'Wilf tore him off a strip – said it was a responsibility, having a garden like this.'

'What did Keith Doyle say?'

'He said he didn't like fish anyway. He told Wilf to eff off, and he said for Wilf to take his "spastic" with him off his property.'

The two of them watch as, at the top of the garden, Wilf and Oscar rouse themselves after their smoke and set to work again.

'You like him, don't you?' Brendan says.

'Who?'

'Wilf.'

Joyce looks at him, then nods. 'I wondered how I'd cope without Jim, but Wilf's been good to me this last month.'

'Have you asked him out?'

'Oh, we're too old for all that nonsense now.'

'You think?'

'Course we are. Anyway, you get to the stage in your life where you're too stuck in your ways to change.'

'Maybe you're right.'

'Of course I'm right. What would you know about it – you're a *man*!'

'It's just that I came across this in my morning news-paper.' Brendan reaches into his jacket pocket and passes a cutting to her.

'What is it?'

'You are Sagittarius?'

She nods.

'It just seemed relevant, that's all.'

Joyce reads through the horoscope. 'SAGITTARIUS: This is the time of year when you tend to receive proof that marvellous things really can happen. Although it could be wishful thinking to expect all your prayers to be answered to order, the planetary picture indicates that one of them is ready to be realized, as Jupiter, your planetary ruler, suggests that the time is right for you to form a stronger bond with an emotional partner.'

At the top end of the garden, beyond the pagoda that Wilf long ago erected on the side of the outhouse, and where the summer honeysuckle is now heavy with scent, he has begun to kindle a fire to burn the rubbish. He shouts down the garden to ask if Brendan will give Oscar a hand removing the last of their belongings from the outhouse.

Oscar is gathering into a pile in the middle of the outhouse floor anything that belongs to him and Wilf – a couple of screwdrivers left in a drawer, a half-used container of fertilizer, Oscar's watering can.

'Wiff Wooder,' Oscar says, pointing out of the door towards Wilf.

Brendan nods. 'Stuff for Wilf,' he says in confirmation. 'Tell you what – if you carry that lot over to Wilf, I'll finish checking in here to make sure there's nothing left.'

Oscar lifts up the contents of the pile he has assembled and manœuvres out through the door. Brendan begins to work his way through the remaining shelves and cupboards. At the back of the outhouse is an old-fashioned tallboy with a series of deep drawers. He works his way through each of them, checking they are empty. In the bottom drawer is a pile of old Sunday supplements. He lifts them out. Underneath them he finds a brown envelope with the name 'Oscar Brigg' written on it. Inside, there are two sheets of old, heavy-duty yellowing vellum paper. Both parchments, like the ones found around the town, contain a single fourteen-line verse. Each one, written in Hebrew, also has Jacob Baum's now familiar inscription, translating as 'Letter from God' heading in the top left-hand corner.

Out in the garden, Wilf is standing over the fire. Oscar is packing the last items onto the trailer. Brendan wanders out of the outhouse into the sunshine. He looks around for Joyce. She is in the greenhouse, admiring the orchids. Brendan walks over to Wilf. He is carrying a Corn Flakes box.

'I used to keep my ground pegs in there,' Wilf says, seeing the box.

Brendan smiles. 'Plenty more cereal boxes to be had, Wilf.' He peers inside, checking the contents. He has folded up the two remaining parchments and pushed them to the bottom of the box so they won't be seen. He waits for an appropriate lull in the flames, which are licking up the side of the frame, and then lays the box on top of the burning wood. Instantly, the fire begins to curl the box and char it black. Within half a minute the trail, which has led him finally to this garden, and these remaining verses, and to that gaunt and gangling man loading the trailer, is reduced to ash. Brendan watches the fire for a while, working out gradually in his mind what it is that he will tell the Maslows.

'Wilf,' he says eventually, 'do you eat out much?'

'Not really. The lads and me get a takeaway once a week from the Indian. Mind you, we'll need a new partner now that Jim's gone. I suppose I'll have to teach Oscar how to play brag.'

'It's just that I still have this. I wondered if you'd have any use for it.' He takes a voucher from his wallet.

'What is it?'

'It's for a meal at the hotel I've been staying at. Three-course dinner for two. It's a complimentary thing they do for guests who stay for more than a certain length of time. I checked with them and they said anyone could use it. Perhaps you could take Joyce.'

'You think?' Wilf says.

'You can only ask.'

Wilf nods and takes the voucher. 'Thanks, Mr Moon.'

'Brendan,' Brendan says.

'Brendan. Thanks, Brendan.'

'Ben-dan Moon,' Oscar says. He has walked up from the trailer and stands there with them, watching uncertainly for a reaction.

Brendan nods. 'Brendan Moon,' he repeats back to Oscar in acknowledgement.

'Oscar Brigg,' Oscar says, as if introducing himself for the first time.

Brendan nods. 'I know,' he says. The two men shake hands, and Brendan feels Oscar Brigg's warm, comfortable palm pressed against his own.

12

The Bells of Parte Vieja

His apartment in San Sebastián has a narrow stone balcony that juts out over a courtyard cluttered with women's washing and tubs of bougainvillea. Each morning, with the mist still lifting off the bay, Brendan walks into the old town and drinks coffee in one of the bars on the Plaza de la Constitucion and reads a newspaper. Each evening, he leaves his apartment and, in the cooling sun, heads for the sea. He walks between the blue- and yellow-fronted houses with their rows of green shutters, down the avenues of tamarinds beside the river and through the narrow streets of the Parte Vieja with its pattern of cupolas and towers. When he reaches the Paseo Maritimo, he makes for the bar he has found, where he has a view of the waves hitting the rocks below. He can see the two hills that enclose the curve of evening lights around the bay. Until the last of the light drains away, he watches the moored sailing boats bobbing at the far end of the bay, and the line of fishermen's vessels littered with their damp, sea-smelling nets and ropes.

This morning, Brendan is searching for the church. Each evening, as he has walked through the Parte Vieja, he has heard bells somewhere in the neighbourhood, sounding

out the hour. Yesterday he asked Abel, the apartment
supervisor, which church it might be. Santa Maria del Mar,
the supervisor told him. Abel gave Brendan directions and
this morning Brendan has set out to follow them. He weaves
between tall buildings and across boulevards but eventually, somehow, he loses his direction. Unworried, he
continues walking, taking random turns until eventually his
path opens out into a small open square, dotted with trees.
In the middle of the square is a circular stone fountain with
water running steadily from the centre and plopping on the
white stone. There is a café-bar in one corner of the square.
Four tables are set out on the pavement, sheltered by white
sun umbrellas and covered with red and white-checked
tablecloths. An elegant young woman in casual trousers and
a white T-shirt is smoothing out one of the tablecloths as
though she has just finished setting out for the day's trade.
Black hair falls over her shoulders as she leans over the
table.

At the far end of the square is a different church to the one
Brendan has set out in search of – a plain white building
with a series of rough steps rising up to the entrance. The
sun makes the high flat walls of the church seem luminous
against the cornflower blue of the sky. Brendan walks up
the steps and through the wooden doors. The interior of the
church is dense with shadow and suddenly hushed. The
layout is plain and unadorned. It feels to Brendan as though
he is entering a warehouse or a barn. The only other person
he can see in the church is a woman in her fifties or sixties,
wearing a headscarf, who is lighting one of the candles in
the rack by the door as he walks in. Brendan nods to her.
The woman smiles. She indicates the candle in her hand,
suggesting he might be wishing to light a candle of his own.

Brendan shakes his head. She nods and says something to him in Spanish as she returns to her task. He walks on up the side aisle, past a series of murals depicting the Stations of the Cross. Halfway down he stops and edges into a pew.

Brendan sits quite still. He is conscious only of the steady pull of his breathing and the stillness around him that invites him to reflect. After a while he pulls from the side pocket of his jacket the notebook he has carried around since he arrived in San Sebastián. On the cover is the smiling ginger cat, Marmaduke, and the title – *Jack's Story*. He sits in the gentle hush of the church, flicking through parts of his son's story, and then through some of the additional entries he himself has made since Jack's death. There are still three pages empty at the end of the book. He sits looking at one of the blank pages. He runs his fingers over its textures. He turns back to the front of the book and reads out loud the first sentence of his son's story. The woman in the headscarf at the back of the building looks across momentarily as Brendan's words rise and hang in the dry church air.

A little later, he stands and walks back towards the big door at the rear of the church. The woman has gone. He stops by the rack of candles, takes one from the box and lights it in memory of his son. As he is fixing the candle in place, half-glancing down the line of pews, he notices the figure by the side door. He feels his heart being grabbed.

The pale-faced boy half-turns his head. Brendan sees Jack's face glance towards him down the length of the church. He takes a step forward. The figure turns, then slips away. Brendan continues to edge forward, curious.

'Hello?'

He moves cautiously down the aisle. Ahead of him, the side door of the church bangs shut. The noise rings around the building. It takes him several more hesitant steps to reach the door. He pulls at it, but the door will not open.

'Wait!'

He is trying the handle. It still will not move. He twists the handle the other way. The door swings open. The exit leads out into an empty, narrow cobbled street. Brendan walks to the end of the street which leads him back into the square. The boy has gone. Brendan stands on the edge of the square looking around. The sun is bright in his face after the shelter of the cool white church. His heart is beating fast. He walks slowly across the square, looking down each of the narrow avenues. At the far end, for want of anything better to do, he sits down at one of the tables of the café.

The young woman who appears a few minutes later says something to him that he doesn't understand.

'English,' he says.

'Ah.' She nods. 'Can I get you something, English?'

'A beer,' he says eventually.

'A beer.' She is watching him closely. 'Are you OK? You look like you see a ghost.'

'Do you have ghosts here?'

'Football players and bullfighters,' she says, ' – that is all. Do you see a ghost?'

'I thought I saw one – in the church. A boy. Pale. This tall.' He indicates. 'He wouldn't answer me, and then he disappeared.'

'I have nothing to do with the church, but my mother will know. You want me to ask my mother?'

Brendan shrugs helplessly.

'*Mama!*' she shouts. 'Is OK,' she says to Brendan, 'Mama will know. Is to do with the church, she will know.'

In response to the shout, a woman appears in the doorway of the café.

'Maria?' she says, wiping her hands on a cloth.

It is the same woman Brendan saw earlier inside the church, wearing the headscarf. She sees Brendan and says something to him in Spanish.

'Inglés,' Maria says to her mother.

'Ah, si.'

The two women hold a rapid conversation.

'She says she saw you in the church earlier.'

Brendan nods. 'Just to look at the building,' he says, 'not to pray.'

'Me also,' Maria says. 'Is all superstition. My mother is full of superstition. My mother always tells people when she was a girl she saw angels in the church. Not once but four times.' She shrugs and laughs out loud at the idea. 'Four times!'

'In the church over there?' Brendan asks.

'Sure – my mother's church! This church should be *named* after my mother, the times she is in it.'

'Do you and your mother both work here?' Brendan asks.

'The bar is mine,' Maria says. 'Since Papa died, my mother helps. Also Miguel.'

Maria's mother speaks to her again.

'My mother she asks your name.'

'Brendan.'

'*Brendan*,' Maria explains to her mother in response.

'Bren-don,' her mother repeats.

Maria speaks again to her mother in Spanish. Her mother answers. Maria translates for Brendan. 'My mother says, might be Antonio. She isn't sure if he is in the church today. Antonio is one of the altar boys at the church. He has no hearing.'

241

'He's deaf?'

'Deaf. Si. Sometimes he does jobs for Fr Bernard around the church. Maybe is Antonio who doesn't hear you? Maybe not. Maybe is one of Mama's angels – you think?'

She grins to show she is teasing. He feels his heartbeat steadying, and the momentary rush of hope he is helpless to control subsiding one more time.

'You know, my grandfather persuades me, when I was little, that those who see the dead would be better off considering only the living.'

'I think your grandfather was right.'

'So – you don't think it was a ghost?'

'No,' he says to her, ' – I think it was Antonio. But tell your mother thank you.'

'Sure.'

Maria and her mother speak again. Not Jack. Antonio. It can never be Jack, and yet he knows that the hope can never leave him, that such a weight must be carried through each day and into the next for eternity.

While he waits for the drink, Brendan wanders across the road and sits on the low, flat-topped stone wall that runs around the square. The stone feels warm on his hands as he presses them to it. He looks across at his jacket, hanging on the back of the chair over the road at the bar, and then remembers that in leaving the church he has left behind the notebook with the ginger cat on the front cover. It is no matter, he thinks, as he sits in his shirtsleeves in the sun, feeling the comforting heat of the stone on his palms – he can go back in afterwards for it; or perhaps this time, finally, he will choose not to go back for it at all.

A group of people arrive and occupy another table. A man appears from inside the café and one of the group calls

'Miguel!' to him. Miguel acknowledges the man. They talk amiably. Miguel takes the group's order. Brendan walks back across to his table and sits down. Maria appears with Brendan's beer on a small tray. He likes how gracefully, how silently, she walks. He feels a pang of resentment over Miguel. He walks back to his table and Maria serves him the drink.

'Miguel is your husband?' Brendan asks as he sits down.

'My brother,' she says. 'My *little* brother. My *big* brother is in Maryland, America. Computers. My big brother knows everything about one thing and nothing about the rest. That is big brothers for you! Is not a way to be – you think?'

Brendan takes the glass from the tray Maria has brought out for him and begins to pour the beer.

Elsewhere in the world, Joyce McCready is practising the oboe in her kitchen in the house in which she was abandoned when her husband took off with his seven-stone beauty from Warrington. As she plays, she is aware of the geometry of sunlight falling on the window sill, of the sun warming her face, and of feeling her breathing, for once, to be even and relaxed. The sounds of the rich, single, unsyncopated notes of George's Gershwin's 'Someone To Watch Over Me' swim from the room, rising through the open window and out into the neighbourhood, wavering and fading by the wall of the cricket ground. In the hills above the town, Wilf Wardle and Oscar Brigg are in transit, moving between gardens on narrow English lanes, with Duke Ellington tunes rattling off the tin sides of the battered Lada Estate. The people of Heslop Bridge leave posies and stuffed animals by their children's memorial stones and contemplate hopelessly what kind of people these little ones would have become, and they wonder still about the unaccounted-for parchments bequeathed to them in the aftermath of their tragedy. In the streets where once Fr Wynn was guardian to the weak and poor in spirit, boys on bicycles are peddling smack. Lone men talk sex and masturbate on Keith Doyle's premium phone lines. People drink too much, and cry alone. And who can believe that in such a world as this, a world in which, without giving notice, men may walk into bars and offices and schools and shoot and shoot to cast their demons out, who can believe – no matter that it may come to nothing in the end – that a single moment's sublime and unencumbered happiness could be won by the realization that Miguel is her brother?